The Kahills of Willow Walk

A Novel by
S. K. Hamilton

**Stepping
Stones
Press
Ltd.**
www.familybookhouse.com

© 2007 by Sylvia K. Hamilton

This novel is a work of fiction. No similarity to individuals living or dead is intended. Any such resemblance that may occur is coincidental.

All rights reserved, including but not limited to the right of reproduction in whole or in part in any form.

Author's Cover Art by Sylvia K. Hamilton

Cover Design: Linda Lane

ISBN: 0-9769989-2-0

ACKNOWLEDGEMENTS

Editor and publisher - Linda Lane
   First and foremost without your expertise and your wonderful kindness I would not have a published novel. You made it all possible. Thanks, Linda, you're the greatest.

My friend and Author. - Jenny Turner
   Without your help and encouragement in my beginning years of writing, I would have quit. You made me hang in there. You've led me here. Thanks, Jenny.

All my friends in Writers Village University
   For almost two years, we went through much work and effort together. You probably don't know how much you helped—but believe me, you did. Too many names to mention, but you know who you are. Hugs!

A special thanks to
   Best writing buddies Phax and Herb, Charlie and Maria. We've come a long way, good friends. Thanks for the time you took away from your own work to help me with mine. I owe you. Hugs!

And many thanks to the folks who helped me with research.

Weep, my willow trees, and bow to drink
    cool, clear, creek water
        while Willow Walk
            soars skyward atop a knoll
                proud and tall.

Dedicated to my hubby, Ralph G. Hamilton, whose encouragement for me to keep on keeping on led to the completion of this book. Thank you, Honey, for your steadfast support and most of all, thank you for you.
        Pee Wee

Last but not least, I want to remember my family: Daughter Deborah Kaye Woods; son-in-law Charlie Woods; granddaughter Bonny Kaye; grandsons, Ashley, Jarrett, and Bo; and my great-grandbabies, Macin, Trey, and Cade. Remember me — I'm the one who loves you.

CHAPTER ONE

Cable slapped his cap on his head. Shoving his hands in the pockets of his jeans, he spat on the ground and started down the long, dusty road that led to the small Mexican town.

Dawson forced himself to the rented shanty's kitchen window. He cleared a small circle of grime with his shirttail and watched his father walk away. Puffs of dust flew up with every footstep, hiding first Cable's ankles, then his legs, and finally his hips. Soon, all Dawson could see was dust.

Maybe his dad would be gone for days, maybe not. Who knew? Who cared? Not him. Tears surfaced, but he fought them back. He was thirteen, almost a man, and men didn't cry.

Besides, he had a bigger problem now—an almost-seventeen-year-old blond maniac. What she had in mind terrified him, but he understood. And he wanted no part of it.

Polly Dee stood up, grabbing the kitchen chair for support and knocking it over. She smelled like gin mixed with sweat; the odor made him sick. He'd felt that same awful queasiness ten months earlier when his dad dragged him away from his step-mama, Suzanne, and little sister, Kat. He thought then he'd rather have a tooth pulled; he felt the same way now.

I gotta get out of here. She's serious this time.

"Ya never liked me at all, did ya, honey? Or maybe ya just wanna' get to know lil' ol' Polly better. I can teach ya some grown-up stuff. And I bet you'll like me then. Ever'one does. You'll see. You'll be my little man."

"Get away from me, Polly. You're drunk and you're dirty. Dad'll be home soon." That was debatable. "You want him to see you like this?" Stupid question. Polly didn't give a hoot, and Dad didn't care.

"That's okay, sweetie. Come to Polly Dee." She crooked her finger, motioning him closer.

He couldn't move. He couldn't even breathe. *Oh, please, pass out. Anything. Just leave me alone.*

Polly staggered to the left. He charged to her right.

Faster than lightning, she dug her nails into his arm.

"Leave me alone, Polly! Get away." He planted both hands on her chest and pushed.

She tottered backward and fell. Her head bounced off the edge of the overturned chair. A broken rung sliced into her cheek and forehead. She groaned. Sweaty blonde hair swung across her face and stuck there.

He opened his mouth to scream, but nothing came out. Tears rushed to his eyes.

Polly covered her face with both hands. Blood drizzled between her fingers and down her chin. She stopped moving.

His feet wouldn't obey his brain. After what seemed an eternity, he reached her motionless body.

"P-P-P-Polly?" he stuttered in a stifled voice. Then louder he said, "P-Polly?"

He bent down and nudged her arm. He did it again, harder. Her finger twitched. He thought he heard a murmur.

At least she's alive.

He ran out of the kitchen and returned. Then he did it again. Looking down at her, he knew he needed to get help. *Don't cry like a baby. Think like a man.* Stupid place—not even a telephone.

He grabbed Polly's liquor money from the coffee can and stuffed it in his pocket. Then he knelt by her side and touched her one more time. She wheezed and stirred. He'd find a pay phone and call for help.

"Run," he told himself aloud, "now, before it's too late."

Rushing out the open kitchen door, he leapt over the fallen screen and jumped down the steps. He bounced on his bike and peddled for the border.

What if the guards wouldn't let him cross into Texas? They'd gotten real strict about illegal aliens. Oh...it'd be okay because it was obvious, with his light hair and fair skin, he wasn't Mexican. What if they were looking for an American boy on a blue bicycle? He peddled faster.

How he hated Polly Dee. But he didn't mean to hurt her. She just kept coming at him. Didn't the law call that self-defense or something? What if she died? He'd be arrested for...for...for...

Murder!

They'd find him and take him to jail, and he'd be there for the rest of his life. He might never see Mama Suzanne or Kat again. On the other hand, what if they sent him to the electric chair?

Please, no!

He couldn't think about it now. He peddled even faster, his tires sending up cyclones of dust that put Cable's flying puffs to shame.

He was getting closer and closer to home. Texas was just a bridge away. Then came the long haul to West Virginia, but he'd make it. He had to.

He approached the bridge. His friend Pedro, who was on duty, waved him on. Dawson waved back.

Once across the border, he bounded from the seat and stood beside his bike. His muscles quivered; his knees shook. Eyes wide, he gasped for breath. Everywhere he looked loomed larger than life, not like before when he'd spent afternoons here. Now it was different. He was on his own. He had to use his senses.

Finding a pay phone nearby, he dialed the bar where his dad worked. Some girl answered.

"Tell Cable Kahill to go home right away. Polly's hurt." Hoping his dad would get the message, he hung up without waiting for a response.

Texas rested a far piece from West Virginia, but at least he was on his way. He'd make it back in spite of Cable. What was that expression Granddad Kahill always used? Oh, yeah, *come hell or high water*.

He'd promised his little sister he'd be home, and he aimed to keep that promise. He wouldn't disappoint Kat for the world and everything in it. He loved her.

CHAPTER TWO

The bus eased to a stop in the terminal. Dawson stood and looked out the window. He spied Mama Suzanne and Kat straining their necks—they must be trying to find him through the tinted glass. He wanted to holler at the bus driver to hurry and open the door.

Tears stung his eyes. He was home. Nothing could hurt him now.

After what seemed like forever, the door swung open. He bypassed the step down and jumped to the ground. Mama Suzanne's arms wrapped around him and closed him inside. He rested his head on her shoulder. Now he could cry.

"Daw, it's my turn. It's my turn." Kat jumped up and down, tugging on his shirttail. He'd thought he would never hear her little girl voice again.

They hugged, they kissed, they chatted all the way home. He didn't tell them about Polly Dee. He couldn't.

Why hadn't he stayed to help her? The thought had nagged at him all the way home on the bus. But he'd called to let his dad know, hadn't he? Dad would know what to do. That didn't make him a coward, did it? Squeezing his eyes shut, he forced the image of her lying on the floor from his mind. He'd worry about it later. And someday he'd return Polly's money he took from the coffee can to buy his bus ticket home.

But for now he was safe. The green hills and valleys of his hometown never looked so good. Nobody would ever take him away again, most of all not his father.

Dashing into the house, he took the stairs two at a time. His room was just as he'd left it. He glanced in the mirror on his dresser. Somehow he appeared older. Smarter, too. Forget Mexico. Forget the way his dad had changed into an evil giant and the dumb things Polly tried to do. Forget the whole mess. He'd be okay now.

"Daw, hurry! Let's go to our tree!"

He flew down the stairs. "Come on, Sis." He grabbed her hand. Together they ran out the door and down the grassy hill to the white board fence across the dirt road. Dawson lifted her over.

Out of breath but not out of talk, she cocked her head toward him.

"I don't know something, Daw. How come you're my brother, but Mama Suzanne isn't your mama?"

"Well...that's because we're half-brother and sister." He landed beside her and mulled it over. "We have the same daddy."

"Oh. You mean half of you is my brother, and half of me is your sister?"

"Something like that."

Holding hands, they ambled through a field full of clover. She frowned, tilting her head from side to side. Did she understand? He couldn't be sure.

On the way to their secret hiding place under the weeping willow, Dawson told her about Mexico, but only things he thought a six-year-old should know.

"You know something, Daw? I missed you every day you were gone." She swept a strand of hair from her face and dug in her pocket, handing him a tiny photo of her blowing a kiss from her fingertips.

Dawson looked at the delicate frame covered in colorful plastic butterflies. She looked like a princess, smiling from it at him like no one else ever could.

"You like it?"

"Sure do. I'll keep it always. Thanks, Kat."

She stopped jumping up and down and beamed as he bent down to kiss her cheek.

By the time they reached their secret place, Kat had run out of words. But she could have talked all day, and it wouldn't have bothered him.

In the cool green meadow, they sat under the weeping willow, side by side, where no adults could enter. Hundreds of yellow meadow butterflies circled them.

They took tiny, quiet breaths, afraid of shooing the butterflies away. The little flying creatures landed all over them—on their heads and arms and faces. When they couldn't stand the tickling any longer, they burst out laughing and fell back on the grass.

"Oh, Daw. We got lots of butterfly kisses, didn't we?" Kat giggled. "Here's one from me. Catch it now." She kissed her fingertips and blew on the palm of her hand.

He grabbed at the air, put his fingers to his cheek, and smiled. "I got it. Here's yours."

Except for the meadowlark's call echoing over the hill and valley, silence surrounded them.

It was *so* good to be home.

CHAPTER THREE
15 YEARS LATER

The Sunday sky grew purple and soft. A gnawing chill in the air promised that winter wouldn't be late. Kat didn't care about cold, snow, rain, hail, or sleet. She concentrated on her dream, the reason she'd studied day and night instead of dancing and dating.

Filled with hope and determination, her heart fueled her dream to succeed in the fashion industry and nudged her on. She vowed to become the best in West Virginia, maybe even New York and Europe and...well...plenty of time for that later.

"I've waited so long for this, Daw." Standing with her brother outside the boutique, Kat took a deep breath. "Hope I haven't made a mistake with my share of Mama's inheritance."

"Now don't go thinking negative. You can do anything you set your mind to. You always could."

Dawson's undying faith in her never failed to pick her up.

"Where would I be without my big brother? Sometimes I think I depend on you too much."

"Don't be silly. I'll be here for you until the day I die."

Kat valued his support above all else. "Just think, Daw, tomorrow morning these double doors will open and welcome everyone who enters. My grand opening!" She looked toward him. "Did you remember to put a poster in the gift shop window and one in the beauty salon and..."

"C'mon Kat. I got them out a week ago."

She gave him a sidelong glance and grinned. Shading her eyes from the sun, she looked up at the sign he'd made for her.

"It's beautiful, Daw, so...so *right*."

The sign stood for much more than a name on a board. Its message of hope, expectancy, and promise shouted from every inch of loving craftsmanship. In the lower left corner, the black silhouette of a cat looked up as though to read the calligraphy lettering: *Fashions by Kat*.

"I *love* it. Thank you." She leaned over and kissed his cheek.

His gaze fixed on her. "I'd give you the moon if I could."

"I know you would, Daw. Have I ever told you that you're the best brother a girl could have?" She dabbed at the love in her heart that was welling up in her eyes.

"Uh-huh. Sure. You're just saying that because it's true."

He stretched his hand and fingers taut and swung his hand to his eyebrow. Grinning all the while, he paced backward down the sidewalk to his truck.

"You're insufferable!" She displayed a fist. "But I love you anyway."

He threw her a butterfly kiss. She plucked it from the air and threw one back. Then he gave her his signature look.

Dawson had a way of tilting his cowboy hat low on his forehead and looking out from underneath. In spite of her intention to do otherwise, she had to grin every time he did it. She watched him open the door and toss his hat on the seat. He would sweep a lock of sandy hair from his forehead like he always did before he glanced over his shoulder and waved.

What would I ever do without him?

As he drove out of sight, a mist of uncomfortable memories floated into her consciousness. The same uneasy feeling that had haunted her for years lashed out at her.

She was six again, running after the camper trailer that tore out of the driveway and sped off down the road, ripping her brother from her life. Tears streamed down her cheeks now as they had then. She blinked and the vision faded, along with the fear of losing him.

Inside the boutique she headed to the refrigerator in the lunchroom and poured a glass of tomato juice. Then, wandering through the racks of clothing, she touched the fine silks and soft rayons, making sure everything hung just so. Still, she couldn't let go of her thoughts of Dawson.

He'd grown from a gangly boy into a solid, tall man of twenty-eight. He was handsome with strong, muscled shoulders and a dimpled smile that could melt an iceberg. He found pleasure among simple things. But something imbedded deep within him—something she couldn't identify—crept out at times, and he became uneasy, edgy, confused.

Kat wanted a man like him. The unexpected thought jolted her. Sometimes it seemed as though they weren't related at all. Then she felt ashamed, frightened at the thought. But what woman wouldn't want such a kind and handsome man? *Perfectly natural*, she assured herself.

She spent the rest of the day seeing that the gowns hung according to size and color and arranging folded garments on shelves for ease of shopping. She moved a vase of flowers from one stand to another, stood back contemplating, then moved it again. Switching on the waterfall in the atrium, she checked the water pressure and the lighting. The artful displays, more of Dawson's creative handiwork, still amazed her. Last minute housekeeping chores ensured that everything was in order.

At sundown she dimmed the lights and plopped down on the lounge in the showroom to look over it all one final time. Bathed in a soft glow, the beautiful décor and the fashions she'd created for the grand opening would bring fresh elegance to the neighborhood and new style to the industry.

But what a job it had been! Thank goodness for the enormous amount of help she'd had. In addition to Dawson's contributions, she'd enlisted the management and creative assistance of Bonny and Deborah, her two best college friends.

Satisfied that Fashions by Kat met her exacting standards, she walked out the back door to her car. When it came time to expand... there she went again, planning too soon for the future.

Dawson's often repeated words of encouragement whispered to her as she drove down the country road toward home.

If you must dream, Sis, dream big. Hitch your wagon to that proverbial star.

And she had.

CHAPTER FOUR

Lost in thought, Dawson didn't see the hills and valleys in the distance or the ravines along the roadside as he drove toward Willow Walk.

If only things could be different, like when we first married.

Love hadn't played a significant role in his relationship with Valorie for a long time—though he tried to protect and advise her when she would listen. His hands tightened on the wheel. The woman who now shared his home and bed bore little resemblance to the stunning woman he'd married.

Dappled rays of sunlight peeked through aged weeping willows that lined the quarter mile drive to the main house. Each bend brought him closer until the three-story structure towered in front of him. Sitting atop a wooded lot, level for several acres before sloping to the road, it always made him feel as though he were seeing it for the first time. He marveled at his great-great-granddad's architectural achievement. If it took the rest of his life, he'd create a masterpiece like this. Already on the drawing board, a ski lodge located at the base of the large hill on the acreage at the back of the property loomed in his imagination. Then it faded.

Willow Walk, Kat's project, and the sorry state of his marriage demanded all his time and energy. His architectural accomplishments would have to wait.

He drove to the rear of the house and parked under the spreading maple tree. Its leaves had already started to yellow. The truck door opened without the usual squeak, and he stepped out, still wondering why he stayed in this hopeless situation with Valorie. But deep inside, he knew. It went back to the time he left Polly lying on the floor in a pool of blood. Leaving Valorie in her condition now would be the same as abandoning Polly had been then.

Clippings of mowed grass, still damp from last night's rain, stuck to his boots as he cut across the lawn. He waved to Granddad Jedediah sitting on the swing that hung from the back porch rafters. Next month, the old man would paint, patch, and repair this most important piece of furniture at Willow Walk.

Dawson and Granddad had long ago mastered their own form of communication, and he'd more than once shared with the old man his desire to avoid Valorie whenever possible. Now Granddad raised his hand and poked a finger in the direction of the house.

Dawson gave him a thumbs up.

Quiet days and nights never lasted long at Willow Walk. Tranquility turned to mayhem without warning when Valorie lurked inside, making sure all her hidden boxes of chocolates were safe. He hoped her other obsession, photography, might find her developing pictures in the dark room. Otherwise, he might not make it to the swing without being seen or heard.

Stopping to remove any remnants of grass clippings, he used the rusted boot scraper while the old man nodded his approval. Not to clean your boots before entering Grandma Emma's kitchen had been forbidden for as long as he could remember. The center of Willow Walk even after she was gone, its polished floor reflected the image of all who entered.

He tiptoed up the wide stairs and onto the porch, then removed his hat and hung it on the hook by the door. Shading his eyes with his hand, he peered through the screen, looking past the kitchen into the living room.

Just as he feared, Valorie reclined on the couch, engaged in her favorite pastime—eating chocolates and doing nothing. No one could do *nothing* better than Valorie. But she didn't look up.

He made his way to the swing and sat down beside the old man, a bleak smile passing across his lips and disappearing.

"How you doin', Sonny?" Granddad's low voice still rang strong.

"I'm okay, just don't feel like contending with you know who."

"Yeah, I know who." He slapped Dawson's knee, then cast a wistful look out over the countryside. "Too bad your step-mama died so young. She was kind, just like my Emma, and she raised you kids right." Dawson saw his faraway look. "You know, Sonny, this time of year always gets to me. Em's been gone ten years next week. Sometimes I wish that autumn death had taken us together."

The loneliness in Granddad's expression tied a knot in Dawson's stomach. His search for comforting words came up empty, so he said nothing.

"Remember how particular your grandma was? She wouldn't tolerate a speck of dirt on her shiny kitchen floor. She wore out more brooms on me than I can count." He paused and blinked hard. 'Get out there to that scraper, Jed Kahill, and wipe your boots. You're dirtyin' my floor, and I won't stand for it'. That's what she'd say." He smiled, but Dawson saw the moisture in his tired eyes. "Then I'd give her a pat on the rump, and she'd pretend to scold me again. She was a tough ol' bird, that grandmother of yours. But how I loved that woman."

Dawson sighed and put his hand on Granddad's arm, staring beyond the porch toward the faces of the fields and hills that often comforted him more than the faces of men. An unwelcome memory—one of Mexico and a worn down, filthy shanty— struggled to surface. He forced it back with the agility acquired from years of practice. Some things were better kept in darkness.

His eyes twinkling, Granddad broke the somber silence. "You know, Sonny, I'm ninety now. This black hair's turned silver. Everything I have is headed toward the ground. Kitten says I'll be jawin' till they put me in the dirt. You believe that?"

"Sure do. Did she say you'd carry a big stick, too?" A grin relaxed Dawson's face. "That cane of yours is as mean a weapon as Grandma's broom."

"You know I just use it to put the fear into ya. I'd *never* hit anyone." He winked at Dawson. "I'll tell you one thing for sure. It's about doggone time you get me that baby boy for my namesake. Otherwise, I'm goin' to have to fight the grim reaper off with this." He raised his cane high and swiped the air.

Dawson sighed. "Someday, Granddad." Naming his first-born after Grandfather Jedediah in exchange for Willow Walk was a small price for such a huge gift. He wanted to fulfill the old man's wishes, but he couldn't even imagine Valorie with a child. "I just can't promise when."

Granddad gave him a sly smile and shot a cagey look in his direction. "I know somethin'—that if you knew—you might not say that so fast. An *old* family secret."

"Stop it! Why do you do that?" Dawson frowned. No matter how he begged, Granddad would never divulge the mystery to which he often alluded. Probably nothing to it—just one of the games he liked to play. "You've been taunting us with that for years. I've guessed everything but..." He paused. "Twins? Twins run in the family? Is that it?

"Maybe. Maybe not. I'm not sayin'."

They sat in silence for a long while. Dawson wondered what Granddad was thinking and figured Granddad was doing the same about him.

"Time for my nap, Sonny." The old man pushed himself up and ambled to the door.

"Okay. Try not to worry the devil the way you do me." Dawson chuckled in spite of himself.

Granddad swung the cane in his grandson's direction, pushed his eyebrows together, and pranced into the house. Sporting only a slight limp, he hadn't lost any of his spunk. His walk had slowed a bit, but his legs were still strong and his mind as sharp as ever.

Please let Granddad live long enough to hold his namesake in his arms. That's all I ask.

CHAPTER FIVE

Dawson stretched out on the swing, thinking about Kat. She had grown into a beautiful woman. Thick loose waves replaced black pigtails and framed her oval face. Azure eyes shone beneath long lashes. Strong willed, she was a lot like Granddad—naïve maybe, but smart. She'd make a terrific businesswoman and, one day, a great wife.

Kat's falling in love wasn't something he wanted to think about. When it happened, the man'd better be worthy of her. A feeling far deeper than the need to protect her stirred within him. He forced it out of his mind the same way he left his past behind.

Valorie intruded on his thoughts. After the wedding, she'd become insanely jealous of Kat. Sure, he'd known Valorie wasn't the happiest person, but he thought that would change—that he could prove all men were not like her father. It hadn't worked. Even therapy didn't help. He wanted to walk away, yet he couldn't. She had no one but him, no family, no friends. He'd walked away once before, but he'd never do it again. But if Valorie did anything...crazy, he'd feel responsible. What a trap!

The screen door opened, then banged shut. Still wearing bedroom slippers and looking more like a bag lady than the lady of Willow Walk, Valorie shuffled across the porch. Her drab housedress needed a good pressing. She leaned against the big round column near the steps, crossed her arms, and stared.

His good intentions had not materialized. The harder he tried to make her forget, the more she remembered. Her pain and rage had festered too long, he supposed. She was on her own path of destruction, and he was powerless to intervene.

Now, unexplained incidents at Willow Walk haunted him, the latest one the most bizarre to date. The excuse she offered for the headless chicken found in the barnyard? A fox got into the pen. He'd never known a fox to eat just the head.

Dawson sat up in the swing and watched the sun slip behind the mountain. A nippy breeze warned of a coming weather change. He zipped his jacket and stuck his hands in his pockets.

Valorie moseyed over to the swing and sat hunched over; she crossed her legs. Neither spoke for a long time. He glanced at her scowling face and then out over the rolling land. He couldn't help feeling sorry for her. She looked sadder than the Raggedy Ann doll he remembered Kat playing with when they were youngsters.

"What do you say we go to town tomorrow? I'd like you to see what I've done with the boutique. We could have lunch and—"

Her contemptuous laugh interrupted him. "Looks like for once in your life you'd get enough of your husband stealing half-sister. Don't you think I know what you've been up to?" The pity he'd felt for her a moment before turned to disgust.

"What did you say?" *Why do I even bother to try?* "I'll tell you one last time, Valorie." He clenched his fist and wished she'd been a man. "Don't *ever* talk that way about Kat. You understand?"

She sneered and looked away.

"She's never been mean to you. In fact, she's gone out of her way to be friendly."

Valorie raised both brows. "If you love her so much, why don't you sleep in her bed?"

"You have a filthy mind, Valorie. I can't take this anymore." Dawson stood up and started toward the kitchen.

She leapt to her feet, grabbed his arm, and pulled him around to face her. Fire blazed in her eyes. He felt her breath on his face. "Yeah? So, what're you gonna do about it? Whine to your little *sister*?"

Rage churned his stomach. "Stay out of my way, Valorie." Blood and a body on the floor of a shanty raced in front of him. He marched to the door, hoping to end the confrontation.

She must have picked up the magazine from the swing and hurled it toward him, for the sharp edge of its corner hit the middle of his back. His anger exploded. He wanted to hurt her.

Forcing himself to remain calm, he turned. "Valorie, I'm going into town tomorrow to see my attorney. Our marriage is over. You can have as much money as it takes to provide comfortable living quarters and—"

Valorie began to laugh, first in an undertone, then harder until her body shook. It went on and on until she appeared crazed.

Dawson's lips parted, but he said nothing. He watched the blood drain from her face and her expression harden.

"Over my dead body, you jerk. If anyone goes, it'll be *you*. Willow Walk will be mine—all of it. And the inheritance you got from your Mama will be mine—all of it. I'll get it if I have to lie in court." Her voice took on the defiant tone of a nineteen-forties movie queen. "Don't forget, darling, I'll be an abused, misused, black and blue wife that the judge will pity. And oh yes, your incestuous relationship with that slut of a sister will be on everybody's lips. I'll tell a story that will have them running you right out of town—or put you behind bars."

Neither of them moved. He didn't know the woman standing in front of him. In a heartbeat, her face turned from stone white to blood red.

Dawson yanked the screen door open and stormed into the house. She would stop at nothing to get her way. A judge would have to be as crazy as she was to believe her lies.

He opened the refrigerator and pulled out a beer, then sat at the table by the window. One sip, two sips. Swallowing past the lump of grief and rage in his throat took almost more effort than he had to expend. How he loved Willow Walk and the surrounding land, yet he could claim no happiness in his heart. He wanted children, love, and peace. He possessed none of them.

Someday he'd fulfill Granddad's dream, but at this moment he didn't know how. His wife would never be the mother of his children.

Valorie slithered into the kitchen, opened a huge box of chocolates, and began to stuff her mouth. Dawson glanced at her out of the corner of his eye. At least her full mouth kept her quiet while she devoured one piece after another.

The strained silence unnerved him much more than usual. A line had been crossed. Threats had been made. Ground rules had changed.

He sensed it the same way he perceived gathering clouds to foreshadow a storm.

Valorie continued her mechanical chewing. The awful smacking noise was less disgusting than the line of brown sludge flowing unchecked down her chin. That turned his stomach. He stood and walked away.

Once again, he sat on the porch swing. The sun had disappeared over the mountain, and a thin moon rose into the black sky.

The will to save his marriage died within him. He knew in his heart that nothing would bring it back again.

CHAPTER SIX

One-eared, one-eyed Teddy Bear, blobbed with old stains of chocolate ice cream, gooey candy, and sticky chewing gum, had never forsaken his place on top of the French Provincial headboard in Kat's bedroom.

Beneath the blue lace canopy, Kat hovered somewhere between sleeping and waking. The quiet just before dawn drove her deeper into slumber, further into space and time.

Wrapped in a vapor of memory, she was a six-year-old listening to a vehicle clank up the gravel driveway. She peered out her bedroom window and saw her father behind the wheel of his rickety pickup. Polly Dee sat so close to him it looked like they were one person with two heads.

The next thing she knew, Cable stood just inside the screen door, bellowing, "Dawson! You and Kat better get out here if ya know what's good fer ya!"

Dawson's young boy voice echoed in her head. "Run, Sis! Hide in the pantry. I'll go see what he wants."

She trembled in her half-awake state, tears stinging her eyes. "Go away, Daddy. Go with that other girl. I don't want you anymore."

"Don't cry, Sis. It's okay. I'll talk to him. You stay here, promise? Cross your heart and hope to die?"

She envisioned herself crossing her heart. As she wiped her eyes with the back of her hand, she sucked in a fast, deep breath.

* * * *

Her head turned from side to side, ruffling the case half off the pillow. "Daw come back, come back."

The dream merged into a happier time after Dawson returned. She rolled in bed toward the window and felt a butterfly kiss on her cheek. Early morning sunlight spiraled through the branches of the old elm outside the upstairs window.

A smile played at the corners of her mouth. Stirring slightly, she placed a hand to her cheek. She and Dawson sat under the weeping willow while yellow butterflies drifted toward her on a gentle breeze...

The jangling sound penetrated her dreamy state. She rolled away from the window, trying to block the noise, but the ringing persisted. She opened her eyes and remembered what day it was. Yawning, she reached over and picked up the phone.

"You still in bed, sleepy head?" Dawson asked. "Are you okay?"

"Yeah, just trying to get past the butterflies." She yawned again and plopped her head back on the pillow.

"Come on now, don't worry. Those butterflies are a sign of our good luck."

She giggled. "I was dreaming about them. Remember?"

"How could I forget?" He laughed. "Better stop dreaming and get dressed. This is your big day."

"I know. But now that you mentioned it, I think some of them stuck in my stomach. But I'll get over it. I better go now...and Daw, tell Val and Granddad I hope they'll come to the opening."

"Yeah, the last thing Granddad said was, 'Tell Kitten I wouldn't miss her grand opening for a skinny dip with a buxom blonde.'" It was a few seconds before they stopped laughing. "But I know Val won't be there. She has the weird notion that you're trying to take me away from her. She's convinced herself that we're having some kind of affair. I don't know how much longer I can live like this."

His breaking voice echoed through the phone, and she, too, wondered how much more he could endure.

"Daw, I know how you feel." She was filled with emotion she couldn't express. "Val's not dealing well with whatever happened to her. I feel so sorry for both of you."

"What am I going to do? She won't go back to her doctor, and she's losing touch with reality. She hates me one minute, but won't consider divorce the next. She threatens to take Willow Walk if I file." He paused. "That can never happen."

"I know." Kat sat on the edge of the bed, facing the window. A line of gray storm clouds floated across the sky and into her heart.

"Sis, I married her for the wrong reason." He sighed. "It's my own fault I'm in this predicament."

"Don't blame yourself." Kat sensed his pain. "Let's talk later. We'll find a solution together."

Kat sighed. Nothing could be harder than living with an emotionally unbalanced person.

"Okay. We'll talk later. For now, get your rear in gear, girl. You've got a boutique to open."

The black note in his voice had threatened the perfection she so desired for this day. She wanted Dawson to be as happy as she was now. His inexhaustible goodness took a beating every time Valorie opened her mouth. Little by little, she was destroying him.

"I'll see you soon...and...hang in there. I love you, Daw."

"Love you, too."

Dawson had been a beacon of light for her after Mama died. Now she needed to be one for him, and she didn't know how.

Leaning on one elbow, Kat clicked off the cordless handset and lay back on the bed, staring at the canopy overhead. Could Val really take Willow Walk away from Daw? Surely, no judge in his right mind would let her—but stranger things had happened. If only Granddad hadn't deeded the place to her brother on his twenty-first birthday. To lose Willow Walk... Shaking her head, she tried to focus on her new boutique, but Dawson's sadness kept seeping into her happiness. He was right about Valorie. Fair or not, the woman always seemed to get her way. If she set her heart on Willow Walk, she just might get it.

How she wished she could say the same thing to him that he had so often said to her. *This is your dream, a new beginning for you. Concentrate on it, and never let go.*

The next time she saw him, she would do exactly that. But for now, she would do exactly what he expected her to: Make the most of her own opportunity.

Taking a deep breath, she sat up to greet her grand opening day. Meeting the demands for unique and elaborate fashions from the wealthy would be tough, but she had spent years preparing for the challenge. Many from the older generation, the blue-haired upper class ladies around Wheeling, would pass through her doors today. The younger generation from New York, wrapped in furs sporting large brimmed hats, would come later—after word of her exclusive designs spread. She stood, chin up, full of confidence. It felt good. Daw would help her if she started to fall. Like always, he'd be there for her. But she wanted to stand on her own feet, make her own decisions. And now, more than ever, she wanted to be there for him.

Sliding her feet into fluffy slippers, she scuffled to the open window and pulled the sheer curtain aside. Her vision fogged, and she saw herself and Dawson at the swing. It seemed like yesterday.

"Push me higher, Daw! See the white kitty in that cloud? I wish I could catch him and put him in my pocket."

"Don't be silly, girl. You'll fall and hurt yourself and..."

She sighed and turned from the window to get ready.

After showering, she splashed cologne on her wrists and neck, slipped into a winter white gauze dress, and added black cat earrings, her fashion symbol. A quick look in the mirror pleased her. "That'll do," she said.

Grabbing her purse from the hallstand, she hurried out the door. The magnitude of her new adventure hit full force when she reached the porch steps; she stopped to acknowledge the moment. This was her dream. This was Daw's dream for her. She'd make it work, no matter what.

Dawson took the last sip of coffee and placed the cup in the sink. He was about to tell Val that he was leaving for the boutique when he spied her standing just inside the archway leading into the dining room, her back to him.

He opened his mouth to speak, then closed it, watching in bewilderment. Valorie appeared to be communicating with someone. But no one was there. Her mouth moved like a drowning person gasping for air. The more gestures she made, the more agitated she became. He eased closer. What came from her was a whisper so low it sounded like a hum rather than words.

"Valorie?" Dawson said.

She turned, her complexion as pale as her lifeless dress.

"Who are you talking to?"

"No one, why?" She gave him a searching look as though she didn't know what he meant.

Dawson didn't know what to say. "Well, I...are you sure you won't come with me?"

"No, you go on. I don't feel welcome around your sister. Besides, you two ignore me."

"Oh, come on, Val. That's not true." Her unpredictable mood swings worried him. Was it safe to leave her alone? Granddad would be going with him.

Her eyes turned cold, stubborn. Whatever window of opportunity he might have had banged shut.

"I'll be late getting home. Kat's going to keep the doors open until nine or so."

Valorie rushed to him, her hand on his arm as if to hold him there. Her countenance switched from angry pursed lips to pleading, childlike eyes.

"Don't go. Please don't go and leave me here by myself."

He hesitated, feeling her anguish, remembering Kat in pigtails and a pink dress, saying the same thing.

"Val, I promised I'd be there for the opening. I can't let Kat down. Please come along. She issued you a special invitation." Her expression changed; she stood statue-like, unresponsive. "Okay. Call me if you change your mind, and I'll come for you." He turned and walked out the door.

Granddad was waiting in the truck when he jumped in. "We're gonna be late. Let's get a move on, Sonny."

Tears stung Valorie's eyes as she watched him go. Why didn't he love her anymore? She wiped the moisture off her cheeks with the hem of her dress. Men were like that...just like Daddy. Her stomach hurt. She stomped into the kitchen and rummaged through the cabinet.

Ah, her chocolates. They always made her feel better. She popped the sweets in her mouth, one after another, but this time they didn't work. Her sorrow turned to anger, then to rage.

Dawson had broken his vows, his promises to her. She didn't have proof he cheated on her, but he didn't touch her anymore. What more proof did she need? He catered to his sister's every whim. He cared only for her. A man shouldn't care more for his sister than he cared about his wife. He should love his wife first.

She'd make them pay. Kat's dream of a lifetime, that hoity-toity boutique she'd sunk her inheritance into, would never make it. The time Dawson spent using his degree in architecture on that stupid dress store would prove to be in vain. *Yes*, she'd make Kat pay—Dawson, too. She shoved another chocolate in her mouth and thought a bit.

Hearts can be broken...but what really breaks a heart is the death of a dream.

CHAPTER SEVEN

Kat opened the double doors and walked out. Then she turned and stepped back over the threshold, as a customer entering the store would, and looked around. The boutique overflowed with originality and glamour. Stores like this thrived in New York, but would this one work in Wheeling?

Heading to a rack of long gowns, she straightened the pink one she loved so much. It reminded her of the paint color on the walls—the electrifying pink that beamed like a beacon light in a dark night. She remembered the day it was determined by Debbie and Bonny. Every strawberry daiquiri they drank had translated into greater depth of color until the present intense shade found its way onto the walls. Toned down by the abundant white latticework and white wicker, it presented a striking backdrop of assertiveness and sophistication.

In the lunchroom connected to her office in the back, she made coffee. It would be ready by the time the girls arrived.

"Hello! Anyone here?"

"Hi, Deb, Your timing couldn't be better. The coffeemaker just finished its job."

"Are you ready for the biggest day of your life?" Deb walked into the lunchroom.

"I am. Pour us some coffee while I open this package." She snipped the tape and pulled open the box.

"What is it?"

"A special black gown I copied from a dream I had. I want you to model it sometime today." She held the elegant dress up for Deb to see. "You like it?"

"Gorgeous! How much?" Deb's eyes sparkled as she touched the fabric.

"Three-fifty nine. What do you think?" Kat ran her hand over the luscious fabric.

"Why so cheap? I would have guessed closer to five hundred. Give me three of them in different colors." Deb laughed and headed for the showroom. "Is Dawson coming in today, or is that a silly question?"

"Silly question. He wouldn't miss the grand opening for anything. And Granddad's coming, too." Kat hung the black dress among the pink and blue satins, creamy laces, and more daring animal print gowns.

"You know, you've got one good-looking brother. Too bad he's hooked up with a crazy one."

"She's sick—I mean really ill. Her psychiatrist said she has a limited internal self or ego, whatever that means. But I do worry about Dawson."

Deb tilted her head and frowned. "I can see why. You know, it's a good thing he got away from his father when he was a kid and came back to help you through school and smooth out the bumps on life's road."

"I guess that's why we're so close." Kat couldn't prevent the past from invading the present. Images of Dawson's bargaining with Cable to leave her at home and just take him flooded her mind. Deb's voice brought her back.

"You don't see your dad much, I guess." Deb straightened the centerpiece on the refreshment table before downing a cheese roll.

"Nope. He's here and there and everywhere just like he's always been. But it's just as well. I've never forgiven him for taking Dawson away from me. I told him that day I didn't want him anymore. I still don't."

"When I saw him at Mama Suzanne's funeral, he looked bad, sick or something. Didn't you notice? He didn't look as mean as I pictured him either."

"I didn't even glance in his direction when Daw told me where he was sitting." Kat looked toward the door when she heard it open.

Bonny pranced in like a model. "Hi, everyone," she said in a deep, raspy voice. "You needn't tell me how beautiful I look in my new red dress, an exclusive design by Katarina Renée Kahill, the up-and-coming lady of fash—"

"Good morning, Bon. You can stop now." Kat smiled. "We won't mention how great you look. Grab a cup of coffee and help me hang these last minute things." She opened another box.

"Nothing stronger than coffee? How about spiked tomato juice or something?" Bonny sighed. "Oh, well, I guess if you did, Deb would already be into it."

Deb rolled her eyes. "Even *I* wouldn't be drinking this early in the morning."

Kat glanced at her watch. "I wonder where Daw is."

"You worry too much," Bonny said. "He's a grown man, Kat. He can take care of himself."

"When it comes to Valorie, I'm not sure." Kat walked to the doors and looked outside. She'd turned to go back when she heard his truck roar up the street. Granddad waved out the window while Dawson whipped down the alley toward the parking behind the store.

She hurried to the back door. "It's about time you two got here. Granddad! I'm so glad you came."

"You think I'd miss your grand openin', Kitten? Not unless I was six foot under."

He'd attended her high-school graduation, college graduation, and every special event she could remember. At family gatherings he was the life of the party. After a couple glasses of wine, he would recite "The Face on the Barroom Floor." Everyone sat spellbound at his narration of the famous poem.

She hugged the old man, feeling secure in his comfortable embrace. He held his hand out, and she took it. Her grand opening wouldn't be the same without him.

Together they followed Dawson into the boutique.

"Hi, girls." Dawson gave a dimpled smile.

Kat looked at her watch. "We open in fifteen minutes. Are we ready? You think anyone will show up?"

"They'd better if they don't want to be hog-tied and shackled to my truck and hand delivered to your front door."

Granddad eyed him, then looked around. "Don't think you'll be needin' to do that, Sonny. My guess is she'll do just fine on her own."

He walked to the sitting area and plopped down in a wicker chair. "Right smart place you got here, Kitten."

"Thanks, Granddad. It's been fun getting it ready, but it'll be even more fun when it starts making some money."

She opened the doors to a short elderly lady dressed to the hilt. Smiling at her, she peered over her head up and down the street. The sidewalk was empty.

"Nice of you to stop by. Please come in."

"I'm from New York, and I've seen everything they have. My friend said I better come visit her here in Wheeling if I want to see the newest fashions. She's ailing this morning, so she couldn't come herself. Arthritis, you know. I do hope your designs make my trip worthwhile."

"You made the right choice," Granddad spoke up. "And they will." He was on his feet and at the woman's side faster than Kat had seen him move in years. "I'm Jedediah Joseph Kahill at your service. And what is your name, pretty lady?"

"Why...why it's Penelope. P-P-Penelope Weatherbush."

Granddad raised her gloved hand to his lips. Her mouth fell open, and she looked misty-eyed at him. "Nice to meet you, sir...uh...Mr. Kahill. Wherever did you get that daring dimple?"

"Why, Penelope, ma'am, I was born with it. You just call me Jed and allow me to show you around." Granddad grinned and placed the lady's arm on his own as he hung his cane over his free arm. Looking over his shoulder, he winked at Kat and Dawson. Penelope swooned. She couldn't take her eyes off him.

Kat forced back the howl of laughter that threatened to erupt.

At nine o'clock Kat bid good-by to the last customer. Only Dawson and Granddad remained when she turned the open sign to *closed*.

She gave them both a big hug. "Thanks for being here for me. What would I do without you two?" Kat leaned over and kissed Granddad on the cheek. "Will you come visit me again?"

"You betcha, Kitten. Just try to keep me away. But let's talk business. How'd we...uh, you...do today?"

Tears sprung to her eyes. "Not me. *We*, just like you said, Granddad. And *we* did better than I ever imagined."

"So are you going to tell us how well *we* did?" Dawson's eyes twinkled.

"Well, let's see." She watched their expectant expressions.

"Well, nothin', Missy. Out with it!" Ganddad's impatient words forced a smile despite her effort to remain serious.

"Okay, okay. The grand opening exceeded my wildest dreams. I haven't even had time to count the pile of orders. Bonny tabulated the day's sales before she left, and I can't believe how much they totaled. And the compliments just kept coming right down till the last customer left with three gowns." She stopped to catch her breath. "Let's go out to dinner one night next weekend to celebrate."

"Good idea. I'll bring Penelope, and you bring Dawson." He burst into laughter and swung his cane in the air. "Don't think I'm kiddin' either. She's got her eye on me."

"Yes, I noticed." Kat walked them to the door. "See you tomorrow," she said to Dawson.

"Okay. But don't stick around tonight. You look exhausted. Why don't we do lunch tomorrow, and you can fill me in on everything? I'll need to start the bookkeeping soon." Dawson said.

"I won't have time to leave, I'm sure. Why don't you come here and we'll order something in?"

He eyed her for a moment. "See you at noon. I'll bring lunch."

She locked the door and poured herself a glass of champagne. Plopping down on the overstuffed sofa, she gazed around the room. Dawson's special touches had earned almost as many compliments as her designs. Why didn't he use his architectural training more? Well...maybe she understood. Willow Walk kept him busy, and that was his first priority. Too bad Valorie didn't share his love for the beautiful old homestead.

Kat forced herself up onto aching feet and left the boutique by the back door. A sound at her feet made her look down. A black kitten jumped up, raised its back in defense, and glared at her. Kat squatted in front of it.

"C'mon little one...that's right."

Where was its mother? The soft fur and round belly meant the kitten had been well fed, but the little thing was alone. Picking it up, she cuddled it against her chest and stepped into the car.

"You're scared, aren't you, kitty. I think I'll call you Snow White in spite of your color."

Kat smiled and wondered whether the name would match the gender. She rubbed the kitten gently behind the ear. Purring its contentment, it fell asleep in her lap.

Thoughts of her brother filled her mind as she drove home. A long overdue talk about his situation would happen tomorrow at lunch. She'd see to it.

She felt like a huge weight was about to be lifted from her shoulders.

CHAPTER EIGHT

Dawson woke to another morning just like all the others in his recent past. In silence he recounted his blessings to force himself out of bed to face the day.

I'm alive. I function. I possess opinions and a will. I have honor.

Yet it seemed he'd lived without love forever. He felt the life draining out of him, and he didn't know how to stop it.

I don't know if I understand—all I know is, I need love.

Scolding himself for his selfishness, he made a perfunctory trip to the kitchen for buttered toast with strawberry jam. Despite the restoring power of sleep, he dreaded the day. The fear that his wife would snap and do harm to him or to Kat hung like a black cloud over every other thought.

Valorie's ability to hide the venomous wrath inside her worried him most. He could never determine her exact state of mind. If only he could commit her...but he couldn't take that step, not as long as one thread of hope existed for her recovery. That would be a coward's way out.

But each day, she became more paranoid, more frightening, more calculating.

He sighed and pushed himself away from the table. He wanted to get away from the house before Valorie awoke. Even though she often slept until noon, she sometimes rose with the sun and ruined his day before it even started. A hot shower and clean shave improved his outlook, and he slipped into clean clothes and hurried back to the kitchen. Swallowing the last sip of coffee, he placed his cup in the sink and headed for his pickup, dodging raindrops on the way.

Why hadn't he listened to Kat? Before he married Valorie, she warned him not to give his heart to someone who wouldn't protect it.

Be careful, Daw. I don't have a good feeling about this.

You don't have a good feeling? What's that supposed to mean?

His words had been sharp. He could still remember the hurt expression on her face.

I can't explain. It's just that something isn't right, isn't what it appears. I don't know...maybe my female intuition is working overtime.

Female nonsense is more like it. I know what I'm doing, Kat. I'll be good for her. We'll be good for each other.

With tears in her eyes, she had patted his arm. *Sure you will, Daw. And I'm behind you one hundred percent, you know that.*

Now he knew how right Kat had been. Valorie wasn't at all the way she had appeared. But it didn't matter anymore. Although he didn't believe in divorce, deep down he felt relieved that he'd made the decision. He hadn't been good for her, no matter how hard he'd tried. They hadn't been good for each other.

Driving down the long drive from the house, he glanced out over the small portion of Willow Walk where he planned to build a few elegant spec houses on one-acre lots. Granddad Jedediah had every right to expect a return on Dawson's degree in architecture since he'd put his grandson through college. Dawson wouldn't let the old man down. Besides, he was good at what he did. And he'd be even better when the burden of his marriage had been laid to rest.

Until then, he was glad to help Kat with the boutique, glad to have somewhere to go. Glad to have his sister around.

He pulled into the parking lot and jumped out of the truck.

Kat spotted him dashing through the boutique door and hurried over to greet him.

"I thought you were bringing food."

"As hard as you've worked, you deserve to get out of here for lunch." He grabbed her hand. "Let's go."

"I can't leave, Daw. I told you I need to be here. It's only my second day open."

Deb stepped up on one side and Bonny on the other.

"I think we can manage without you for an hour or so." Deb looked indignant.

"We did study business and design with you if I recall correctly," Bonny reminded her.

"But I suppose you still might feel that we aren't good enough to run your business during the lunch hour," Deb said, sniffing.

"All right, you two, you win." Kat laughed. Grabbing her purse and sweater, she stepped from the climate-controlled boutique into a chilly, drizzling rain that dampened her enthusiasm for going out.

Dawson opened the door of the truck for her. "How does the Seafood House sound?"

"Ummm...good idea. I've been craving lobster."

Neither spoke on the way to the restaurant, but Kat knew from his scowl that he wasn't thinking happy thoughts. He gripped the steering wheel with white knuckles, something he only did when he was upset or worried.

Leading them to a corner booth, the hostess handed them a menu. Candles and lanterns cast a golden glow over the area. Seashells and driftwood filled the fishnet draped from the ceiling. Rough board walls finished the rustic atmosphere that made the trek through the rain almost worth the discomfort.

Dawson smiled and looked at Kat as the cocktail waitress stood ready to take their order.

"Would you like wine, Kat, or maybe a margarita?"

"Please. I'll have a margarita on the rocks with salt."

"I'll have the same."

The waitress left, and Dawson twisted in the booth to watch her derriere disappear around the corner.

"Daw!" she scolded, trying to hide her smile.

"What's wrong with a little look?" Dawson's devilish grin and waggling eyebrows made her giggle.

"Oh, you!" The rascal in him always popped out at the strangest times.

She wanted to talk about Valorie, but didn't want to be the first to bring it up. Nor did she want to break the humor of the moment. Leaning back in the booth, she let her gaze rest on his face as he looked around the restaurant. He drifted back to her and caught the question in her eyes.

"What?"

"Nothing much. I was just wondering what's going on with Valorie and the divorce?"

"As you know, she threatened to lie in court, even make up stuff about us if she had to."

"Do you think she'd actually do that?"

"My attorney said even if she tries, she has very little credibility. She's shrewd though. He doesn't know her like I do."

Or like I do, Kat thought.

"I've thought of moving my office to the guesthouse," Dawson continued. "I'm not sure I'd know how to act with that much peace and quiet though. What do you think?"

"Great idea, but what about Granddad? If he fell or something, do you think Valerie would help him?"

"He's agreed to move into the guesthouse with me. Claims I need company." Dawson grinned and shook his head. "He's still very independent. Makes his own way, even cooks his own meals when he feels like eating."

"I think this is just what you need, Daw. Granddad, too."

The waitress returned with their drinks.

Kat looked at the glass set before her, not really seeing it. The full impact of Dawson's dilemma touched her, overwhelmed her. He would never have a happy marriage while Valorie remained in his life, never have the children he dreamed of. With Valorie promising to cause him future pain, Kat knew his days of suffering had just begun.

She reached out and laid her hand on his. "Be careful."

Dawson looked past her and grimaced. "Speak of the devil."

Valorie sauntered to the table. "Fancy meeting you two here. But I'm not surprised since this is your favorite place. What a cozy little out-of-the-way table. May I join you?"

Kat held her breath, waiting for Dawson to extend an invitation that didn't come. She'd witnessed one of Val's rages and never wanted to endure another, especially in public.

"Of course, join us, please." She forced a smile. "I haven't seen you for awhile. Where've you been hiding?"

Dawson cast a glance of disapproval in his sister's direction, and slid over. Valorie scooted in beside him and kissed him on the cheek.

The waitress appeared, bearing cheese and hot garlic biscuits, and glanced at Valorie. "May I get you something from the bar?"

Valorie turned toward Dawson. "My usual, sweetheart."

"A martini for the new arrival." He ordered the drink and removed Valorie's clutching hand from his arm.

Kat nudged his leg under the table with her foot and hoped he'd get the message not to antagonize his wife. He nodded. In his place she'd feel the same, but her understanding didn't mean she wanted to see them fight.

Dawson cleared his throat. "Kat and I have already ordered. Were you planning on eating?"

Valorie's hand shook as she raised her glass. "Oh no, I'm not here to eat. I came to tell you, Dawson, that I've seen my attorney about the divorce."

Dawson's wary expression made Kat ache for him. To be forced into politeness for her sake had to be difficult She wished she had followed her instincts and stayed at the boutique.

Valorie glared at Kat. "Don't tell me, my dear, you didn't know about the divorce. I thought Daw—oh, I mean Dawson—told you everything."

Dawson sighed, scrutinizing the polished silverware as though he were an inspector for the board of health.

Kat opened her mouth to answer her sister-in-law, but Dawson intervened.

"Valorie, why are you here? I know it's not just for small talk." Dawson rubbed his forehead.

"Can't your wife join you for lunch? After all, we aren't divorced yet." Giving Dawson a dismissive look, Val downed her Martini and turned to Kat. "How did your grand opening go? Make much money?"

Dawson watched Kat over the rim of the glass; she felt a warning delivered on the wave of his stare. She stiffened "It went well, and we did well. You should've come."

"I understand my husband helped you quite a bit."

"Yes, he did a wonderful job. As I said, you should come see for yourself sometime."

"He's always helping you while the ranch and I go neglected." Valorie put on a pathetic face and cast a sidelong glance at Dawson.

"The ranch has never gone neglected, and neither have you."

Dawson looked like he was about to choke. Kat glanced toward the patrons sitting close by. So far no one seemed to notice the tension at their table.

"Don't get testy, Dawson. Katarina will think we don't get along." Valorie's mouth narrowed. "You want the truth? Fine, I'll give it to you. My attorney was very interested in what you've done to me. You'll be hearing from him. Have a wonderful lunch and whatever else you do when I'm not around."

Valorie was gone before Dawson could counter her accusation.

"How could she!" Dawson hissed, his fingers so tight around the stem of the glass, Kat thought it would snap. They watched Valorie retreat through the maze of tables. Kat leaned forward and lowered her voice. "She's up to something."

"Yes, she is" With a crisp move of his wrist, he drained what was left of his drink. "She's threatened to make me sorry I ever met her, which won't be hard to do."

The waitress reappeared with the steaming lobster, melted butter, baked potato, and sliced tomatoes. Kat waited until she left.

"I'll help any way I can. Just say the word." She reached across the table and again placed her hand over Dawson's. A flash of light startled them. Kat jerked her hand back, almost spilling her margarita. Valorie stood beside a post several yards away with a camera in her hand.

"Ta, ta." Val waved her fingers and dashed away.

"What's that all about?" Kat asked.

Dawson frowned. "You can't guess? She thinks she can use our having lunch together as a criminal offense." His voice was expressionless; his eyes sparked. "That woman is dangerous."

She wanted to comfort him, take him in her arms and hold him, but with strength from years of practice, she buried what she had always felt and shook her head in disgust.

He picked up his knife and fork, and she followed suit. They ate in silence.

"Are you ready to return to the slave pit?" Dawson's voice pierced the black cloud hanging over them.

Kat tried to smile. "Can't call it that yet. Maybe by tomorrow. If the boutique keeps doing well, I'll be able to pay Bonny and Deborah to manage it full time."

"Seems a little early to make that call. Do you have plans to do something else?" Dawson brushed breadcrumbs from his shirt.

She had wanted to discuss the letter she received from Lincoln Colter Wolf of Wolf International Fashions last week, but this didn't seem the time.

"Nothing, really."

"Okay, out with it."

He knew her too well. "Here goes nothing. Remember when I went to New York for that designer's convention last month?"

"Yeah, so?"

"I received a letter from the owner of Wolf International Fashions. Mr. Wolf asked me to New York for an interview. Said he was impressed with my designs and wanted to take a closer look. The company is searching for a lead designer."

"A closer look at your designs—or you?"

"Don't be silly. What do you think about the offer?"

He scowled. "I don't know—that's up to you. I thought you were happy now. Good grief, Kat, the boutique's been open less than forty-eight hours."

"Well, I am. I mean...the interview has nothing to do with that."

"It has *everything* to do with that. Have you thought about what you would do with the boutique if he hires you?"

"I could commute back and forth. With Bonny and Deb looking after the shop, I could still run the designing end. And I could split my time between the two. Besides, I wouldn't obligate myself for longer than a year's contract, sort of a trial period. Dawson, don't you see...with an opportunity like this, I could make a name for myself. If I'm hired, the details will fall into place. I'm not worried about that."

"Sounds like you've made up your mind. Do you know anything about this...this Mr. Wolf? Is he married? Is he legit? Do you know what you're getting into?"

For the first time she could remember, she felt irritated at her brother. "Look, Daw, I don't do crystal balls. I can't foresee anything. I can only wait for whatever comes." She tried to soften her words. "Wolf International Fashions is known and respected around the world. A monumental fashion show is held every year, and the company won four years in a row. But it came in second last year. I'll find out more about him before I make any decisions, I promise."

"Sis, I don't mean to put a damper on your plans, but you've got to be careful. Don't you read the paper or watch the news? Powerful men can be dishonest, and...fast. I don't want to see you hurt. I don't want you tied up in something you can't get out of and—"

"I'm only going for an interview, Daw. Give me credit for being able to handle myself." She glanced away, unwilling to let him see how hurt his lack of confidence made her feel.

She heard him sigh and turned back to face him. He'd lost the stern look, and his dimple made him look even younger than his twenty-eight years. "Want me to go with you?"

She smiled. Under different circumstances she would have enjoyed his company, but this was something she wanted to do alone. "No. I'll be fine. I don't think the interview will amount to much. I've got to include a few new sketches aside from those he saw at the convention."

"When's the interview?

"Wednesday. And don't worry, I'll be home the next day."

"Okay, but if he pulls any funny stuff, you call me."

She grinned and rolled her eyes. "My hero. Save me from the big bad wolf."

"It's not funny, Kat. Those corporate types can be ruthless and you're not—"

She interrupted him. "Experienced?"

"Just be on your guard."

"I'll knock his block off if he tries any funny stuff. And then I'll call you." She hid her grin with her hand.

Dawson looked dubious as he searched her expression. Smiling broadly, she lowered her hand. He laughed.

"You about ready to go, toughie?" Dawson stood up.

Silence filled the truck on the way back to the boutique just as it had when they headed for the restaurant.

Lost in her own thoughts, Kat debated the pros and cons of becoming the lead designer for Wolf International—if she were offered the position. Could she trust Lincoln Wolf with her designs? She'd find out soon enough about this Wolf man; but whatever he was, she could handle him. And while she couldn't attest to his character, she knew he was without question one of the best looking men on the planet. That made little difference, she told herself. She was trying out for the lead for one reason only: to learn as much as possible about the fashion world and get her designs in front of the right people. So she'd give the handsome Mr. Wolf her best effort.

She finished the day with Bonny and Deb and locked up, letting her mind wander back to Lincoln Wolf. He had been a perfect gentleman the day she met him, and she'd trust her first impression. After all, she seldom misjudged people.

What could possibly happen if she was careful?

CHAPTER NINE

"Be there in a minute, Lil. I can't find the corkscrew."

Lincoln Wolf stood behind the bar in the great room, scratching his head. Where had he put that blasted thing? If all else failed, he'd open the wine with his teeth. He began the frenzied search again. Paraphernalia from the last six drawers flew everywhere. At last he found the elusive fugitive in the center of the clutter.

He ran his fingers through his thick black hair and smiled before jabbing the corkscrew into the top of a bottle of French Château Mouton Rothschild, the winning bid at a wine auction. He'd been hoarding it for a special occasion or an excuse to drink it, whichever came first.

The thought of dismissing Lillian wasn't anything to celebrate, but opening the expensive bottle of French wine in her behalf lessened his guilt. He shrugged his shoulders and made a helpless gesture with his hands. *C'est la vie.*

"Linc, what are you doing?" A short pause followed. "If you can't get the wine open, bring anything. I'm dying of thirst."

"Be right there." The distance from the bar in the corner of the great room with its cathedral ceiling to where Lillian sat almost echoed their voices.

Curled up in a catlike pose, she thumbed through a magazine. "I hope so. You've been fiddling with that bottle forever. It'll be evaporated by the time you get here with it."

Ah, beautiful Lillian—but it happened every time. Top-notch designers stayed on top for four or five years before burnout rendered them useless. Nothing to do with him, he rationalized, not his fault; he didn't invent death to a designer.

He took a tray of cheese and crackers from the small refrigerator behind the bar, grabbed the wine glasses and bottle with his other hand, and ambled over to Lillian. He heard her humming along with the CD as she fiddled with her long red fingernails. She wore the transparent creamy negligee like she had been born in it. He couldn't tell where the gown stopped and skin started.

"At last." She reached for the wine, looked up at him through long lashes, and patted the seat beside her. The spark in her eyes burned a hole straight through him.

"Lillian, there's something I need to..." He hesitated. Giving her the bad news tonight made no sense. She might cry, or, worse, she might storm out the door. Neither reaction fit his plans for the evening.

"Not now, Linc. Let's enjoy this evening together. We never know when it might be our last."

"You're right."

What was that all about? He hadn't said anything to alert her about what was coming, and he hadn't told anybody else. Oh, well, it didn't matter because he knew how to distract her. Running his hand through her short-cropped hair, he let his fingers linger on her neck before moving them to her shoulders. Funny, she didn't seem to respond.

"I've been meaning to ask about Rebecca. She lifted his hand from her shoulder and held it for a moment before putting it back. "How's she doing with her drug problem? I know how hard this is for you."

Hard? She didn't know the half of it. Nor did anyone else.

"She's a little better. I had her released from The Comfort House yesterday. Mrs. Oliver will care for her. At least, she'd better for what I'm paying her...although I'll be letting her go soon. Rebecca is getting better every day." He brushed his lips across her forehead.

"I don't understand why she's in and out of that place so much." Lillian nuzzled his neck. A little grin played around the corners of her mouth while her fingers toyed with his ear.

Now this was more like it. "Let's not think about it now."

She rested her hand on his face. "If anyone ever tries to take you away from me, I swear I'll rip her eyes out."

He set her glass on the end table and placed his beside it. Ignoring her threat, he took her hand, and she rose with an angular grace. The aroma of musk perfume sent him reeling. His hands moved to the small of her back, pulling her against him. He held her, kissing her eyes, her cheeks, and her mouth. They twirled, turned, and touched to the rhythm of the music.

City sounds, softened by distance, echoed far below the open window, but the core of life existed only in this room, this instant, with this woman.

"You're beautiful, Lillian."

"I'll never forget you, Lincoln."

Her kisses held him like high voltage.

Dawn's quiet filled the room. Streaks of the rising sun slanted through the east window, suffusing the room with a brightness that nudged Lincoln awake as it did every morning. Eyes half open, he observed her and wished things could be different. She was a lovely thing. The best he'd ever had.

He left her sleeping and tiptoed to the bathroom, where a warm shower and a shave finished waking him. He slipped into a bathrobe and followed the beckoning aroma of coffee.

Filling a cup, he took a quick sip and settled into the oversized recliner. He picked up his day-planner and studied it. How was he supposed to do everything his secretary had scheduled for him? Carla was another one whose days were numbered if she didn't get it together.

First she had scheduled Katarina Kahill before he had even intended to get to the office today. Hmm...Katarina Kahill, now there was a classy lady. Who could forget those azure eyes that said "look but don't touch"?

And her sketches weren't bad either.

If the rest of her portfolio proved as good as what he'd seen at the convention, he would have no need to look further.

"What are you doing, Linc?" Lillian called from the bedroom.

"Nothing, Lil. Just having coffee and looking at my schedule."

"Well, get your sweet buns in here."

"Not now, Lil, I'm busy." *Why couldn't she act more like a lady?* "Don't you ever think about anything else?"

"You'll be sorry." She said more, but it was too muffled to decipher.

Lincoln slammed the schedule on his lap. "What?" he shouted and glanced out the window. "I can't hear you from in there."

Lillian appeared in the doorway. "I said...will I see you tonight?"

"I'm not sure."

"It's my birthday, Linc.! I'd like to make plans."

"And I've got a big day ahead of me. I don't know yet when I'll finish."

When I need her, I'd fight dragons to be with her, but when I don't need her, she won't go away.

He wanted to get on with the day's work. Even more, he wanted to get to the interview with Katarina Kahill.

Lillian showered and dressed in black leather slacks and a white silk blouse. At thirty-four, she stood tall and thin, sleek as a cat. Her eyes could buy the soul of almost any man.

She stood in front of the full-length mirror for a long time, letting thoughts she'd avoided wander through her mind. She'd seen Lincoln's schedule. Why was he interviewing Katarina Kahill and those others? Were they being considered for positions beneath her? She reflected on her performance over the last year and reached a sobering conclusion. She was being replaced.

Not long ago everything was perfect. What happened?

Reflections didn't lie. Her fingers touched crow's feet in the corners of her eyes, and laugh lines appeared deeper than she remembered. The figure in the mirror blurred from tears. It was over. Her days with Wolf International and nights with Lincoln were history. Everything was slipping away. Within days—weeks at the most—it would all be gone.

She covered her eyes to stop the tears. *Why couldn't he love me?* She'd been in tight places before, but never like this, never without hope.

When would he tell her?

In the kitchen she poured coffee. The penthouse suddenly felt cold, threatening its blanket of silence. She glided to the big picture window, passing Lincoln as though he weren't there. The platinum sun appeared over the New York skyline and illuminated the sadness in her ghostlike reflection. Never again would she look upon the mammoth city at sunrise from this room, maybe not from any room.

She turned from the window and caught him watching her. The pondering look, the frown, the way he sat there left her wanting to stop time and drown in his arms. She would have cried if he hadn't been watching. Her eyes met his for a brief, guarded moment and returned to her coffee cup.

"Will I see you tonight?" The question echoed between them, then sought refuge in the corners of the room.

He sighed. "Yes, Lil, tonight. We'll have dinner in the Harbor Room. Is that good?"

"That'll be nice. And don't worry, Linc. I understand," she lied. She didn't understand. How could he write her off like a tax deduction or worse, like last season's flop? She'd been good for him. She deserved better.

The goodbye is coming. It's just a matter of time.

Her years with him had been a mixture of agony and ecstasy. She never knew where she stood while he played around—until he came back to her. *No more.* She went to him and placed a soft kiss on his lips. It held no passion, no promise, just affection, warmth, and a touch of finality.

She hurried to the door and turned before he could move. "See you tonight, Linc, and thanks...thanks for everything."

Lillian rode the elevator to the ground floor and walked without purpose from the building. She squinted at the bright sky. The rapture of the autumn morning, the billowy white clouds rushing across the blue sky, the glow of the sun on skyscrapers—she would have enjoyed it all had she not been dying inside.

It was getting colder. The world blurred like her hopelessness, and she wondered about the names on Lincoln's calendar. Which one was coming in this morning? Ah, yes, Katarina Kahill. Was she the one?

Would Katarina Kahill succeed Lillian Rae as lead designer for Wolf International Fashions?

Would Katarina Kahill succeed Lillian Rae in Lincoln Wolf's life?

If so, what was left for her?

CHAPTER TEN

Kat's stomach high-jumped to her throat when her eyes swept the bold black lettering on the frosted glass door: *Wolf International Fashions.*

What an inopportune time to interview for lead designer just when she'd opened her new boutique. But she couldn't afford not to take advantage of it. She ran her damp palms down her skirt. Why so nervous? Because Lincoln Wolf blew the sides out of gorgeous, that was why.

She slipped her portfolio under her arm, turned the brass door handle, and entered. The secretary rose gracefully, standing on legs that went on and on. Kat's eyes followed her up...and up...and up. The model material leaned over the disarray of papers on her desk and extended her hand.

"Hello, I'm Carla. You're Ms. Kahill?"

"Yes. Katarina Kahill." She returned the redhead's smile. Carla was far too striking to waste away in this environment. Her classy knee length dress matched her eyes, and the scooped neck showed just enough cleavage to fry a normal healthy male.

Kat had chosen her outfit for the interview with great care. She wanted to look businesslike when she met Lincoln Wolf—prosperous, but not so much that she didn't have to work for a living. Carla made her wish her choice had been less conservative. A bit of cleavage here, some waistline there, and more leg, something like the sophisticated black and white suit she'd designed to turn the head of any man. But Dawson had warned her that Mr. Wolf might take advantage of her country girl innocence, as he called it; so far she'd complied. Her curve-concealing suit was impregnable. She should be safe from the most roving eyes. Just what she'd always wanted: safety from roving eyes.

"Follow me, please." Carla led the way to Lincoln Wolf's office. Kat imagined the secretary's hips swayed to counterbalance her bosom, or maybe she'd been taking modeling lessons. Carla spoke over her shoulder as they walked.

"Mr. Wolf telephoned and said he'd been detained. You're to make yourself comfortable."

Feeling like Tom Thumb beside the statuesque redhead, Kat nodded a thank you in response to Carla's gesture to take a seat in the black leather wingback chair. She laid her portfolio on the small table next to it and gazed around the well-appointed room. Neat rows of books sat on shelves that reached to the ceiling. She couldn't help but wonder whether these were meant to keep appointments occupied while they waited for the tardy Mr. Wolf.

"Would you like coffee or tea while you wait?" Carla asked.

A stiff brandy would be nice. "No, thank you. When do you expect him?"

Carla's long slender fingers with perfectly manicured nails fiddled with the pens and shuffled some papers around on the polished teak wood desk. Kat glanced at her own nails. *Not as long but just as pretty.*

"Soon. I'll be at my desk if you want anything."

"Thank you."

The large office, though neat and tasteful, offered little insight into the character of its primary occupant. An open beam ceiling complimented the furnishings, and the grass wall covering created texture and warmth. Still, Kat felt small in the room.

She chose the latest issue of *Cosmopolitan* from the table beside her. Thumbing through it, she stopped and stared at an advertisement of a woman sprawled on a couch, watching television and eating chocolates. Shaking her head, she looked again. The model could have been a double for her sister-in-law.

Kat sighed. What was Val up to? Daw'd been the best thing that ever happened to her, and she was too self-consumed to see it. Mentally ill or not, the woman had no excuse for her treatment of Dawson.

And she could forget Willow Walk. Daw would die before he gave her any part of the homestead.

Kat glanced at the clock; she'd been waiting almost half an hour. Was Mr. Wolf trying her patience? No way would she work for someone who had so little respect for her time. She picked up her portfolio and stepped into the reception room.

"Carla, I'm canceling today. Mr. Wolf can call me if he wants to reschedule."

"Oh, no!" Color drained from Carla's face as she jumped up. "Mr. Wolf will be terribly annoyed if you leave. Please, Ms. Kahill, I'm sure he won't be much longer."

Kat ignored the warning voice in her head. "I'll wait ten minutes more and no longer."

Carla ushered her back into the large office. On her way out, she closed the door behind her as though to keep Kat prisoner until the warden arrived.

She remained standing and looked around the room while the clock ticked the minutes away. A framed picture of a chic blonde sat on one corner of the desk, signed, *All my love forever, Lillian.* A yellow memo read, Call The Comfort House regarding Rebecca. The calendar was full of women's names, including her own.

Hanging on the wall across from the desk was a portrait of a stately gentleman, white haired, nineteen hundred vintage sideburns and a bushy mustache. His stern look reminded her of Granddad Jedediah.

After making her way around the room, she stood at the window and looked down on the sidewalks and streets of New York City. Buildings rose out of concrete and asphalt. Mother earth took a back seat to steel and mortar, leaving the green hills and valleys of home on the back roads of her mind.

She looked at her watch; it had been more than forty-five minutes. Mr. Wolf's credibility flew out the window. He knew she'd come all the way from West Virginia; to stand her up was inexcusable. He could have at least given his secretary an explanation. She'd heard that he used his looks and charisma to get his way. If he thought that would work on her, he had another think coming.

She snapped up her portfolio and reached for the doorknob. At the same moment the door swung open, slamming into the right side of her face and knocking her backward. Her purse fell to the floor, spilling its contents.

"Oh!" She pressed the heel of her palm against her throbbing eye and knelt on the plush carpet to return her belongs to her purse. From the corner of her other eye, she saw Lincoln Wolf stiffen.

"Ms. Kahill, I'm truly sorry. Are you all right?" He knelt beside her and helped with the pick up.

"Yes...considering that I've just been smacked in the face with a door."

"Carla!" Lincoln turned toward the reception area. "Bring some ice and a damp cloth."

"Never mind the ice. I was just leaving." She snapped her purse closed. "Making me wait, then bashing my head in—this *isn't* what I came here for, Mr. Wolf."

She lost her balance as they rose, and he grabbed her shoulders. Even though she knew his touch meant only to steady her, she became all the more aware of him. Struggling to turn off her stirring emotions, she realized she had been holding her breath as though this moment and this man were very important in some way she did not yet understand. They stood so close she felt like she could walk right into his eyes. A chill ran through her, or was it an icy-hot heat wave? She broke the moment and stepped back, turning her head to hide her blush from Mr. Wolf.

I must be dazed from the blow to my head. He hadn't had this effect on her at the convention.

Carla rushed in with ice wrapped in a wet towel. Lincoln took it and guided Kat to the chair. He nudged her down, covered her eye with the cloth, and pushed her head back.

"I'm...I'm all right, Mr. Wolf. Stop pushing on me." She stared at Lincoln with one good eye.

He continued to apologize, fumbling to keep the ice in the towel. His clumsiness made the situation almost amusing, like a little boy who didn't know quite how to help. He frowned and gave her control of the compress before seating himself at his desk.

"I can't tell you how sorry I am, Ms. Kahill. Carla said you were here, but I had no idea you were standing so close to the door. Believe me, I do apologize. I'll be happy to take you to the emergency room if you want."

"That won't be necessary. It's not *that* bad." Kat smiled to lighten the tension. She remembered Dawson's warning and stopped her smiling when he responded with a crooked grin. Turning stern, she borrowed on Granddad's strength. "Of course, I might be more forgiving if you tell me why I was kept waiting almost an hour without any explanation."

He leaned back in his leather chair, one eyebrow raised, and studied her. The little boy vanished. "I don't give explanations, Katrina, if I may call you by your first name, and I've already apologized. Now, if you are up to my viewing your sketches instead of analyzing my character, let's begin."

She removed the compress and glared at him. "Of course, and it's Kat-a-rina, not Katrina."

"Kat-a-rina then." Lincoln sighed. "Another blunder."

They stared at each other in a combat of wills. She finally looked off toward the bookshelves to break the intensity. Was he challenging her in some way?

She lifted the portfolio and spoke. "Mr. Wolf, my time is just as valuable as yours. I've traveled a long way for this interview." She read the expression on his face. *He thinks I'm too bold.*

His smile surprised her. "All right, your time is as valuable as mine. Lay your sketches on the desk, and we'll have a look."

Her hand trembled as she undid the clasp on the portfolio. She couldn't tell whether it was the bizarre situation, the man himself, or the idea of exhibiting her work. She removed the sketches and laid them on the desk.

"You've got talent," he murmured as he leafed through the sketches. "Some very unique designs here."

They spent the next hour viewing and discussing her layout. His politeness put her at ease until she remembered this man ruled in a world she knew little about.

He leaned back and rubbed his chin. "I like what I've seen so far. Leave your sketches with me. We'll discuss them in detail over dinner tomorrow night."

That's an order, not an invitation. He was much too presumptuous; but in her heart, she wasn't displeased. She answered with the same tenacity. "Sorry, Mr. Wolf. I'll be returning home tomorrow. I have a boutique to run."

"Very well. Tonight then. Eight for cocktails, dinner at nine, and please call me Lincoln. Where are you staying?"

"The Regency, room two-twenty-two. But I...I haven't..."

"I have a previous engagement, but it can be canceled." He closed the portfolio and gave her a devilish half grin. "It's more than your layout that impresses me."

Daw had been right. The name Wolf obviously fit his character, but he was howling up the wrong tree. His eyes danced as though he knew what she was thinking.

"I'm flattered, Mr. Wolf. I'll appreciate knowing something concrete this evening." Unable to keep from digging at him a bit, she added, "I try not to keep people waiting without a good reason."

Lincoln's eyes widened and he smiled that crooked grin. "I'll let you know."

She returned his smile and left.

"Thanks, Carla, for the compress," Kat said as she walked out the door.

What was it about Lincoln Wolf that put her on the defensive? Was it his amusement at her expense or that charming half smile? Instinctively, she'd wanted to rebuff him, even when he was pleasant and considerate. He gave her a headache, or maybe it was her eye. No matter which, he was responsible.

She refused to assign importance to unimportant things. Either he liked her designs or he didn't. Mama Suzanne would say she was being wishy-washy; one minute she didn't care about the position and the next she hoped to win it.

At the hotel, she decided a hot bath should put her in top condition for the evening sparring match with Mr. Wolf. She slipped out of her suit, looked in the mirror and gasped. Beneath her eye, a blue half-moon discolored the skin. She filled a washcloth with ice and lay down on the bed.

The blonde face in the frame on Lincoln's desk flashed past her and back again. She wondered if she'd been his date for the evening. What was her name? Lillian. Lillian with no last name. She'd heard that name before. Maybe at the convention or on the society page of the *New York Times*.

No matter. Whoever the blonde was had nothing to do with her.

CHAPTER ELEVEN

For years, she had left Lincoln's penthouse happy, smiling, content to be Lillian Rae, lead designer for Wolf International Fashions and mistress of its wealthy, handsome owner. Not today.

Her claws had bled more times than she could count as she climbed the ladder to the top. But she'd made it. She earned the position Lincoln offered her. And it had benefited them *both*.

Emerging from a dung heap of designer wannabes, she rose above them all. Oh, Lincoln Wolf was good all right, but even he had never trumped her. Now, stepping into the taxi and giving her address, she knew what it was like to be on the edge of losing. Leaning back in the seat, she closed her eyes.

I did my best, Lincoln, and you know it. You approved the designs for the show. Now you want to blame me because we came in second. What's wrong with this picture?

This business was a killer. Either you had it or you didn't. *Close* didn't count. Who cared that her designs placed first for four years straight? Or that she'd secured accounts for Wolf International that Lincoln never dreamed possible?

You seem to forget that I've kept you on top for almost half a decade. Don't I deserve a little credit for that? Or is your memory as short as your attention span for women?

She could almost hear his response. *I won't accept second best, Lillian. Not from you or anyone else. You've lost the edge. This won't work for Wolf International Fashions. I'm sorry.*

And he was right. She'd lost it.

But her dismissal would not be all her loss. She'd looked the other way when the tell-tale signs of his womanizing surfaced—lipstick on his shirt collar, perfume on his suits, a note from a lady in distress in his pocket. She never mentioned that she knew. And he always came back to her. But these indiscretions compared to the way he looked at her now—the lack of confidence in her, the indifference, the lost admiration for her expertise—couldn't be controlled with smart little female tricks. This was the grand finale.

She shuffled over the tiled steps to the front door of the apartment house. She used to feel fulfilled when coming home after being with Lincoln. Now her heart felt empty. It seemed she'd aged from thirty-three to ninety three overnight.

With one hand on the banister, she climbed the squeaky staircase to her apartment. No hurry. Nobody was waiting. She undressed just inside the bedroom, slipping into the warm and fuzzy terrycloth robe that should have been retired long ago.

A healthy glass of Chardonnay and a couple pain pills might ease this hurt in my heart. Anything's worth a try.

The wine sloshed in the glass as she opened the walk-in closet. The black gown, ageless, demure—sexy—would be perfect. And the color suited the occasion.

Lincoln was so predictable. He'd deliver a well-rehearsed dismissal followed by a hug, a pat on the rump, and an invitation to make love. Then he'd look away and refill the wine glass.

But she'd be one jump ahead of him, making the evening special, one he'd never forget. Some electrifying looks, special touches, and she'd be calm, cool, and lady-like—opposite her nature. He'd take notice and be thrown off guard.

She ambled through her large walk-in closet, brushing her hand across the fine silks and rich velvets, and sleek satins.

I've got so much to have so little.

Holding up the black sheath, she cast a critical eye over its classic lines and hung it back on the rack. The right choice for tonight had to be a different black number, Lincoln's favorite, the one she'd designed for the New Year's Eve dance last year that Lincoln called off, claiming a family crisis.

"Sorry, Lil. Can't make it tonight of all nights. Rebecca's sister is in the hospital. I'm sorry, baby. I love you."

A family emergency? Yeah, sure. More likely an irate wife...or an irate husband. Whatever the case, she never knew, didn't ask, didn't want to know. But for all the broken dates she'd endured, New Year's Eve included, he'd never missed her birthday, not in the years they'd known each other.

The sequined gown sparkled as she stood in front of the full-length mirror, holding it up to her. *This is nice.* She circled again—and again.

"Stand still," she heard herself saying, and all the while her legs kept moving, twirling, as though they needed practice for some journey yet to come.

"We'll have dinner, maybe a show afterwards, and the best part of the birthday celebration later."

Who was she fooling? If he didn't love her by now, he never would. It was time to move on to a new game.

"One more night and that's it. I don't need any more heartaches from you, Lincoln Wolf."

She laid her dress on the bed, smoothing it with her hand. Her forced smile faded into the tears she'd been holding back. They cascaded in a torrent down her face.

Don't do this to yourself, Lil. No man is worth it.

She walked over to the dresser and picked up the diamond bracelet he'd given her on her last birthday. Lying down on the bed, she held it up to the large crystal chandelier above her, envisioning that night. Prisms of reflected light bounced around the room.

Hold me, Lincoln. Hold me tight. Don't ever let me go. They'd swayed to the music, their feet barely moving.

The phone rang, jerking her out of her reverie. With reluctance bordering on apprehension, she reached for the receiver. Lincoln's voice greeted her even before she spoke.

"Hey, Lil, I meant to call you earlier, but...I got busy. You know how hectic this place is." He sounded rushed.

"I was getting some things together for tonight. What time will you be—"

"That's why I want to talk to you. Something has come up. I'm not going to make it, but we can celebrate tomorrow if that's okay with you?"

A scream rose in her throat. Tears wet her cheeks. She bit her tongue.

"Lil? Lil, are you there?"

"I'm here." Lillian's voice caught somewhere between her larynx and her mouth.

"Honey, I'm so sorry, but it can't be helped. There's this designer in town. She's leaving tomorrow, and it's essential we get together this evening. It means so much for the company. You understand, don't you?"

She swallowed angry words. "More than you know. Tell me something, Lincoln, and please be honest. Is this interview with someone who might replace me?"

"I'll tell you all about it tomorrow. I'm in a rush now."

"A simple yes or no will do. I have a right to know, and I don't want to wait until tomorrow."

"All right! I didn't want to do this now, but since you demand to hear it—yes. But don't worry. I thought you could assist—until you find something else. You know, show her the ropes...work with her."

"How nice. And when did you plan to tell me?" How dare he be so insensitive! Her palm itched to strike him. She could almost hear the sound the slap would make, exploding against his jaw.

"I don't have time to go over all this now, Lil. I said we'd discuss it tomorrow. I won't leave you out in the cold."

"Really?" She paused, placed her hand over the mouthpiece, and swallowed back tears of agony. "What about us?"

"Come on, Lil. We can still see each other. And you'll have *no* problem finding a new position. Not with your reputation."

"I see." Her breath rose to her throat and throttled any further words.

"I'm glad you're taking this well. I expected you to be angry."

She heard the smile in his voice, the smile that dealt a death blow to her heart.

"I'll do anything I can to help you and the company."

"Thanks, baby. I knew I could count on you. Now listen, we'll celebrate tomorrow, okay? I've got to go now. Talk to you later."

"Sure, Linc, maybe tomor—" The phone clicked in her ear.

She needed another glass of wine. A glass? She needed the whole bottle. No point in saving the Beringer 1997 that she'd planned for this special occasion. What could be more memorable than a celebration alone? She opened the bottle, filled her glass to the brim, and shuffled to the balcony off her bedroom. The old wicker rocker almost swallowed her, but comfort didn't matter. The evening gathered up the day, suffocating it. The moon and stars hung as silent eulogies to the death of dreams. Suspended in the past, she sat motionless for a long time. What she had, this life half built, now abandoned, was a shell that would never see completion.

Somewhere, sometime—he must have wanted me. If not, why did we begin?

Shivering, she forced herself to her feet and walked inside. Lincoln or no Lincoln, the night would not go to waste. She lit candles and filled the whirlpool tub with lilac scented water. Dropping her robe to the floor, she stepped into the warmth. How good it felt as she slid down. Resting her head against the bath pillow, she closed her eyes and let the water embrace her.

I know what makes a baby cry when it's born Her mouth turned up on one side. *It's leaving the safety and peace of the womb for the unknown world outside.* She would have been content to slip down into the water and never come up.

But it wasn't yet time. She lifted herself from the tub and dried. Maybe she'd go out on the town by herself. She sprayed her favorite cologne all over and slipped into her sequined gown. With meticulous care, she applied makeup and fastened the diamond bracelet. Looking in the mirror, she heard Lincoln's voice from yesterday. *You're beautiful, Lillian.*

If I'm so beautiful, Lincoln, why don't you love me?

She sat on the edge of the bed, swirling the wine around the bottom of the glass. The partial bottle of sleeping pills on the nightstand stared at her. Why not? Maybe it was time after all.

She poured the pills into her hand, popped them into her mouth, and washed them down with the last of the wine. Lying back on the bed, she closed her eyes. She had one reason for living, and now he was gone.

The room faded away, and she floated in space. She could feel their lips touching as his arms enfolded her. A bright tunnel of light appeared, drew them in like a whirlwind, and carried them down... down...down...

CHAPTER TWELVE

Kat slipped into a simple off-the-shoulder silk dress. Her trademark black cat earrings and necklace lay on her blemish-free skin. She piled her long black hair on top of her head and fiddled with two loose curls to frame her face.

Five till eight.

"Oh, my goodness," she said, checking her reflection in the mirror. The bruise that circled her eye couldn't be disguised with her makeup. With a chuckle, she put on the garish sunglasses she'd purchased that afternoon. They settled on her nose, giving her the look of a celebrity trying to dodge the paparazzi.

At eight o'clock sharp, Lincoln arrived. She smoothed a hair back into place, took a deep breath, and sashayed to the door. With slow, fluid movement she opened it.

"Good evening, Lincoln, come in."

He blinked. His jaw tightened, his gaze stuck on the sunglasses. "Should I extend sympathy, humor, or pretend not to notice?"

"It's not my place to tell you what to do." Kat turned and hid a smile. "I'll get my purse. It matches my eye."

His laughter followed her through the room, and the mood for the evening began on a friendly note. With a light step, she followed him to the waiting taxi. All the way to the restaurant, Kat fidgeted, her gaze leaping from one New York landmark to the next. She hardly noticed the small talk Lincoln made about the traffic, their reservations, and the weather. When they arrived at their destination, she slipped her sunglasses into her purse. Maybe people would think she'd smudged her eye make up.

Stranger things had happened.

Kat caught her breath as they entered the famous doors of '21' Club—a former speakeasy that now topped the list of New York's finest restaurants. Escorted into the soft light of the recently opened Upstairs at '21,' they were greeted by four murals depicting the seasons of New York in the mid nineteen-thirties. She struggled not to squeal with delight—to appear sophisticated rather than overwhelmed.

Distracted by such elegance, Kat forgot about her eye when the waiter approached. She wanted to ask him how long it took to become so well versed in the menu and wines but opted not to call attention to herself. He didn't seem to notice her eye, or maybe he was just being professional.

Her mouth turned up at the corners when Lincoln asked what she'd like to drink. She had never been much of a drinker. Even in college, when beer was the thing, she'd hated it.

"I'll have the same as you, please."

Lincoln ordered a First Growth Bordeaux from the wine list of more than thirteen hundred selections. When it arrived, she sipped and swallowed, letting its velvet smoothness stroke her throat all the way down. He ordered another and then another. Her tensions and her inhibitions melted away.

"You look lovely tonight, Katarina."

"Thank you." She lowered her eyes, not sure whether the blush came from his compliment or from the wine.

As their drinks went down, comfortable conversation came up. Candlelight and romantic music added to the ambiance, and everything fell into place, very different from the tension in the office. She couldn't wait to tell Dawson about Lincoln's impeccable conduct, the opposite of what her brother had predicted.

"What's going on in that beautiful head of yours, Kat?"

She realized she had been grinning. "Oh...just thinking about... this exquisite place," she answered, perusing the menu.

"If you don't have a preference, I'll order for you."

"Thank you. I have no preference."

He ordered two of the tasting menus. They included seven courses, and the business woman in her calculated quickly. The price would buy more than one-hundred-twenty hamburgers at a fast-food restaurant.

While their order was being prepared, she watched him watch her and waited for him to speak.

"I have what I hope will be good news for you, Katarina. I would like you to format my show this year. It will be hard work, but I think you can do it. The job is yours if you want it." He paused, glancing away and then back to her. "Your designs are simple, but elegant. They have the powerful quality I'm looking for. We can work out the details in the next week or two." He placed his hand over hers. Through flickering candlelight their eyes met. "Will you do it?"

For a moment she was speechless. The proposal caught her off guard. Worse yet, the touch of his hand made her weak. She wondered if he could hear her knees knocking together. Her lips shaped words and her tongue wedged them out. "I...I'm not usually tongue tied, but I don't know what to say."

"Say yes."

She loved his blue eyes, now enhanced by golden candlelight that made them appear an amazing green—Paris green, she thought.

They looked at each other in silence for a moment before she spoke again. "Yes...I will...and thank you, Lincoln."

She hadn't done one thing Dawson advised her to do—like checking Lincoln's background or being careful to protect herself from his charm. But tonight's excitement made it seem so unnecessary. Besides, she didn't want to spoil the magic of the moment.

Smiling that half smile that mesmerized her, he raised his glass. "May you and I together knock their collective blue-stockings off."

Unable to think of anything to add, she smiled and nodded. The idea of undertaking a project as monumental as an international show and spending time alone with *this* man shortened her breath and made her heart beat to a tune. He was a strong, all too compelling presence. The feeling unsettled her.

Over dinner they discussed details: salary, designs, time limits, her commute between the boutique and New York, and the general order of things. A thought came from the tiny voice inside her that sounded more like Dawson than her. *Had he brought his previous designer here, maybe to this same table?* If so, she bet the lady wasn't wearing sunglasses.

"Who was your designer before me?"

"Lillian Rae. For the last five years. She shouldn't have a problem finding a new position, of course one with less prestige, but that's business."

His voice hadn't changed, but a sting swept through her at the way he said it. Poor Lillian. She'd been booted out, rather ungraciously at that.

Lillian? Is that the "all my love forever" blonde in the photograph sitting on his desk?

"I see."

And I'm on the verge of stepping into this woman's shoes? Where will I be in five years? In a frame next to hers on that same desk?

She looked down at her plate. The heat of the moment dissipated as reality settled in.

Take it easy, girl.

Her left eyebrow went up, her heart dropped, and she fell back to earth.

CHAPTER THIRTEEN

"Ten-thousand for the show alone."

Did I hear him right?

"What do you say. Kat?"

"Well...I..."

"All right, twelve thousand for the show and seventy-five for a year's contract, plus fifteen for next year's show if we place first this year."

"Because of my boutique, I can't commit to a year."

"Last offer, Kat. Fifteen thousand to see us through the show, payable when it's over and we've taken first place. We'll discuss the future then."

"And if Wolf Fashions doesn't take first place?"

"With your designs, we will."

"That seems a bit presumptuous, don't you think?"

"I call it positive thinking."

"Fifteen thousand...payable when the show is over? And we'll have a contract, right?"

"That's right. Don't think you won't be earning it. I'm going to expect a *lot* from you."

He's going to expect more from me than my designs?

She caught her breath. "It's a *very* generous offer...as long as our relationship stays strictly business."

Why did I say that?

He gave her an unreadable look. "Do you think our relationship will be any thing *other* than business?"

"No...of course not. I didn't mean...I thought...I don't know what I thought." She deserved the embarrassment.

"If I ever want anything more from our relationship than business, you'll be the first to know." His eyes twinkled.

She felt like a precocious child who had been chastised.

"Would you like a cup of coffee, Kat? Or something cold to offset the rising temperature in here?"

She blushed.

Can I salvage at least a shred of my dignity?

"No...no thanks. Uh...uh...what do you think of this for starters?" She pulled a sketch from her portfolio and held it up in front of her face—a midnight blue gown and matching coat. "We could complement the long sheath with a silk chiffon overdress dusted with silver. I thought we could call it 'Starry Summer Night.' Maybe decorate the stage...the backdrop...with shades of navy blue and twinkling lights. An illuminated quarter moon could hang in the sky with a model sitting on it, swinging back and forth. What do you think?"

I hope he thinks it's a brilliant idea. I'll take a good anything at this point.

"Why are you holding the sketch pad in front of your face?"

"So you can see the drawing without any distractions." There she went again. Mouth engaged. Brain out to lunch.

She laid the sketch down and watched him walk around the desk toward her. Her blush deepened. He said nothing.

His light blue eyes couldn't disguise the great darkness behind them. In a flash, she understood it wasn't conceit that made him seem so superior; it was the control he exercised over *the people he owned*.

He bent over her, laying a hand on her shoulder. If he'd been any closer, she would have fainted.

Am I wrong to wonder if he's so close on purpose?

His unexpected look of approval caught her off guard.

"Perfect. I see the same thing. We'll go with it." He straightened and returned to his desk, leaving behind the subtle scent of his cologne.

In another hour Lincoln would be driving her to the airport. In one way she hated to leave; in another, she was eager to return with her exciting news.

So much had happened in such a short while. She'd been hired to lead the design team for one of the largest fashion designers in the country. She'd also made a pleasing impression on the owner, toured the city where glamour and fashion reigned, sported a black eye, and dined in New York City's most renowned restaurant—all in a day and a half and one fantastic night. The incredible, empowering experience made the boutique, the girls, and her brother seem worlds away.

Yet those worlds would meld. She couldn't wait to tell Dawson all that happened. Naturally, she'd leave the part out about not looking into Lincoln's background. Good grief! She hadn't had time to breathe, let alone check up on a man who gave her no reason to doubt his intentions. Dawson would just have to get used to the idea that she was a big girl now and could take care of herself. She smiled...like that would ever happen.

She and Lincoln reached the airport with thirty minutes to spare before she would go through security and disappear into the areas designated for passengers only. His presence felt awkward. She tried to listen to him, but she couldn't focus on his words.

Why am I having second thoughts? Am I doing the right thing to take this position?

The announcement interrupted her ruminations. "Flight 22 boarding at gate nine."

Lincoln looked so deep into her eyes she felt hypnotized. "Goodbye Kat." The tone implied far more than a simple goodbye. It perplexed her to think what she was thinking. "See you next week, but I won't like the wait." He extended his hand, and when she took it, he pulled her closer. She neither protested nor encouraged him. He brushed her lips with a sweet, gentle kiss.

"I...I'd...better go, Lincoln. I'll be in touch."

From her window seat Kat, studied the city while the plane ascended toward the white cathedral of cumulous clouds. Once above the cottony puffs, she drifted in a maze of her own thoughts.

Have I made the right decision?

She couldn't shake the misgivings from her mind. One thing for sure, the choice would benefit Bonny and Deb. By her being away from the boutique, they would have the chance to *manage*, to utilize their expertise, to be productive. But it was more than that.

Her attraction to Lincoln nagged at her. She'd manage the job, no problem, but could she manage him? His apparent need to exercise omniscient control worried her, and she shuddered. Why was he so good looking? So charming? Maybe she should tell him something came up and she couldn't take the position.

That wouldn't be fair to Bonny and Deb...or him...or her future plans for expansion, especially after the generous salary he'd offered. Besides, he'd behaved in a very professional manner—with the possible exception of the sweet but decidedly unbusiness-like kiss at the airport. On the other hand, she had made a fool of herself more than once.

And this black eye! The girls, she was sure, would believe the cockeyed truth of how it happened. But would Dawson? At least it didn't hurt much now—she was grateful for that—and it was fading. She smiled at the thought of the preposterous incident. Never in a million years would that happen again...she hoped.

Her plane landed in Pittsburgh a little after two, but by the time she drove home, showered, changed, and reached the boutique, it was five-thirty. Bonny and Deb hugged her neck. Snow White greeted her with the meow of a lioness.

"Kat, what happened to your eye? Were you mugged?" Bonny looked as though she expected a frightening tale of robbery in one of New York City's infamous dark alleys.

"Nothing that exciting," Kat confessed. "I ran into a door—or rather, the door ran into me."

Bonnie cast a doubtful look in her direction. "Uh-huh, sure."

"Come on, Kat. Let's sit down, and you tell us everything that happened, starting with that black eye." Deb said.

"I'll get us some wine. You hungry, Kat?" Bonny didn't wait for an answer. "I'll grab cheese and crackers...and don't start before I get back." She ran off to the lunchroom.

Snow White rubbed against Kat's leg, meowing her welcome home with the volume of an opera star. She reminded Kat of the days when Dawson pushed her on the tire swing, when she would reach her small hand toward the elusive kitten in the white cloud. What did it matter that Snow White was black? She was just as soft and sweet as that imaginary white kitten in the clouds.

She watched Bonny and Deb fidget while she told them all about New York and everything that had happened—except the part about Lincoln. After explaining the black eye incident to a chorus of chuckles and doubts, she talked about the sketches she'd presented.

"We *know* about your sketches," Bonny chided. "You did them here, remember? We want to hear about *Lincoln Wolf's etchings*. What's he like, Kat?"

Deb lifted her glass to take a sip. "Does he have a girlfriend?"

"Is he gorgeous?" Bonny waggled her eyebrows.

"Is he *married*?" Deb was the practical one.

Kat tried to keep the warmth rising up her neck from blossoming into a full-blown blush. "I swear, you two remind me of high school when you were dying for me to date Karl whatshisname."

Bonny grinned. "Oh, yeah, the big football hero. I can't believe you remember that guy with his cute backside and those—"

"Okay, enough!" Kat said. We're long past schoolgirl crushes and prom nights and—"

"And *what*?" Bonny asked.

"And Lincoln Wolf is absolutely g-o-r-g-e-o-u-s," Kat admitted.

The effusive ahhhs and ohhhs from Bonny and Deb scared Snow White, and she dashed under the sofa.

Kat changed the subject. "Did Dawson come in yesterday?"

Yeah, but he had to leave early. Got a call about a cow bogged down in the creek. Said he'd see you today sometime. Now there's a *real* dreamboat for you." Bonny said. Deb nodded in agreement.

"What am I going to do with you two? Now you're trying to seduce my *married* brother."

"About-to-be-divorced brother," Bonny reminded her with a bright smile and a glint in her eye.

"But not yet available," Kat said, not returning her smile. "So let's talk business. What happened here while I was gone?"

"Customers came in a steady stream, and tallied some fifty-five hundred dollars in sales. I'm coming in early tomorrow and change the window display."

"Already? The one we have seems to be working very well."

Bonny nodded. "Yes, and the next one will work even better."

Deb polished off a cheese-covered cracker. "I'll come early and help."

"Thanks. I'll have your Bloody Mary ready." Deb winked at Kat.

Bonny reached for another cracker. "You know I don't drink before dinner."

"Right, Bonny, but its dinnertime somewhere in the world."

They all laughed.

What enthusiasm! Deborah and Bonny had managed the shop with ease while she was in New York, and they could do it again. All she'd have to do is sketch new designs, specify fabric, color, and so forth, and send them to the dressmaker. The future looked brighter with each passing hour.

"If it's okay with you two, I'll head for home."

Kat wanted to phone Dawson before heading to bed, and her whirlwind trip to the Big Apple was catching up with her. It had been a long two days, and too much was happening too fast.

"Go ahead...and sleep in tomorrow if you want," Deb said.

"Yeah, everything's under control." Bonny agreed.

She hugged the girls and headed home. As soon as she arrived, she went straight to the phone and dialed Dawson's number.

"Did you get the cow unstuck?" she asked, trying to keep her wide smile from showing in her voice.

"Aw, Sis. Glad you're home. Sorry I didn't make it in today, but James and I had a time getting that stupid heifer out of the mud."

"Well...I've got lots to tell you, but not over the phone."

"Sounds serious. Is everything okay?"

"Everything's fine—better than fine—and I can't wait to see you. Seems I've been gone for months."

"Tell me right now. Did you get the job?"

"Sure did, but I'm too tired to talk about it. Can you come by tomorrow?"

"Be at your place first thing. Get some good sleep now."

"Daw?" She thought of her eye and wondered how he was going to take the explanation that sounded so phony.

"Yeah, Sis? What is it?"

She hesitated. "Oh...nothing. You'll see me in the morning."

"I'll be there in time for breakfast. I'll even cook it for you. You just have the coffee ready. Love you, Sis. Now go to bed."

"I'm going, I'm going. Goodnight, Daw."

She took a deep breath, and let it out in one big puff of doubtfulness. Walking over to her bedroom mirror, she looked at the still obvious shiner.

He'll never believe it.

CHAPTER FOURTEEN

This is the longest blasted red light in town.
If he hadn't been in a hurry to get to a phone, it would have been green or at least yellow when he approached. But *that* would have made things *too* easy. Lincoln's prickly mood lightened as he drove up the ramp of the high-rise parking area and took the elevator to his penthouse.

He pulled off his sports jacket as he hotfooted toward the phone on the bar. Slinging it on a bar stool, he dialed Lillian's number.

Where the devil was she? With the phone clutched between his neck and shoulder, he poured a brandy. But why worry? He didn't owe her anything.

With the cordless in one hand and his drink in the other, he walked to the plate glass window in the great room. Peering down at New York City's night lights reminded him of all the times he and Lillian had stood in this very spot, watching these same lights flicker like fire flies. He took a deep breath and exhaled.

Walking over to his recliner, he plopped down. Dostoevsky's *Crime and Punishment* that Lillian gave him found a home months before on the small round table next to his chair. The book had collected dust over countless weeks before he picked it up tonight. Turning to the first chapter, he shuddered slightly. He'd only heard what the book was about, but the title said it all and drove it home. *His* crime—of the moral variety. *His* punishment—long overdue.

His parents had used each other right up to the end. Their lives had been all about who could get the most, the quickest. They played the game of 'Gimme Gimme': hooray for me and the heck with you. The one who surpassed the other won the round. *I'm like Dad, I guess.* He knew no other way.

He dialed Lillian's apartment again. Still no answer. Something wasn't right.

The grandfather clock chimed midnight. She never stayed out past ten unless they were together.

Something's very wrong.

The strange way she'd reacted when he broke their date raced through his mind. Indifferent. Detached. No, something more. He could have understood tears and angry words, but the total lack of emotion was *not* like Lillian.

He looked up from his book, his jaw stiffening.

Oh, no!

Slamming his half finished drink on the end table, he dashed from the apartment.

Don't let it be what I think it is.

The Mercedes squealed to a halt in front of Lillian's apartment. He jumped from the car. His gut burned as he prayed he wasn't too late.

He took the stairs two at a time, not stopping to wait for the ancient elevator that creaked with age older than Methuselah .

So blasted many steps!

He banged on the door, cursing himself for not putting the key in his pocket. "Lillian? Open up, Lil."

Pressing his ear against it, he listened. Silence. She wasn't home. Or maybe she didn't hear. Again, he rang, knocked, and called her name.

Come on Lil, answer the door.

He fought to control his patience and the volume of his voice. He didn't need the neighbors itching to cause a scandal in the society pages...not now.

Try the doorknob, idiot.

She didn't usually leave it unlocked. The door opened. He stepped inside.

"Lillian? Are you here?"

His eyes adjusted to the room's darkness, and he saw the dim light shining beneath the closed bedroom door. He inched his way forward and pushed the door open. Lillian was asleep.

Asleep? No. *Not* asleep.

She never slept on her back...and in an evening gown?

"Lillian? Lil?"

A lifetime passed as he watched for some indication of life, a breath, a twitch of her hand or foot, *anything*. She lay too still. She was too pale. Fear like he'd never felt before coursed through him.

This couldn't be happening. He felt for her pulse, laid his head on her chest and listened for a heart beat. Finally, he heard something—more of a flutter than a beat.

The empty pill bottle lay on the floor. He had no idea how many she'd taken or how long ago.

Please let her live.

His mind raced and his hand shook as he picked up the receiver and dialed nine-one-one. One ring, then two.

How blasted long does it take them to answer?

"This is Lincoln Wolf. I have an overdose victim here. Hurry. She's..."

"Yes...and your name sir?"

"Lincoln Wolf. I already told you."

"What happened, Mr. Wolf."

"Any more questions I'll answer when you get here. The woman is dying, and you're asking me what happened?"

"Please stay calm, sir. Someone will be there shortly."

"And just how long is 'shortly'?" His hand tightened on the handset. "*Hurry*! If the woman dies, it'll be on your head for asking so many stupid questions."

He paced the floor, sat beside her, patted her hand. Talking to her, he tried with all his might to bring her back. Where the blazes were those medics? Maybe he'd given the wrong address. He sat rocking her in his arms.

Looking down at her, he realized she'd dressed to go out for the evening, for the dinner he'd promised her. The black sequined gown she wore made her body look bloodless.

She can't die. She has no right to die.

Blast her for making him feel guilty. He never wanted this. What she did with her life was *her* choice, *her* decision. He wasn't her keeper. She knew from the beginning he wouldn't tolerate a clinging vine. He would come and go as he pleased with no explanations. Just like his father had.

The doorbell rang. He laid her back down and flew across the dark living room to open it.

"Where have you guys been? She's in here."

Lincoln led the way to the bedroom. The medics worked over Lillian, administered an IV, asked Lincoln more questions, and finally lifted her onto a stretcher. Outside they hoisted her into the ambulance and closed the door.

The night hung dark—the sky starless—as Lincoln followed the racing vehicle to the private hospital where he'd asked that she be taken. Again, he prayed for a miracle. It had been many years since he'd prayed twice in a day or even twice in a year, but Lillian needed all the help she could get.

Except for occasional muffled cries punctuated by sirens delivering more poor souls to be patched up or cured—or to spend their final moments—the emergency room seemed deathly quiet. After waiting interminably, Lincoln made his way to the intensive care unit where he finally learned she'd been taken. He waited again, this time in a small room designated for family members of ICU patients. Finally, a man in green scrubs with a stethoscope hanging around his neck approached.

"I'm Dr. Fletcher. Are you the husband?"

"No, but she has no relatives. I...I'm all she has."

"Well, I'll be truthful with you, Mr...."

"Wolf. Lincoln Wolf."

"Mr. Wolf. We've done all we can. It's up to her now. If you'd been a few minutes later, you could have been too late. We don't normally allow non-family members to visit ICU patients, but you can see her since she has no one else. Maybe she'll respond to your presence. Five minutes. That's how long you can stay."

"Thank you, doctor."

The dim light above the bed cast an eerie glow on Lillian. Humming, beeping, hissing machines monitoring her motionless body and delivering oxygen formed a distinctly dissonant chorus.

He stood at the edge of the bed, conscious of her cold, unresponsive hand's dead weight in his warm one. He bent down and brushed her forehead with his lips.

The abominable snowman couldn't have been any whiter or colder. He felt like vomiting.

"Lillian, can you hear me? I'm here."

No response.

"Come on, darling, say something."

Nothing.

"I love you, Lil. I'm waiting for you to come back to me."

Silence.

"You'll have to leave now." The nurse standing at the end of the bed wasn't smiling.

"I'll wait outside."

"You can have five minutes every hour if you're still here."

"Every hour?" He looked at his watch. "I'll be here."

Throughout the night, nurses moved past the sitting room door. When he was with Lil, they hovered. While he was in the waiting area, they brought him coffee. By dawn the color began to return to her face, and her eyes opened. Lincoln smiled, breathing a sigh of relief.

"Thank goodness, Lillian, I'm here. How do you feel, sweetheart?"

But the eyes that had looked at him with devotion for the last five years stared past him, cold, hard as chiseled marble. She seemed unaware of his presence. Her eyelids fluttered and closed.

Lincoln called for the doctor, pacing the waiting room floor until the physician appeared. At first he droned on about tests that meant nothing to Lincoln. Then he put matters in simple lay terms.

"I've consulted with the neurologist. I'm afraid there isn't any easy way to say this. Ms. Rae's in a coma."

"But she opened her eyes," Lincoln argued.

"This happens, Mr. Wolf. It's not uncommon. A person will appear to regain consciousness for a moment and then slip deeper into the coma. I'm truly sorry."

"What are her chances?"

"Her chances have been significantly reduced because she was overdosed for such a long time before medical intervention. Fifty-fifty at the most, and that may be too optimistic."

"No better than that?"

"I wish I could be more positive. Let's wait and see. We'll be running more tests later. We'll do all we can."

"Thank you. If there's any question of payment—please—I'll assume responsibility for anything that isn't covered by her health insurance."

I can't afford any negative publicity about this. Wolf International will have a tough enough time getting back on top without being blamed for the demise of its former lead designer.

Doctor Fletcher patted him on the shoulder and left the room.

Lincoln returned to Lillian's bedside, hoping that maybe she could hear him despite her comatose state. "Baby, I'm so, so sorry. You don't deserve this."

And neither do I.

Seeing her like this sucked the energy right out of him. He turned and walked back to the waiting room.

What would happen to Lillian? She had no one but him. Her parents were dead; she had neither children nor siblings. And now she was in a coma, maybe dying. None of this had anything to do with him. Or did it?

She wouldn't be here if not for him.

Maybe he'd been ruthless at times, but how else did one get ahead? This affair with Lillian was never intended to be anything more than a brief encounter, like all his other affairs. But it hadn't been brief. For the last year, she'd been clinging to him, smothering him. He couldn't tolerate that. She had to go. Still, he could have celebrated with her one last time. He could have talked to her about the reasons for her replacement and given her another position. He could have done a lot of things. But he didn't.

No, he was true to himself if nothing else. He'd used her for his own gratification, which had been his one and *only* intent.

Neither Lillian nor Rebecca did he love. But one made him rich and the other quenched his sensual thirst.

Now maybe Katarina Kahill would pull him out of the trouble he knew was coming.

Ah, yes, Kat. That one was different. As lovely a woman as he'd ever met, she seemed totally unaware of her effect on a man. She might even have turned Dad's head and made him change his ways. She sure was making his son rethink some things.

Was it possible that true love would be his at last?

CHAPTER FIFTEEN

Granddad had hit the genius mark when he urged Dawson to move into Willow Walk's guesthouse and use it for a live-in office.

"Get away from that shrewish woman," he'd said, "who won't do diddly-squat to help herself."

Dawson smiled, remembering his tone. Granddad was right.

Not waiting for the coffee to finish dripping before he grabbed the pot handle and poured a mug, Dawson took a big swig and leaned his backside against the kitchen counter. He couldn't remember the last time it felt so good to be alive. His elation was no doubt due to the absence of Valorie's chocolate-dribbling mouth and her cruel accusations.

At long last, he could work on the designs he'd started in his last year of college. With a few finishing touches, they'd be complete, and he could start on his long overdue project. The rolling back portion of the acreage would be the perfect spot for a ski slope with a lodge on top of the hill. He'd once planned to subdivide and build spec houses—and he still would someday—but the lodge now fueled his creative fire.

One last obstacle had to be overcome, and he could proceed with the construction. Hannibal West, longtime friend and attorney for the Kahills, warned him at their last meeting: *"Whatever you do, Dawson, you mustn't alter, begin, or undo anything until the divorce is final."* Then he'd added the final incentive. *"If you don't do as I say, I may not be able to keep Willow Walk for you."*

Hannibal didn't say such things without good reason. Dawson had waited this long to pursue his dream; a few more weeks or months wouldn't make any difference.

He carried the cordless phone, coffee, and a bowl of fruit salad to the oak pedestal table and pulled a napkin from the holder to set his mug on so it wouldn't leave a water ring. Grandma Emma Kahill had hand finished it when she was the lady of Willow Walk. Her stern voice still hid in the corners of every room, haunting family members who even *thought* about going against her will. But her smile was as sweet as her rules were strict.

He had to call Kat. Since he couldn't make it over to fix her breakfast because he had a cow calving for the first time, he wanted to tell her about Cable's calling. She took longer than usual to answer, and when she did, she sounded sleepy. He grimaced. "Did I wake you?"

"Naw." He heard her noisy yawn. "Deb and Bonny suggested I sleep in this morning, so I did. I've been drinking orange juice and reading the *Times*. I tell you, Daw, I got my shock for the day. There's an article about Lillian Rae, Lincoln's ex-designer. She tried to commit suicide. And she did it while I was there, just a couple days ago."

"Tried?" News like that he didn't need, not with Kat prospecting work with the same company.

"She's still alive."

"Is the suicide related to her being replaced at Wolf International?" He couldn't believe Kat would consider taking the job under such circumstances.

"The paper doesn't say, but I suppose it *could* be. Lincoln said he was letting her go because she burned out."

She stopped speaking. For a moment he wondered what she was thinking.

"I guess it does make me a little uncomfortable, but it isn't connected to me, is it? How do I know that she wasn't dumped by a husband or a lover, and that caused her to try to end it all?"

Yeah, right. Make excuses rather than accept the obvious, Kat.

"So tell me how things went in New York, other than the suicide drama."

"They went well. Lincoln and I got off to an...unusual start. Then we were so pushed for time he suggested we talk over dinner. I didn't get much sleep."

"Didn't get much sleep?" Dawson frowned.

"It was a long evening and a short night. We had a fantastic dinner at '21' Club, the most wonderful wine, and then a carriage ride around the city till the wee hours of the morning. I love New York at night. I felt like a debutante." She laughed. He visualized her twirling around the room with the phone to her ear.

"Thought you said you went to dinner to discuss business?"

"We did discuss business. And he offered me the position, *if* I want it."

"*Do* you want it?"

"Of course I do. I wasn't sure at first, but now—"

"I guess you discussed business on the carriage ride, too? Funny, I thought you were happy with your *own* business."

"I *am* happy with my business. That's the main reason I want this job—to make contacts that will advance my clothing line and expand my boutiques in other areas. I'll be getting paid to learn the ins and outs of the business. The more I know, the better my boutiques. I guess in a way I'm using the position for *my* good."

"You don't think that's a conflict of interest?"

"I don't see how it could be. Lincoln knows I'm a designer and I market my designs through my boutique."

"You don't think he'll include a no competition clause in your contract with him?"

"Uh...he didn't mention anything like that." She cleared her throat. "Let's continue this conversation over lunch, providing your cow does her thing by noon."

"Okay, providing...but first I've something to tell you. Cable called while you were gone. He said Polly Dee wants to see us. Said there's something we should know."

"She wants to see us?" Kat paused. "That's strange. So...does this mean we go to Mexico, big brother?"

"Yeah, right. Just like that." He hesitated. "I'll pick you up at the boutique about one, and we'll talk about it."

"Okay, Daw. But please don't be a grump."

"Me? A grump? You know I'm never grumpy."

"Hmm, you sure didn't sound very thrilled about my exciting opportunity in the Big Apple."

"My problem isn't with the *Big Apple*; it's with a smaller one in that barrel that's rotten to the core."

"If you're talking about Lincoln Wolf, you're speaking out of turn, Dawson Kahill. He *always* treats me like a lady."

Dawson bit his tongue to keep from snapping back. What was going on? This wasn't the little sister he'd practically raised. *His* Kat would have been appalled at the suicide attempt of the woman whose position she was taking over. And she'd already have phoned that Wolf character and told him what he could do with his job.

"You're right, Kat. I don't know the man."

"That's right, Daw, you don't. I'll see you for lunch. Goodbye!"

The phone clicked in his ear before he could respond.

He poured more coffee and carried it to the bedroom. For the first time in his life, he wished he didn't care so much about Kat. She seemed determined to go her own way on this one, no matter what he said. Why couldn't she see that she was headed for disaster? Why didn't she realize that he was just trying to protect her?

Wolf's name fit him well if Dawson could believe the reports he'd read, but the man must have worn the proverbial sheep's clothing when Kat was around. She, on the other hand, was an innocent lamb being led to the slaughter.

He set his cup on the dresser and glanced in the mirror. The western jeans he wore were as black as the coffee and seemed a good choice with his red and white checked shirt. He took a second look, and his mouth dropped open. Was his memory playing tricks on him? Or had Polly Dee been wearing a red and white checked sundress the day Dawson pushed her and ran away? He shook the image from his mind and frowned at his reflection.

What could Polly want after all these years? Was it payback time for his leaving her hurt and bloody and scarred for life? Even more curious was why she included Kat.

Dawson needed to see her, to find out for himself what the situation was. Maybe he wanted this more than was wise; he had nothing to offer. No apologies, no excuses, no regrets. What would they talk about? It didn't matter. He had to see her. Whatever happened would...just happen.

Dawson pulled on his black boots and headed down the stairs to have mid-morning coffee with Granddad. They sat for several moments in companionable silence at the table by the window.

"Whatcha thinkin' 'bout, Sonny? That frown don't come naturally on your face, 'specially since you moved out of the big house."

Dawson sighed. "A little bit of everything, I guess. When Dad said Polly wanted to see us, it brought back memories I'd rather forget. I can still see Polly lying on the floor, blood all over her head and face, just as plain as the day it happened. I never should've left her; I was such a coward. But what bothers me even more is I can't seem to muster up any remorse over pushing her away from me."

"Don't be so hard on yourself, boy. You were thirteen. You did what you had to do." Granddad's big thumbs hooked into the suspenders of his overalls. He balanced the chair on two back legs. "What do you reckon Polly Dee wants to see you and Kat about?"

Was he imagining it, or did Granddad sound like he knew something he wasn't saying?

"I don't know. I thought maybe you'd have some idea."

"Dang, Sonny, you know Cable and I don't talk long enough to give each other a hello, goodbye, or kiss my butt. It's just as well. We'd likely kill each other." He gave Dawson a sad look. "My own son ain't nothin' to be proud of."

"Things were never right between you two." Whatever Granddad held against his only son, he kept a secret. "Dad told me after Polly left the hospital, they stayed together for a month. Then she was gone one day when he came home. No note, nothing."

"The girl was just a baby, only sixteen an' makin' a livin' off her good looks." He hesitated. "They must've got back in touch, bein' he's the one that called to ask if you'd see her."

"I guess so...but what if I hadn't shoved her that day? What if I'd fought her off, stood my ground, and waited for Dad to come home?"

Granddad gave Dawson a stern look. "What if she had overpowered you? What if your Dad took her side? Forget the what-ifs, Sonny." Granddad poured himself another coffee and took a sweet roll from the plate. "In a way I feel sorry for her though. Cable ought to be hogtied, takin' a girl three times younger than him. O' course, she's no prize, tryin' to seduce our boy, who was just a tadpole. Must be one of those nympho...nympho...whatever you call 'em."

"Nymphomaniac?"

"Yeah...one of those."

"Dad said he saw her years back, wearing a scarf over her face and with a kid in her arms. But she didn't see him."

"A kid, huh? Don't know nothin' 'bout that. I'm still wonderin' why she wants to see you and Kat."

"Maybe curiosity, or maybe to see if we've forgiven each other...I don't know." Dawson rose and set his empty cup in the sink. "Gotta go to the barn and check on that cow. If we have a calf, I'm going to the boutique and take Kat to lunch. See you later. And try to stay out of trouble while I'm gone."

"What fun is that? You think I'm an old man or somethin'? Tell Kitten I said howdy."

After watching the newborn calf trying to stand on wobbly legs, he backed his truck onto Willow Walk's private road and headed for the boutique.

Trees lining the narrow drive blazed with orange and gold; a gentle breeze blew through the cab's open windows. Across the valley, leftover patches of summer green accented autumn's colorful palette. Willow branches gleamed like sun on glass. Dawson gritted his teeth. Valorie would *never* get Willow Walk.

When he arrived at the boutique, Bonny was showing a girl a gray suit while Deb completed a sale at the register.

"Hi, Dawson." Deb waved. "Kat's making coffee in the lunch room, but wait a minute before you go in. I want to talk to you."

"What's up?"

"I...I don't think you want to...to see her." Deb stuttered and coughed. Bonny disappeared behind a rack of dresses.

"What?"

"I said, I think you *must* want to see her."

The conversation seemed to be going nowhere. "What's going on Deb?"

"Oh, hmm...well...it's something I've been meaning to talk to you about." Deb twisted her mouth in a peculiar fashion, tapped her fingers on the counter, and looked at him as though he were a dragon getting ready to spit fire. "You see, it's...well...it's like this. You know how honest Kat is all the time. You never have any reason to doubt her word, right? You know she really knows how to take care of herself, and...

"Get to the point, Deb."

"Nothing...nothing you'd understand. Oh...go ahead and look at her. I mean...go ahead and see her. You'll find out sooner or later."

"Thank you for permission to see my sister." He scratched his head and walked to the lunchroom.

"Hi. You still upset with me?"

She didn't answer. He walked up behind her and reached around to kiss her on the cheek. Out of the corner of his eye he saw a dark shadow.

"Turn around, Kat. You've got something on your face."

"In a minute. I'm busy."

"*Now*, please."

She turned toward him but didn't make eye contact. Somewhere between shock and fury, he blurted, "What on earth?"

"Now, Daw, don't get in an uproar. I can explain. It's like this..."

"I'll nail the jerk! I'll pulverize him! I'll—"

"Daw! Lincoln didn't do it. Not on purpose anyway."

"Did you say...*not on purpose*? *Why* are you defending him? I suppose you're going to tell me you ran into a door."

"Uh...not exactly...but close. Please listen, Daw. Stop assuming the worst."

"This'd better be good." He'd never known her to lie to him. "Does it hurt?"

"Not anymore. In fact, it never did hurt much. It just *looks* like it hurts. And the door ran into me."

"What!"

She filled him in, laughing as she finished.

"It's not funny, Sis. He could have killed you. Given you a concussion or put your eye out."

"It was an accident, Daw." She cocked her head to the side, stretching her neck to face him eye to eye. "An *accident*!"

The black eye story was too preposterous to be anything but the truth. "Well, I...you know I'm right to be concerned." He couldn't help himself. His grin escalated into a hearty laugh.

When they both regained their composure, she said, "The big thing is the fashion show." She walked to the table and sat down. He followed. "There's considerable money involved, not to mention the prestige. For Lincoln, it's his shot at regaining the top spot in the fashion world. For me, a small town girl, it's the opportunity of a lifetime."

"So?"

"What could I say but yes? *My* business will benefit enormously. And there's a ten thousand dollar bonus if Wolf International wins."

"Have you ever heard that when something sounds too good to be true, it usually is?"

"Give me a break, Daw. He *really* liked my designs. This is a win-win situation for both of us."

"Maybe so, Kat, but tell me, where's Lillian Rae now?"

"I...I don't know. Why do you ask?"

"I wonder if their relationship extended beyond business." He'd thought about this ever since she told him about the woman's suicide attempt, and he'd bet almost anything that they were.

"I can't believe you said that." She turned her head away, her black hear swishing over her shoulder, and then back again as she searched his eyes. "And how should I know? I didn't think to ask, but if Lincoln chose to mix business with pleasure, that's his business. Why are you so eager to dislike him? You know I have to leave in the morning for New York. We've so much to do for the show in so little time." She paused. "Will you take me to the airport?"

"You know I will, and to answer your question, I have my reasons for not liking Lincoln Wolf. The newest one is that black eye. It's a guy thing, and whether you like it or not, I know how guys think."

She shook her head. "You're just being contrary."

"Don't get in a tizzy." He wanted to protect her, not make her feel incapable of exercising good judgment.

"I'd think you were being a social bigot if I didn't know you better than that."

"Yeah? Have you fallen for him already?" He shouldn't have asked, but he wanted to know.

"I...I...it's none of your business, but since you asked, no, I haven't *fallen* for him. Why are you so argumentative today? Lincoln's interest in me...uh, my designs...is nothing more than business."

"Right!" He stomped to the refrigerator and grabbed an orange. "You're being naïve, Sis. I guarantee you that his interest in you—a newbie to the fashion field—extends beyond your drawings. Tell me, why do you think he's paying such big bucks to an unknown, untested designer? You're a beautiful woman, Kat. I would be willing to bet he's already made a pass at you."

"Nonsense." She hesitated. A touch of pink flushed her cheeks. "He was a perfect gentleman. You, on the other hand, sound like a jealous suitor."

Dawson's voice softened. "I'm *not* jealous. I don't want to see you hurt. I want you to be happy, but with the right person. You deserve that. So at least promise me you'll insist on the right to continue your own design business in your own name."

Kat put her arm around his waist while he peeled the orange. "I promise. Now let's not argue. If I want to leave the company after the show next month, I can. I haven't obligated myself beyond that time. So what do you say?" She grinned at him. "Are you happy for me?"

"Yeah, Sis, I am." Dawson glanced at her. "Just be careful. You're not used to that lifestyle, and I don't want him taking advantage of you. For all you know, he could be married, hiding a wife somewhere in the shadows."

"I'll be careful. I promise." She brightened. "I've been thinking..."

"Did it hurt?"

Kat laughed. "Stop it. I'm being serious."

Dawson grinned and popped an orange section into his mouth.

"Why don't you and I take a little vacation down Mexico way after the show is over? We could both use some rest and relaxation. And we could meet with Polly Dee. See what's on her mind. That wouldn't interfere with the court dates for you divorce, would it?"

"I don't think so. But I'll ask Hannibal."

"If he says okay, will you go?" Kat sounded anxious.

"I couldn't say no to you if I wanted to" He grinned and sat straight in the chair.

"It's settled then. We'll have a ball." The light above caught her hair, and it glimmered, black as a crow's wing. She hugged him and took his hand. "But I can't imagine what Polly Dee could want...especially with me."

He wasn't concerned about Polly Dee right now. He opened his mouth to speak, but when he looked at her, he couldn't put the fear he felt for her into words.

He had only to look at his sister as a woman, and he *knew* what Lincoln Wolf wanted.

CHAPTER SIXTEEN

"I'll get Willow Walk one way or another."

Valorie's threat hammered at Dawson. She wanted his soul and everything he owned. But Willow Walk was *his* heritage. She would never get it—not as long as he was alive.

He stood on the steps under the back door overhang and tugged off his muddy boots, dropping them in front of the big kitchen window. He removed his almost new shirt.

Darn! He stuck three fingers through the hole where the pocket used to be and dropped it on top of his boots. That's what he got for not changing clothes after he took Kat to the airport. He let his jeans fall around his ankles and stepped out. Dry autumn leaves rustled past his bare feet. The cool air invigorated him almost as much as skinny-dipping in Willow Creek. He glanced in the window; his near-naked reflection peered back at him. How ridiculous he looked, shivering in the chilly autumn breeze.

One mud hole in the creek filled, one new shirt ruined, and one brainless, highbred heifer out of harm's way for now. Maybe she'd redeem herself by winning the grand prize at next year's county fair. Prize money would buy a boatload of shirts, and a blue ribbon would buy statewide recognition and more. Cattle buyers traveled hundreds of miles for the best of the lot; that's what Dawson planned to give them.

Hannibal West had told him not to worry—no way could Valorie touch the estate, but Hannibal didn't know her. Dawson had learned the hard way. Valorie and the devil were bosom buddies. They sat in the same seat, drank from the same cup, and sang the same songs.

He showered, dressed, and raced to Hannibal's office for the deposition.

"Sorry I'm late, Hannibal, but I've got one stupid heifer that..." He looked around. "Where is everyone?"

"The deposition's been postponed, but—"

All that hurry and worry for nothing? "Why didn't you call me and save me a trip?"

"I wanted to talk to you about something equally important. Sit down, Dawson."

His gut told him he wasn't going to like it.

"Valorie's attorney made a proposal."

Dawson moved to the edge of his chair. "Go on."

"If you give her the house and a couple acres, she won't ask for anything more—money, stocks, bonds, or other—"

Dawson sprang to his feet. "She'll *never* get Willow Walk." Anger burned through his skin all the way to his midsection. He flexed his shoulders and looked back at Hannibal.

The attorney held up a hand as if to silence him. "Pour yourself a cup of coffee and calm down, Dawson. Over there." Hannibal nodded toward the coffee maker on the other side of the room. He waited for the man to return to his chair.

"You know my answer to that, Hannibal." Dawson took a deep breath. "Not one inch, not one cockeyed blade of grass from Willow Walk. Is that clear?" His voice boomed, echoing through the room and probably down the hallway.

"Relax, Dawson. I *know* you're not giving Willow Walk to anyone. I'm just relaying her proposal." Hannibal rose from his chair and leaned on his desktop. "You know I won't let that happen. I told her attorney to get off his duff and accept our offer, or they'll end up with nothing. I also told him his client had a serious mental disorder. He played a poker face on that one."

Dawson gulped the last of the hot coffee. It burned all the way down, but it couldn't match the rage that blazed within him.

Hannibal cast a no-nonsense look at Dawson.

"Valorie's got a darn good divorce attorney. The last thing we want to do is underestimate him." His dark brows arched. "Want to know what her response to our proposal was?" He didn't wait for Dawson to answer. "She laughed."

91

Dawson restrained his anger. "I guess we'll see who laughs last."

"Keep your cool and stay away from her, Dawson. Don't—and I can't stress this enough—*don't* get into a confrontation. If you want to keep Willow Walk, do as I say." Hannibal walked to the window.

Dawson sat back in the chair. His breath caught in his throat. The attorney's words slapped him with the realization that his heritage could, indeed, be in jeopardy if he didn't watch his step.

He took a deep breath and sighed. "I didn't mean to lose it. I'll back off and leave this mess in your hands."

"That's more like it. You've got a lot at stake, and I don't blame you for being concerned. Look...I'm no fortune teller, but take my word—she won't touch the land or the house. As far as your other assets...we'll see."

"Thanks, Hannibal. Just be careful. She's as cunning as she is crazy." Dawson frowned and shook his head.

"I've been doing this for years, and I've seen all kinds—some a lot worse than Valorie. And it's a rare case that I lose. The most important thing now is for you to watch everything you do until this is over. No girls, no night life—an occasional beer or Johnny Red in private is okay. You know the drill." Hannibal grinned. "I understand you're staying in the guest house at Willow Walk."

"Yes."

"Be a good boy and make my day—keep it that way." Hannibal pointed his finger at Dawson.

"Right."

Hannibal shook Dawson's hand and walked him to the door.

"Let me know about the deposition. And by the way..." Dawson smirked.

"What?"

"Try hitting that little white ball on your next golf game."

"Get outta here!"

He turned into the private drive, parking at the front entrance of the guest house and got out. Except for crickets and tree frogs, the late evening was quiet. A dim light shown in the kitchen window at the back of the main house—probably Valorie eating her weight in chocolates and planning her next move against him.

He stood for a moment and stared. The full moon brightened the clearing. She could plan all she wanted, but she'd never get her hands on Willow Walk. He'd see to that.

CHAPTER SEVENTEEN

"Where's the time gone? It's six o'clock, Linc."

Kat rubbed the back of her neck after placing the last of the sketches on his desk. Exhausted but pleased with her progress, she kept her gaze on the completed work—and away from the strong features of his face and the rest of him.

Show preparations were completed. She'd chosen colors, fabrics, and theme; as soon as he approved these, the last of the designs would be on the way to the dressmakers. Over the last month, she had managed to pull from herself more designs than she'd completed in half a year back home. The pressure, the excitement, and the opportunity seemed to have jumpstarted her creativity.

Creativity wasn't the only thing jumpstarted, thanks to Lincoln's constant presence.

As though sensing her thoughts, he looked up from a sketch of an evening gown and sent her an endearing grin. "You look ready for some relaxation. It's not very cold this evening. How about a walk in Central Park?"

She stretched and nodded. "Sounds wonderful."

When he stood, he towered over her. She felt the warmth, the passion, of his presence.

Get hold of yourself. This is the very thing you promised Dawson you'd avoid.

"Have you been to Central Park?" he asked as he wrapped a scarf around his neck and held her coat for her.

She shook her head. "I haven't had time. But I've always wanted to go."

"Well, tonight's the night, little lady."

Although her back was to him, she could hear the smile in his tone and felt a ridiculous grin spread across her own face. As they passed, Carla gave them a strange look. So what if she went for a walk with the boss? It wasn't as though she were going alone...to his penthouse...at night...for the whole night...

They stepped from the office into a busy city that buzzed with energy and entered the park at Sixty-fifth Street, walking past the Tavern on the Green. Central Park enchanted her.

"Except for my home town, I've never seen anything so... so captivating." The city suited her mood, dreamy and surreal. And as they wandered through the park, the magic escalated.

Lincoln took her elbow and gestured toward a bench. They sat under a maple tree, its branches sprawling above the path and into Sheep Meadow—a lush, green meadow that was once home to a flock of sheep and its shepherd. Kat could see for what seemed like miles of skyline. She drank in every inch of the scenery.

"Breathtaking!" She spoke more to herself than to him.

A boy and a girl nearby frolicked in a world of their own. Their giggles struck a familiar chord. She and Dawson had played like this in a place much less crowded. The boy displayed a dimpled smile just like Dawson's, and the girl wore long pigtails. She remembered how happy they'd been as children.

"Why so quiet, Kat?"

She shifted her weight on the bench but kept her gaze on the children. "I was just reminiscing."

"Must have been some memory. You were a long way off."

She smiled. "I was thinking about Dawson and me when we were kids. About the same ages as those over there."

"You and your brother are very close, aren't you?"

"I guess you could say that. He raised me with Granddad's help. We're half-brother and -sister, but I think you know that."

"No, I didn't."

"We have the same father, different mothers. Cable took Dawson and left Mama and me when I was six. Dawson was twelve. He ran away from our father and came home almost a year later."

"I see. Is Cable your dad?"

"My biological father, but he's never been my dad."

"I'm sorry, Kat. And your mother?"

"Mama died when I was twelve. I really don't know what I'd do without Dawson. He's everything to me."

"Everything? Don't you want a man to love and to love you? A home with children running around and a dog lying in front of the fireplace in winter?"

The question hung for a moment in mid-air.

"Someday maybe. I have plenty of time."

His face mirrored his tender intent. She looked away to break the intensity.

Gently, with one finger, he turned her face toward his. She stared into his imploring gaze for several seconds before his mouth met hers. His kiss burned into her blood. She held very still, eyes closed.

Please tell me this is right.

He pulled back. She could feel his eyes staring into her heart. He took her hand.

"It's getting late." He looked out beyond the naked trees. "Are you hungry?"

"I...I'm starved."

He smiled. "I know just the place."

When they reached the Tavern on the Green, Kat stopped and gazed around. The atmosphere sparkled. Every branch and trunk of the surrounding trees in the outside dining area twinkled with tiny white and blue lights—a city substitute of stars in the night. She felt as though she could stay here forever.

Through the meal they stuck to safe topics: talked shop, touched on local news, even the weather. She was grateful for the respite from the undercurrent flowing between them. Without a doubt, this had been a wonderful day, not what Dawson had warned her about at all. Dawson meant well, but he was wrong about Lincoln. Never could she call the man anything but a gentleman.

"Thank you for today. It's been fantastic, but tomorrow's another busy day." The meal, the champagne, and the long hours suddenly converged on her; she yawned into her napkin.

"It's been great for me, too. But we have many more coming."

His promise of a future filled with evenings like this stayed with her as they returned to the hotel. They entered the elevator and pressed the button for the twenty-second floor. Her heart was beating so loud that she was sure Lincoln could hear it. Her thoughts ran amuck. No matter which way she turned, she saw his face in front of her.

Please let me get through this night without doing something I'll regret later.

At the door, Kat said. "Thanks again, Lincoln, for a perfect day. I'll see you tomorrow."

He took her in his arms and kissed her soundly. Temptation weakened her knees. She straightened and pulled away.

"Kat," he whispered, releasing her, "I need to talk to you about something very important. May I come in for a minute?"

"I...I guess it'll be all right...but just for a minute."

Lincoln followed her into the room and walked over to the window overlooking the city. Kat took off her coat before meandering up beside him. Long moments of quiet passed as they stood studying the lights below. She turned from him and took a seat.

"What is it you wanted to talk about, Linc?"

He faced her. "I told you you'd be the first to know if I had any interest in you beyond business. I'm...I'm afraid I'm falling in love with you, Kat." He diverted his gaze away from her, then back again. "But I haven't always been proud of my past actions—much less my conduct—and I'm so afraid for you to know the truth. But...I want to change...for you."

The bewildered look that shadowed his face didn't compare to the confusion in her heart. She wasn't ready for this. And what mistakes in his past did he fear she would learn?

"I've been thinking," he continued.

She rose and stood beside him. "What are you trying to say?"

"Come away with me, Kat, after the show, win or lose. We need time to talk. I need you to understand. Please. We can go anywhere you like. You pick the location."

She turned away from those daring eyes and half grin that would undermine her determination and bit her tongue to keep from shouting her "yes" to the stars. Like ivy on a trellis, Lincoln crawled into her mind, and a vision of sandy beaches and moonlight threatened to destroy her good intentions.

Her heart murmured and her temperature rose. She felt his warm breath on her cheek.

Oh, my goodness, could this be love?

He must have felt her unspoken words. "What are you thinking?"

She took a deep breath and shushed her treacherous heart. "I can't go away with you, Linc. I know what would happen. I would want it to happen...but it can't."

Disappointment clouded his expression. "I know I'm not getting the words right; but every time I look at you, there's love inside me." He gave her that lopsided grin. "We've known each other such a short time, but I've never felt this way about a woman, *any* woman."

She stood frozen, staring into his tempting eyes, and then suddenly she was against him.

He sought her mouth with his own. She returned his kiss with all the passion that was in her before she pushed away. He let her go, and she sucked in gulps of air, trying to cool the fire within that threatened to break a promise she'd made years before.

Mama Suzanne's words echoed in her mind. *Save yourself for your husband on your wedding night, Kat. You have a special gift just for him, but it's a gift you can give only once. I know that sounds old-fashioned, but trust me on this one. If you do it, you'll never be sorry. If you don't, you'll regret it for the rest of your life.*

She remembered her response. *I promise, Mama. I won't ever do anything to make you or Granddad or Dawson ashamed of me.*

Mama Suzanne smiled. *This one you do for yourself, child, and for your husband. Not for anyone else.*

Kat took another deep breath. The fire flickered and went out. She wouldn't give in for anything less than the marrying kind of love, the kind that makes two people one, the kind she would share first on her wedding night.

Lincoln stood very still, never taking his eyes from hers.

She wrapped her arms around herself to reinforce her position. It didn't work. Each time she glanced at him, she weakened.

"Kat, I'm sorry. Only...when you're ready...and now, I think it's time for me to leave."

Kat saw him to the door. "Linc, don't give up on me...please. Give me time."

"I won't give up. Take all the time you need. Now get some rest. I'll pick you up in the morning. Another day should put us in good shape for the show."

He leaned closer. She thought he was going to take her in his arms again, but he didn't. Instead, he caressed her cheek with his finger and walked out the door, his footsteps fading down the hallway.

She wanted to stop him, came close to stopping him. Watching him round the corner, she felt an epiphany wash over her. The confusion lifted. She was ready to fall in love.

But with Lincoln?

Oh, she was attracted to him, all right. But the only thing she knew about him was that she *didn't* know enough.

CHAPTER EIGHTEEN

Lincoln wandered the streets of the big, cold city. Hands in his pockets, coat collar turned up, he bumped shoulders with strangers who knew those streets, who lived in the limbo there. He had wondered what it was like to return to this side of the tracks, but he never imagined he would find out.

Was he here where he didn't belong to empathize with the low life, the life he knew before he married Rebecca? He'd vowed to get ahead no matter what the cost, to never revisit his past. The price of that vow had been Rebecca's money. Lillian's body and soul had come as an unexpected but welcome bonus.

Now all that seemed of little value. Kat, without even knowing it, had shown him the real treasure, the one he'd never had but was willing to sacrifice everything else for.

Love.

Even if I win her love, she'll never accept me, especially when she learns the truth about Rebecca.

He shuffled along the littered sidewalk, lights and music from a nearby tavern reaching out to pull him in. Two bar stools stood empty; he squeezed onto one of them and eyeballed the bartender. The row of men and women sitting side by side could have been computer generated animations, the women looking as though they had nowhere else to go and the men staring into their beers or shot glasses. He peered into the huge mirror behind the bar and watched synchronized elbows raise glasses toward mouths. He lowered his gaze and shoved a filled ashtray away from him.

"What'll it be, fella?"

Lincoln looked up into the smiling face of a bartender whose gold front tooth dominated his features. He marveled. Staying alive in this neighborhood with all that gold flashing was a miracle.

"I'll have a brandy."

He sipped slowly, letting the liquid warm him all the way down.

His mind insisted on revisiting the past, the time when he'd been part of this not-so-wonderful side of New York. Despite the hard times he'd managed to keep his conscience clean and clear. That was before he climbed the social ladder, every infected rung of it. Back then, he had been one of the good guys. No more. And he didn't know how to get back there from where he was.

Money talks, his father had preached. *Unfortunately, Dad, it also corrupts. But you never learned that. And I learned it too late.*

After the fourth brandy—and after being approached by two prostitutes and a man with a Cocker Spaniel puppy hidden under his trench coat—he decided this place, the booze, the people weren't the answer.

The answer was simple, the attainment almost impossible. He needed Katarina Kahill. More than hope or money, wisdom or drink, he needed her love. His gut burning like a red-hot coal, he gave up the useless attempt to obliterate her from his brain and ambled back the way he'd come. Once in his car, he started for home. His trip into the past had accomplished nothing. He was no longer the man who had left behind the hopelessness of the streets for the glitz of the city.

Falling into bed, he allowed the black, timeless night to suck him in like quicksand.

The alarm clock buzzed. He woke up longing for Kat. While he shaved and showered, he planned. This morning, before Kat boarded the plane for home, he'd tell her again how much he loved her. Later, he'd divulge his sordid past and hope she'd understand. What else could he do?

Kat rambled on and on about the show on the drive to the airport. He listened but didn't hear very much. She was saying something about "...if the stars don't twinkle..." and "...colors are perfect..." Instead of paying attention, he searched for what to say and how to say it.

The hustle and bustle of people and luggage carts and loud speakers killed his hopes. Wrong time...wrong place.

She looked toward the security gate and back to him, lowering her head as though she wanted to say something. He had no idea what it could be.

When it came time to go, he tucked a knuckle under her chin and lifted it until she looked straight into his eyes. He bent to kiss her. The rosy blush of her perfect complexion and the scent of her perfume set his yearning heart ablaze. She returned his kiss, then backed away and looked at him.

"If you need anything while I'm away, Linc, give me a call." She ran her forefinger along the line of his jaw.

Need anything? That's an understatement.

"I will. Take care of yourself. I...I'll be waiting." It was the wrong time to say I love you.

She boarded the plane. Once again she was leaving one life for another as she had done often in the last months.

Resting against the seat, she allowed the show to fill her mind—with Lincoln as the main attraction—yet something was missing. A void nagged at the edges of her consciousness. She escaped her thoughts by falling asleep, waking when the stewardess touched her shoulder after the plane landed.

She walked into the afternoon's unexpected warmth, welcoming its temporary respite from the season's chill. Gliding in and out of clouds, the sun splashed the barren hills with hints of gold.

Coming home always felt better than leaving, even more now than before. She loved every inch of this country, and two weeks seemed much too short a time before returning to New York. But then she'd have only three days to tie up loose ends before the early January show.

The first week flew by, and she caught up on everything at the boutique. She began the second week by spending time with Dawson, Deb, and Bonny.

With just a few days left, she treated herself to sleeping in on a Wednesday morning, something she hadn't done in years. The ringing telephone roused her from pleasant dreams of her childhood after Daw's return from Mexico.

"Sure is good to hear your voice. I was wondering if you're ready for the big day?"

"Oh, Linc, hello. Yes, I'm looking forward to it. Is everything in order?"

"I believe so. Any chance of your coming back early?"

"Not this time. I'm...I'm catching up on things here, but don't worry, I'll be there as planned."

"I miss you. I'm counting the days. Take care, Kat, and know that I'm thinking of you every minute."

"Uh...me, too. I'll see you soon."

In a way she missed him, too. But the distance had somehow become more comfortable than the closeness.

Kat retired to the porch glider at the old homestead where she still lived, waving to Dawson as he pulled up in the drive. He came often to visit, and she prepared the meals he had liked best when they were growing up.

"Hey, big brother."

"Sure smells good." He sniffed the aromas wafting from the kitchen as they walked inside. Slipping out of his jacket, he hung it on the old hall tree.

After supper they sat in front of the fireplace.

The afternoon sunshine that had given way to a gray, drowsy rain with hints of sleet made the fireplace feel even cozier.

Dawson stretched his legs and smiled. "I made our reservations for January twenty-second. Will you be able to get away then?"

"Sounds perfect. I can't wait to get my hands on those gorgeous gauzes and cottons I can't get here in the States. I phoned a shop down there to let them know I'm a designer and want to consider their fabrics for my new line. I got the owner's home number in case they're closed when we get there."

"Great. Hannibal said, because of the divorce, it would be better if it looked like a business trip, something I'd be helping you with."

"It'll be the truth. I do need your help."

Dawson walked over to the window and looked across the meadow. She followed his gaze. The sleet had turned to a down-like snow, which was leaving a white blanket across the ground.

"I've been trying to reach Dad, but so far, no luck. I was supposed to let him know if we'd be willing to see Polly so he could set up the meeting. But you know Dad. I'm not surprised he's not home. He probably worked to save up enough money to blow on what he calls a vacation." Dawson shrugged.

"We still have plenty time to contact him before we leave."

Dawson nodded. "So how did it go with your new boyfriend?"

"He's not my boyfriend, Daw!" She drew a deep breath. "I appreciate your concern, but I think you're being obsessive. Linc treats me with the utmost respect. I like him. In fact, I more than like him."

She looked away, wishing she'd kept that to herself.

"You can't be serious, Kat. There's something dishonest about this guy, and I aim to find out what it is. You're jumping into something you know nothing about."

"Talk about jumping *into* something. You know less about the man than I do. You've never even met him. How can you judge him that way?" Kat stiffened.

Dawson pressed his lips together, then relaxed them. "I'm surprised you haven't been keeping up with the society pages. His picture's plastered all over. You know who's on his arm in those photos? That Lillian woman, the designer you replaced. The one who tried to kill herself. Do you think I want you involved with a guy like that?"

Kat covered her surprise. "The pictures were probably taken during a show. Please, I don't want to talk about this any longer. It's been a thorn in our sides ever since I applied for the job. He's a prominent man in the industry. He's bound to be photographed with attractive women, and bound to have attractive women hanging on his arm. I understand that. Why can't you?"

"I don't care about his women as long as they don't include a pretty black-haired lady who happens to be my sister."

He had always been protective. In the past she had appreciated it. "I do understand how you feel, and I promise to be careful."

After several moments, Dawson spoke up. "I'm sorry. I just...I can't explain how I feel."

"I know. I feel the same. If we weren't years apart, I'd swear we could be twins."

Dawson covered her hand with his, engulfing it. "You're too darn sweet."

And you, dear brother, are too argumentative. She smiled and looked straight at him. "Daw?"

"Yes."

"Please take care of yourself while I'm in New York."

"I'll be fine. You're the one we should both be worrying about. If you want me to go with you, you know I will."

"I know. But it's best I go alone." She smiled. "How about some hot chocolate? I picked up a bag of those little marshmallows we loved as kids."

"No thanks. I'd better get going. I've got to hibernate with five pounds of coffee and find an error somewhere in my books. Hannibal says they'd better be in order before the divorce. If I don't see you before you leave, I'll see you as soon as you get back. Remember, I love you." He hugged Kat and gave her a peck on the cheek. Half way to his truck, he turned and blew a butterfly kiss. She caught it and blew one back.

An error in the books? That doesn't sound like Daw. He's a math whiz.

He wasn't fooling her. The man was up to something. She watched the truck until it was out of sight.

The maple trees stretched naked arms against the sky. In a few months they'd wear new green outfits, but now the soft snow had robed them in white. They stood silent in the peaceful night.

The same air of quiet prevailed within her. Like the trees, she stood against the night. Dawson's words sang in her ears.

You're too darn sweet.

CHAPTER NINETEEN

Dawson flew to New York, the name of a private investigator scribbled on the back of Hannibal's business card tucked in his wallet. He signed the register at the hotel, picked up his room key, and went directly to the elevator.

The room was far from fancy, but it looked comfortable and clean. He sat on the bed, read the name on the card—Benny Bryant—and dialed his number.

"Bryant here."

"Mr. Bryant, this is Dawson Kahill. Hannibal West gave me your name and number."

"Hannibal? Well, how's the old boy doing? Haven't heard from him since our last golf game. Probably 'cause he lost." The voice boomed, and Dawson held the phone away from his ear.

"He's doing fine, but I need some help."

"What sort of help?"

"Some information about a certain man in town."

"What's his name?"

"Lincoln Wolf, owner of Wolf International Fashions. I just need a brief run down on his background. Nothing in depth."

"You've come to the right man. I know one thing without even leaving this chair...well...I won't go into that. Maybe you better come to the office where we can talk. I have a couple hours open right now."

"I'll be there shortly."

Dawson took a taxi to Bryant's office in an old tenement neighborhood. Symmetrical brick buildings, which once housed waves of immigrants, stood against each other. Now they were being renovated. A few residents remained, Benny among them. An ancient—probably homeless—man slept on the doorstep. Dawson wondered whether he was in the right place.

Stepping over the old man, he entered the dim hallway that led past several doors on both sides. Sheets of plastic hung from the ceiling to separate construction areas from those accessible to the public. At the end of the hall, on the right, he found Benny Bryant's office. He knocked, then turned the knob.

"Mr. Bryant?"

"Come on in," a voice replied from somewhere in the shadows of the dingy room. "You Dawson Kahill?"

"Yes."

Dawson's eyes darted around the room. Benny's office looked like an overstuffed storage unit. If not for the cigar smoke swirling upward above the boxes and papers piled on the desk and around the room, Dawson wouldn't have found the man.

"Pull up a chair, Mr. Kahill."

A yellow cat occupied the only chair in the office. Dawson nudged the feline. It growled like a dog and took a swipe at him before jumping down and running under the desk.

"Don't mind Hotshot; she's a rat killer." Benny laughed. "Saves me money on cat food and mouse traps. Move that chair over here where I can see you. Now what do you want to know about this Wolf man?"

"Just basic background. Married, single, business dealings, you know, the regular."

"Okay. Give me a day or so." Feet on a small clear spot on his desk, he leaned back in his large chair and looked Dawson square in the eye, his bushy eyebrows furrowing up and down. "This guy running around with your wife?"

Dawson suppressed a grin. Benny was obviously sharper than his surroundings suggested. "It's about my sister—"

"Sure, they all have sisters. That story is as old as Dick Tracy. But don't matter to me."

"I only have until tomorrow, Mr. Bryant, so 'a day or so' doesn't work very well for me. I know it's short notice, but I'll pay extra—whatever that may be."

"Fee's two hundred a day, plus expenses for footwork. For the kind of stuff Hannibal has me do, which is mostly assets checks, I charge a flat fee of fifty bucks plus whatever the service bureau charges. Usually comes out to seventy-five or a hundred total. Add another fifty for a legal profile; double that for an all-states check. Don't need to pay more'n that."

"Do as much as you can by noon tomorrow, and we'll see where we stand. I got a plane to catch."

"Right. Three o'clock work for you?" Benny flopped his feet on the floor and the cat jumped in his lap. "Stupid cat loves me."

"What's not to love?" Dawson grinned. He could understand why Hotshot was so plump. The office must have harbored mice galore. "Three's great. I don't have to be at the airport till seven-thirty." He liked Benny despite the shabby surroundings. *The man's smart like a fox.* He stood and held out his hand.

When Benny rose, Hotshot jumped off his lap and shot behind a file cabinet, leaving behind snags in his owner's pants. Benny grimaced. "One of these days I'm gonna have that darn cat de-clawed and throw her to the mice."

Dawson laughed, doubting the feline was in any danger. Only then did he realize that Benny Bryant couldn't be taller than five feet. But if Hannibal's glowing recommendation was even close to accurate, the man was ten feet tall when it came to producing results.

He recalled Hannibal's parting words: *Benny's not a typical New Yorker. Dealing with him is sort of...well...like dealing with Sherlock Holms while observing Watson.*

"See you tomorrow," Dawson said.

"Where you staying, Kahill?" Finding a pen but no paper, he jotted down the hotel on a section of the blotter along with a hundred other notes. "Got it."

Dawson walked out, leaving Benny behind his mountains of clutter. Outside, with his hand still on the doorknob, he stopped and rolled his eyes upward. *Only in New York...*

He spent the rest of the day and a sizeable wad of bills cruising the area in a taxi. They passed the building where Lincoln worked, then took in some of the city sights. He thought about visiting that designer, Lillian Rae, but decided against it. What would he say to her?

Besides, he had no idea where she resided...or whether she was out of the hospital...or even whether she had survived her suicide attempt.

"I'd like to drive by Lincoln Wolf's home," Dawson said to the cab driver. "But I'm not sure where that is. I didn't find his address or number in the phone book."

"Sure. And you can call me Mel. Most of us cabbies know the 'Wolf man.'" Mel hee-hawed, and Dawson grinned. "He's got two places. A penthouse downtown and a mansion called Winslow House. He rarely drives himself around in that Mercedes of his. Takes taxies a lot of times. Which one you wanna see?"

"Winslow House? I wasn't aware he had two places of residence."

"Oh, yeah! He comes and goes between the two. You're not on some kind of vendetta or somethin', are ya? I can't afford no trouble."

"Nothing like that. I just want to be sure he's on the up and up for reasons of my own."

"I doubt we can get in 'cause it's a private drive. You realize how big that place is?"

"Drive by and we'll see." Dawson's determination to get a glimpse of the mansion mushroomed, and he had time to waste.

Mel slowed at the gate. "Wow. This gate ain't usually open. Wanna drive in? He's a very private guy even though he's in the limelight a lot."

"Sure. Why not? You can always say you took the wrong drive if anyone asks."

"Not necessary. Taxies come and go through here all the time. But we have to announce ourselves, and then the gate opens. You know, one of those fancy communication things."

Dawson nodded. "Figures."

Mel turned to the right and entered the drive to the house. The Victorian mansion dwarfed the small buildings around it.

"That building over there must be the guesthouse," Dawson said.

Mel hee-hawed again. "Naw. That's the quarters for the servants. I think the guest house is on the other side." He pointed to the east end of the house.

They drove around the circular drive but didn't stop.

"Totally different, Mel, from the big farmhouses around Wheeling."

"Wheeling? Where's that? "

"The panhandle of West Virginia."

"Oh, yeah, I knew that—and I bet they're more comfortable and friendly than this place could ever hope to be."

Mel was right. Winslow House was magnificent. Grandeur and European sophistication reigned, but it lacked the quiet charm Willow Walk offered.

"Seen all you want to see?" Mel asked.

"Yes. Some place, isn't it? Does he live here all alone?"

"Don't know m'self, but the grape vine has it his visitor is one particular blonde who comes and goes through these gates a lot. That'd be Lillian Rae, his lead designer. Brought her here myself a few times. She tried to do herself in not long ago."

So it does have something to do with Wolf.

"I'm ready to call it a day, Mel."

They arrived at the hotel. Dawson added a generous tip to the fare, handing the driver several bills. "Take it easy."

Mel counted the money and smiled appreciatively. "I'll do that. Might see you tomorrow if you're still here and needin' another ride around."

Dawson went to his room and ordered a pizza, chowing it down while he watched the evening news and then a movie. In a way, he wished he hadn't started checking on Lincoln. If Kat found out, she'd be boiling mad. But he needed to know for his own good as well as hers. Guessing about Lincoln's credibility wasn't good enough. Following his gut instincts, he was driven to learn the facts.

At three o'clock he arrived at Benny's office.

"Sit down," Benny said, "Coffee, Kahill, or maybe something stronger?" Dawson shook his head. "Well, I got as much as I could in the time you gave me." Benny smiled and leaned back in his chair. Hotshot jumped up in his lap.

"Just tell me what you've got, Benny."

"You betcha. Wolf has a wife named Rebecca—maiden name Winslow—who owned a huge estate called Winslow House. Wolf somehow got her to sign it over to him, and that was the end of her ancestral heritage."

"A wife? I knew I was right." Dawson's stomach churned. If he could've wrung Lincoln's neck and gotten by with it, he would've.

"That's what I said. She's been sick for years. Couldn't find out an exact diagnosis on such short notice. Seems to be some drug addiction there, too. Wolf apparently got her to sign *everything* she owned over to him. Wouldn't doubt if he was the cause of the drugs. But that's pure speculation. Know what I'm saying?"

"You mean Wolf has something to do with her drug addiction?"

"That's the scuttlebutt on the street. I get lots of useful info living in tenement housing. May look shabby, but it pays big dividends. Anyway, Wolf first put her in Oaks Mental Institute, then moved her to The Comfort House, one of those hoity-toity places rich people stay when a hospital isn't good enough."

Dawson jumped from the chair and paced the floor. "Are you sure this is true?"

"Look, Kahill," Benny hesitated, giving Dawson just enough time to realize he'd said the wrong thing. "I'm speaking English. If you doubt my word, get yourself another eye."

Dawson inclined his head by way of apology and allowed his voice to become gentle. "No, no, sorry. I'd expected something—just not *something like this*."

"Yeah, well..." Benny took a swig of coffee and puffed on a cigar. "That's not all. Here's the weird part. Mrs. Wolf is kept separate from the others, and there's a private doctor who's seeing her. He's not one of the staff. Very weird set up." Benny drew a blank look and stared at the wall across the room. "Very weird," he repeated. "I spent some of your money talking to the people over there. They think something stinks. Every time Mrs. Wolf's husband leaves, her blood pressure shoots way up, and she gets delusional. You keep that part under your hat, Kahill. I don't want anything bad bleeding back"

"Don't worry. I never heard it from you."

"Something else strange—Wolf gets her released periodically. So she's in and out. And, oh yes, he maintains a penthouse here in the city. It's worth a couple mil. I got the address if you want it. One more thing, it seems he owes the IRS a good amount of back taxes. My contact isn't available to pursue that till next week, but I'll do it then if you give me the go-ahead."

"Won't be necessary. I know enough to know I don't want him anywhere near my sister—and she really *is* my sister—but if I change my mind, I'll let you know." Dawson gritted his teeth and held a hand over his fist.

"Kahill? You okay?" Benny regarded him with concern.

"Yeah, I'm okay"

Benny stubbed his inch long cigar out and lit another. "Want one?" He held the box out to Dawson.

"No thanks."

Dawson pulled out three one hundred dollar bills and handed them over. "Thanks again, you did a fantastic job in such a short time."

"That's not necessary, Kahill. I asked for two hundred."

"I know, but you deserve more. Just smile and say thanks. I'll look you up if I'm ever again in need of a good private eye."

"Well...I can get more if you ever want more. Thanks for coming. I appreciate your business. And tell that old buzzard, Hannibal, to give me a call. Tell him if he can't see that little ol' white ball any better than he used to, I'll beat the pants off him again." Benny's laughter bounced around the room.

Dawson left Benny just like he found him, behind the stack of papers and boxes and smoke.

He jumped in the cab at the curb, closed the door, and leaned back on the seat, knowing exactly what he had to do.

"Where to Buddy?" the cabby said, looking over his right shoulder.

"Wolf International Fashions."

Dawson clenched and unclenched his fists as the taxi brought him ever closer. Just one wrong word, he thought, staring out the window, and I'll wallop the tar out of the dog. Kat likely wouldn't understand, no matter what he said. Either way, a big hurt awaited her. That alone infuriated him.

He had taken a chance that Lincoln would be in his office to receive his surprise visit. A smile crossed his face at the thought of the shocked look on the man's face when he made his neither short nor sweet demand that he'd better inform Kat about his wife and his other misdeeds.

The taxi stopped. Dawson hustled through the rotating door and into the elevator. Normally, he climbed stairs, but not today. Punching in floor seven, he watched the numbers climb.

When the elevator stopped, he stepped out, following the arrow that pointed in the direction of Wolf's office until he stood in front of the firm's frosted glass doors. He'd be as coolheaded as possible. With his divorce in process, he couldn't risk an encounter with the law. Valorie would do legal handsprings. Any loss of control on his part could support her fraudulent abuse claims and give her credibility in her fight to get Willow Walk.

He paused at the door. Mouth set firm and eyes narrowed, he studied the lettering on the glass. Sheer energy charged through him, igniting every fiber of his being. He stopped.

Don't go there, Daw, a voice inside him whispered. *A wise man thinks before he acts.*

His clobbering Lincoln might backfire. Kat had always sided with the underdog. He didn't dare give the man that edge.

So what am I doing here?

Dawson took a deep breath and counted to ten. Turning, he walked away. Outside, he haled a taxi to take him back to the hotel.

Kat would learn the truth—he hoped from Lincoln. She'd take it better that way. Meanwhile, he could plant a seed in her mind that might lead her to ask the right questions.

Why couldn't he walk away and let Kat take care of herself. She was a grown woman. But he couldn't...and he wasn't sure why.

He pounded his fist into his hand. With a couple hours to spare before heading for the airport, he stopped in the hotel lounge for an equalizer to counter his anger. He seldom drank, but for the last few weeks he'd made more than an occasional exception.

"I'll have a brandy," he told the bartender.

Kat would depart for New York an hour before he returned home. For now, he'd give Lincoln Wolf the opportunity to do the decent thing...even though the man's track record seemed to suggest that he fell significantly short of "decent."

A word of warning, Mr. Wolf–if you don't tell her by the time the show's over, you're won't get a second chance.

CHAPTER TWENTY

Kat marveled at the countryside from her bird's eye view as the plane left the ground.

This might be my last trip to New York if I leave Wolf International after the show.

Part of her couldn't wait to see Lincoln. Another part looked longingly toward home. Their mutual attraction was obvious, but all other aspects of their relationship remained unresolved.

The closer the plane came to her destination, the more Kat's enthusiasm waned. She couldn't shake the feeling that something wasn't as it should be.

Anything that seems too good to be true usually is.

But that was nonsense! She was entitled to happiness and a bit of fairytale romance, wasn't she?

New York, the show, meeting Lincoln—it all resembled a fantasy. But reality would set in soon enough. In the meantime, she intended to enjoy every minute of their relationship.

Yet something nagged at her. What was it? Maybe she'd feel differently after a good night's sleep. After all, she loved Lincoln—didn't she?

"I've missed you," he said, arms opened wide as she came into the waiting area. They hugged and went to collect her luggage. Lincoln rambled on and on about the show as they walked to the cab.

Not once did he ask about the boutique or how *her* life was going. She decided to tell him anyway.

"My boutique's doing well, Linc. But I feel sorry for my brother. He's going through a difficult divorce, and his wife isn't in her right mind. Now she's telling stories that he's unfaithful and abusive." Snowflakes thickened the air.

"Is he?"

"Is he what?"

"Unfaithful and abusive."

"Of course not! How can you think my brother would do a thing like that?" He studied her as though some question remained unanswered. "What is it?" Kat asked.

"Nothing. Just—just wondering if you'd like a nightcap in the lounge. I want to talk to you, Kat, but if you're too bushed..."

"Not at all. In fact, a hot buttered rum would hit the spot and take the chill off." Something was indeed bothering him—she could see it in his eyes. Shivering, she stepped out of the taxi. "Brrrrr. The air's so cold, but the snow's beautiful. These flakes must be as big as quarters."

Lincoln took her arm without responding. He led her into the hotel lounge and chose a table in the corner.

He ordered their rums while the waitress lit the candle on the table. Alone again, Kat placed her hands in his.

"It seems a lifetime since I saw you."

A tender look flooded his face. She wanted to tell him she'd never leave again, but was that true? She didn't know.

"I need to tell you...some less than flattering things...about myself. I just don't know where to begin. I'm so afraid you won't understand." Kat kept silent as he paused and looked away. He lowered his eyes. His shoulders slumped.

"What could be so bad, Linc? I don't care about your past. I care about *our* future. Whatever you've been hinting at for weeks now...out with it, *please*. I'm not into playing games with the emotions, and this is beginning to feel like that."

She'd never seen him so nervous. He seemed to have lost his confidence. Was it something about the show? Her designs? His ex-designer, Lillian Rae?

"Well...it's...just that...no...it'll wait until...until after the show. We'll discuss it then."

"Go on," she said, frustration adding shortness to her tone. "Don't be afraid to tell me. I might imagine worse than the truth if you keep putting me off like this."

He looked away again. "It's just that...that you asked about Lillian Rae before you left the last time, and I wanted to tell you she's going to be okay. She's gaining strength every day."

"I'm glad. But is that *all* you wanted to tell me?"

"For now, yes. When I'm ready, I'll tell you more." He eyes turned cold. "Don't push." She heard the edge slip into his voice. What was that all about? *He* was the one with the problem he wanted to share. Or maybe he didn't. She shifted in her seat. An uncomfortable silence hung over them for several moments.

"Sorry," she said, not smiling.

Lincoln's face showed no emotion.

She wanted to know more about Lillian, and the only way to learn was to ask. Despite his reluctance, she needed to quiet the warning bells ringing deep within her. Her voice was soft, controlled, but her manner was bold. "Why did she do it, Linc? Was losing her job so important that she wanted to end her life?"

"No. No, that wasn't all. She had other problems." His eyes shifted to the couple across the room, then back to Kat. "You look wonderful to me, Kat. Maybe a little tired though."

What other problems? His change of subject told her they would no longer discuss Lillian Rae. The warning bells rang louder.

The waitress arrived with their drinks. The conversation became impersonal, but his scrutiny of her was not.

They discussed the display for *Starry Summer Night*. Could they make the moon shine brighter? No. Had they used the brightest light possible for safety? Yes. Would the music be the perfect choice? Yes. Did the apparel fit properly? Yes. Kat hid a yawn with her hand.

"All right, sweetheart, let's go. You're about to fall asleep at the table." He grinned and pushed back his chair.

"I'm sorry."

"Don't be. Come on, I'll walk you to your room."

At the door, he pulled her into his arms. She tried to avoid the sensation his kiss sent through her. He backed away and pretended to tip his hat while she gave a mock curtsey.

"See you tomorrow, pretty girl. Wear comfortable shoes. We'll do the town."

Kat smiled and closed the door. She unpacked and showered before making a cup of the hotel's complimentary hot chocolate. She'd had better, but it soothed her. Turning out the light, she lay wide-eyed in bed and thought about Lincoln's strange behavior.

What could be so *distasteful*—yet so vitally important?

Once in bed, she tossed and turned, crinkling the pillowcase until it felt like straw against her face. The sleepiness that overcame her earlier had disappeared. Now questions raced back and forth through her mind with dizzying speed. Why did Lincoln keep taunting her with his big secret? Why did he start to divulge it and then changed his mind? Surely, whatever he had to tell her wasn't something that couldn't be worked out. Didn't they love each other? Wasn't that all that mattered? And how did Lillian Rae figure into all of this? What had she been to him? What was she *now*?

The next two days, after spending the mornings tying up loose ends, they toured New York.

"You'll learn, Kat, that New York City is not only a playground for the rich and famous, but it's the stomping ground for subcultures from street bums to starving artists to Wall Street's financial wizards." He took her arm in his, and they strolled through Greenwich Village. Awed by its many street fairs and performers, she felt like Alice in Wonderland.

"If you're hungry, I know a great place to eat." Lincoln said.

"I'm starved. Let's go."

Exhilaration ran through her as they wandered the area around the United Nations, sampling international cuisine and mingling with people from all over the world.

"I've heard all about Broadway, Linc. Can we go there, too?"

"Sure. There's so much more to see, and I want to be the one to show you. Maybe after the show we can take it *all* in."

Kat took a deep breath. When should she tell him about her and Dawson's vacation plans. Lincoln was sure to think she preferred going with Dawson to accepting his offer. *Did* she? It seemed they were hiding something from each other. She'd tell him right after the show.

"Tonight, it's champagne and dancing under the stars for the prettiest lady in New York," Lincoln said.

The thrill in his voice, the romance in his eyes, swept her up and locked her in his arms.

* * * * *

The next day they closed the books, filed the sketches, and locked the office door.

"Tomorrow's the big day. Do you feel ready, Kat?"

"Ready as ever, I guess."

"Where for dinner? You name it."

Lincoln's wide grin showed his eagerness.

"Linc, I'm sorry, but I want to be fresh for the show tomorrow. I'm going to turn in early. Maybe order room service for a bite to eat. Do you mind terribly?"

He looked disappointed, but not as much as she expected. "I don't mind as long as you dream about me. You can be sure I'll dream of you."

He winked and kissed her before walking down the hallway to the elevator. She watched him go. The physical attraction between them was dynamite, but...

Maybe there was *too much* attraction and not enough closeness. She enjoyed every moment she spent with Linc. But in all honesty, she couldn't say she knew any more about him than she had on the first day they met.

Stepping into her room, she locked the door behind her. Tomorrow morning she would have her gown steam pressed. Then she would get her hair and nails done before going for a facial and massage. She looked forward to the massage to loosen some of the tension she couldn't seem to shake.

Life in that crowded fast lane wasn't where she wanted to spend the next few years. Hop-scotching from one project to another and commuting back and forth was no way to live. And fighting the urge to wrap herself around Lincoln with every kiss grew more exhausting by the day. Her hotel suite, comfortable at first, had begun to close in on her. Thinking of all she'd done, she decided her salary wasn't so generous after all. She was earning every penny of that large paycheck.

A vacation with Dawson to Mexico would be the perfect way to dump the stress she'd been carrying around. Days with Daw were always fun. And they came *without* stress.

Melancholy draped over her like a shroud. In the city, concrete and steel hid the season's glorious sights, scents, and sounds. Could

Lincoln be happy in a small town? Or would he feel like the proverbial fish out of water? She already knew life in the city would starve her soul. To never watch the songbirds fly south, to never feel the nostalgia of autumn's aging beauty would be akin to a death sentence.

Why hadn't she been satisfied to remain a small town success? Wasn't the boutique enough? No, one boutique *wasn't* enough. But a chain of boutiques...now that was a challenge. And wasn't that why she was here? To earn enough money to open a second shop and then a third...maybe even franchise Fashions by Kat across the country? Her attraction to Lincoln Wolf—the means to this end—confused and frustrated her. It also jeopardized her plans, putting at risk everything that was dear to her.

Past the highest building, beyond the busy city, the sunset fought for recognition. At home, sunsets harmonized with the mountains and all nature. True, challenges kept the blood coursing, but harmony brought true happiness.

She had to be careful. The challenges could easily make her lose sight of that harmony.

The ringing phone broke her concentration.

"Hi, Sis, you doing okay? I've been thinking about you."

"I'm fine...and glad you called."

"You ready for the show?"

"Yes, but I don't know what I'll do if we don't win."

"I guess you could always come home to the people who love you. Hey, remember what you said? You'd do your best and then forget about it, win or lose? Keep that in mind. But I've got a hunch you'll be on top tomorrow."

"Thanks. I wish I shared your confidence. So how are you doing?"

"Couldn't be better."

He was pretending, but she knew him to well to be hoaxed. "How are things going with the divorce?"

"Not bad, not good. Hannibal says to sit cool and bide my time. I wish I were there with you."

"Me, too. I could use your moral support."

"You name it, Kat, I'll take the first plane out. What do you think about that?"

He and Lincoln would lock horns with her pinned in the middle. "What do I think? I think you're dying to treat me to a lobster dinner when I get home."

Dawson laughed. "What a con artist you are. It'll be my pleasure to treat. Don't worry about anything; just come home safe and sound."

"I promise. I'm going to get some shut-eye now. I'll talk to you soon. Love you."

"Me, too. Be good—you hear?"

After talking with Dawson, she felt like she could whip the world. It had always been that way. Any thought she might have had about living in the city seemed ridiculous. She could never live that far from Dawson and her hometown. They were beacons of light that protected her from the rocks beneath life's surface.

Without warning, Bonny and Deb flashed through her mind. How could she leave her two dearest friends behind? They'd no doubt be at the apartment they'd shared since college—unless they went gallivanting after they closed the boutique.

A few minutes later, Kat nestled into bed and drifted off to the vision of Lincoln lost in the backstretch of Willow Walk.

CHAPTER TWENTY-ONE

By nine o'clock, the snow had covered the ground. Glistening specks of silver dotted the white blanket and brightened the dreary gray day.

She'd better get a move on if she wanted to accomplish everything she planned.

On her way to the massage parlor, she stopped in the beauty salon in the hotel to arrange an up-do and a manicure.

"Let me see what I have open." The receptionist scanned the appointment schedule. "It looks like we're booked until...did you say your name's Katarina Kahill?"

"Yes, but if you're booked up, I can do my own hair. I've done it lots of times before. Just felt like splurging a little."

"That won't be necessary, Ms. Kahill. Mr. Wolf called yesterday and asked that you be given top priority."

"He did?"

Nothing like putting the salon on the spot. Gallant of Lincoln in one way, but...

"Oh, yes. His wish is our command. He's very nice and handsome, too." She blushed.

"Yes." Kat lowered her head and tried to hide her grin. "I'm sure Mr. Wolf will be pleased with your efficiency."

"For what he pays us, I sure hope so. Oh...I mean...oh, dear, I mean...for what he...uh..."

"Don't worry. Our girl talk is just between us."

"Thank you, Ms. Kahill."

"Call me Kat." She liked this down to earth girl who came across as refreshing and genuine in this world of what-you-see-is-not-what-you-get people.

Back in the room, she wanted to nap, but she felt far too keyed up to sleep. And why risk undoing the exquisite hairdo that made her look so sophisticated, so stylish?

She paid careful attention to every detail of her appearance. Her black velvet floor-length sheath with matching long coat lined in emerald green satin had been fashioned just for this night. The black cat necklace with emerald eyes, her trademark, accentuated the emerald studded bodice of her gown.

Lincoln arrived at seven o'clock—a dashing escort in his black coat and tails and bow tie. She doubted she'd ever forget the sight of him, standing in the doorway and looking like Prince Charming. He stepped in and handed her a box tied with a pink ribbon.

Kat opened it and gasped. "It's lovely, Linc. I've never seen a miniature white orchid before." Kat kissed him on the cheek. "Please pin it on me. And by the way—we *are* going to win."

"I hope so. Losing is *not* my style."

Not his style? She fought the urge to shudder.

He fumbled with the corsage. "I'm not very good at this."

"Why, Lincoln Wolf, I would have expected you to be an expert at pinning corsages on girls."

His devilish grin punctuated the touch of his hand against her skin. A tremor swept up her arms and enveloped her body. She stepped back. Plucking his gift from the table by the window, she handed him the small box wrapped in black paper and tied with an emerald green bow.

Fidgeting while he unwrapped it, she wanted to jump in and help him. Would he like it? A slow smile spread across his face.

"I don't know what to say. Where in the world did you find cuff links with the Wolf International Fashions logo? I don't think we ever included anything like that in our lines."

"I had them made when I was home."

"Thank you, sweetheart." He paused, looking from the cuff links into her eyes, "I love you." The kiss he offered was soft and sweet.

Kat wanted to drown in the moment, to remain immobile and let the world and time roll by. Whether or not Wolf International Fashions took first place, she was on top of the world.

"Let's go, Kat. Don't want to be late."

Falling from her cloud to earth, she walked over to the couch to pick up her purse and stopped with a start. Her mama's voice rang in her ears, clear as crystal and full of devotion. *Love can be wondrous—but it can also break your heart. Be cautious, Kat, not to love too easily or too soon.*

She turned a puzzled look toward Lincoln.

"What is it, Kat? You look like you've seen a ghost."

Words came slowly. "I...I think I *heard* one." She shook her head and smiled. "Never mind. We'd better leave."

As they entered the crowded hotel lobby, she watched heads turn toward them and conversation stop. Kat checked the front of her gown. Was something amiss?

"Why is everyone staring at us?" Biting her lip, she looked at Lincoln.

"Because you're beautiful...and we make an extraordinarily handsome couple.

"Oh."

For a lifetime? Or for just one beautiful night?

In Lincoln's seldom used Limo, on the way to Radio City Music Hall where the big event would be held and televised, he took her hand. "I wish," he said, "that we will always be as happy as we are this moment."

They arrived just in time enough to meet and chat with Harry Steinbeck, well-known designer for Katherine's Love. He kissed Kat's hand when Lincoln introduced them.

Just wait till Bonny and Deb hear about this!

She tried to act sophisticated; but she could only be herself, whatever the consequences. Either people liked her or they didn't.

After obtaining programs, they were ushered to their reserved seats. Kat took a deep breath and let it out, but the tension in her neck and shoulders remained.

This may be grand, but give me my country any day.

"Never in my wildest dreams did I ever expect to be in the same room with Harry Steinbeck, let alone have him kiss my hand. I wish I had a photograph of that."

Lincoln laughed. "You'll meet all the others after the show."

The Master of Ceremonies introduced the judges and alluded to previous competitions and winners. The assemblage pointed fingers. A low buzz of gossip could be heard around the theater.

"I never imagined anything this outstanding...this gigantic," Kat whispered

"We'll be rubbing shoulders with the buyers after the show, and I'm hoping there will be many," Lincoln said.

"I'm glad our presentation is last. It is, isn't it?" She scanned the program.

"In this business, the best goes last. "We were runner-up last year, so this year we're second to last. We lost first place. Lillian failed me."

She turned and looked at him. What a strange thing to say.

"What if I fail you?"

"That's different."

Different how? What exact part had Lillian played in Lincoln's life? Was theirs a working relationship or much more?

"Then Lillian *was* disappointed at not being chosen to work with you again this year?"

"I suppose."

Lincoln's unconcerned response about the woman who had been his top designer for half a decade disturbed her.

"I imagine it was quite a let down to her."

"Would it have been a let down for you?"

"In the beginning, no. But after working with you these last months...yes!"

"Should I take that as a compliment?"

"If you wish, but don't put words in my mouth."

"Why do you assume I'm doing that?"

Kat cut her eyes to the right then back to him. She hesitated for a few seconds. "Shall we go in circles all night?"

"Sorry, Kat. I'm a little on edge."

Fine—and what do you think I am?

CHAPTER TWENTY-TWO

The theater lights dimmed.

Kat turned her gaze from Lincoln to focus on the stage. Spotlights flashed on. The curtain opened.

Kat gasped.

"Magnificent! Gorgeous!" She pressed her hand over her mouth, looking around to see if anyone heard her outcry.

"Honestly!" the woman in front of Kat blurted.

Ooooops! I'd better act more sophisticated, at least for tonight.

This event spelled money, prestige, recognition, and a much higher form of entertainment than the simple circus that always came to her hometown in the spring of the year.

"I'm getting the impression you're delighted with the show so far," Lincoln said.

Whatever gave you that idea?

"Oh, Lincoln, it's all so stunning." She caught her breath and clutched his arm. "Just look at *that*."

Three life-size faux unicorns circled the stage in slow precision. The models, wearing elegant gowns and matching headdresses, rode bareback. Each unicorn stopped center stage, allowing the model to slide off and walk the runway.

She looked at Lincoln, nudging him with her free hand. "How do they make those unicorns look so alive?" She kept her voice low so not to disturb Ms. Hoity-toity sitting in front of her.

"Many tricks go into staging. You'll learn if you stay with me long enough."

He wants me to stay with him? Is that really what he meant?

She thought of Lillian Rae. Had he said those same words to her at one time? Did it matter tonight?

Let it go, silly. Deal with it another time.

Turning her attention back to the stage, she saw billowy clouds appear to float in the sky. They reminded her of the times Dawson had pushed her on their swing back home. She'd coaxed him to swing her higher and higher so she could pluck her little white kitten out of the cloud and stick it in her pocket.

She felt Lincoln flinch when she squeezed his arm tighter.

"I'm happy you're enjoying the show, sweetheart, but I'm afraid my arm doesn't agree."

"Oh, I'm sorry," she released her grip and patted his arm.

Each creation equaled or exceeded the preceding one. The displays, the backdrops, the models, the fashions awed her.

A blue-haired elderly woman sitting beside her tapped her arm and whispered, "Beautiful, isn't it, honey?"

Kat smiled and nodded in agreement.

The Frenchman's set was a wonder. She studied the five gigantic white candles.

"Look Lincoln. Have you ever seen a more beautiful water fountain? It's shaped like a rose."

"Yes, it's nice."

Nice? Try to control your enthusiasm, Lincoln.

Delicate arcs of water reached high into the air, dancing with rainbow colors from hidden stage lights. *How did they do that?* The imagination, the range of thought it must have taken to gather these elements into such a presentation humbled and excited her.

"Have you ever seen anything so elegant?" she asked.

"Would you believe *Starry Summer Night?*"

She closed her eyes and remembered another moment as precious as this one. Back home when she and Dawson sat under their weeping willow tree—the day he returned from Mexico—a little girl's voice...*Oh, Daw. We got lots of butterfly kisses, didn't we?* The corners of her mouth turned up when she heard her inward giggle. *Here's one from me. Catch it now.* She had kissed her fingertips and blown on the palm of her hand. Dawson grabbed at the air. *I got it. Here's one for you.*

From this indelible memory in childhood she returned to the theater just as the curtain closed on the Frenchmen's display.

The theater rocked with applause. She and Lincoln stood and joined the cheering appreciation for great talent.

"Do we stand a chance, Linc?"

"Hey, pretty girl, have more confidence in yourself. In *us*. We're unbeatable."

"We are, aren't we?" Kat doubted that *Starry Summer Night* would top this one.

Wolf International was next. The Master of Ceremonies introduced them.

"Designer for Wolf International, Ms. Katarina Kahill. Let's welcome the newcomer into the world of fashion."

Heads turned. Exchanged looks among the audience puzzled her. Low murmurs crept through the crowd.

"What happened to Lillian Rae?" someone mumbled.

"Did Ms. Rae leave Wolf International?" another asked.

Lillian's name floating around the auditorium in a whirlwind of not-quite-silent queries landed on Kat's ears. She cast a sidelong glace at Lincoln. Had he heard? What was he thinking?

The emcee continued. "Ladies and gentlemen, we've seen, *Spring in Bloom, Early Summer, Color Me Summer, Candlelight and Roses, Forever Summer,* and now—from Wolf International—*Starry Summer Night*. Mr. Lincoln Wolf, please stand and be recognized for the many years of excellence you've contributed to the world of Fashion."

"Stand, with me, Kat." She bristled at the order, but she obeyed. He took her by the elbow and guided her up.

If he thinks I can't stand on my own...he's right. One leg buckled no sooner than the thought entered her mind.

He whispered in her ear. "Pretend all the people standing out there are in their underwear."

"Polka-dotted boxers and all?"

"Whatever it takes."

Granddad had told her almost the same thing right before she made her college graduation speech. But he added spice to the idea. "Picture them naked," he'd said. Then they both burst into laughter. It worked once again. She could stop holding her breath.

"You're doing fine, Kat," Lincoln whispered.
I might be doing fine, but I wonder how Lillian is doing right now.
Why was she thinking again of Linc's former designer?

"I'm going. That's all there is to it," Lillian said aloud. She turned down the volume on the television, watching for Lincoln as the spotlight and cameras panned the audience.

Why should I sit here and not be a part of it? I put five years into thrusting Wolf Fashions to the top.

She needed to be there, to see the people, to feel the excitement, to hear the whispers and the applause. After all the years of being in the limelight, she couldn't turn off the thrill of winning with a *bon voyage* party and a farewell kiss to the audience. That was *her* place, where *her* heart was—with Lincoln and with the show. The pretty little thing hanging on his arm tonight could never fill *her* shoes.

Lillian opened her closet, pulling out several elegant gowns and laying them on the bed she had shared with Lincoln at least once a week since she came home from the hospital. That little upstart had better not try to take *her* man.

Lincoln had come through just as she knew he would. Her rent and utilities were paid. The cupboard was full. Weekly visits to the psychiatrist were covered by Wolf International Fashions' health insurance. No longer the *former* top designer for Wolf International, she'd been placed on extended leave with full company benefits. Of course, Lincoln hadn't made that public information.

Granted, she'd been a fool to try to kill herself. Her pride and courage had slipped. Never again.

After careful deliberation, she chose Lincoln's favorite gown, applied her make up, and touched up the stubborn spots of her short hair with a curling iron.

"Not too bad for somebody who almost died not long ago," she said, looking in the mirror, a wry smile on her lips.

Hurrying out of the apartment building, she flagged down a passing cab. "Radio City Music Hall. And hurry, please."

The taxi pulled to the curb. A few of the guests mingled out front, smoking and chatting.

"Go around to the stage entrance please." She'd slip in unnoticed and sit near the front but behind Lincoln. That way she could keep an eye on him and his country bumpkin *protégé*. Blending into the milling crowd during the intermission, she found a seat just three rows back from Lincoln and Kat.

That was her name wasn't it? Kat? How fitting!

The lights dimmed. She'd made it just in time for the second half of the program.

The curtain rose. The presentation began.

Kat gasped at the results of the last few months. "Oh, Linc! Our display couldn't be more beautiful."

Her eyes welled, and she put her hand to her mouth as the models strode up and down the runway, turning one way and then another to show each design to the best advantage. Casual beachwear, sleek lines, innovative fabrics, and flowing gowns elicited ohs and ahs from the crowd; and applause erupted after each model's appearance. Finally, the finale was upon them.

"Ladies and Gentlemen, model Silka Sinclair presents the feature design, *Starry Summer Night*, for Wolf International Fashions. This gown, fashioned from midnight blue satin with a silk chiffon overdress covered in silver dust, was created by Ms. Katarina Kahill."

The model, who had the blackest hair Kat had ever seen, moved like a panther stalking its prey. She sauntered down the runway and back to the stage. A handsome man in a tuxedo waited for her. He held the full coat as she slipped into it. She stood still for several seconds with her back to the audience, then turned in one flowing move and spread the fullness into wings. Spotlights caught the silver lamé lining. Like a disco ball, it reflected into the audience and all around the auditorium.

Special lighting effects created the illusion of shooting stars. A faux moon glowing with inner lights came down from the ceiling. The model slid onto it and ascended upward as the curtain closed.

Kat's mouth dropped open. Speechless, she turned to Lincoln.

"We've won," he asserted. "Nobody else's presentation came even close to ours.

Surprised by the presumptuousness of his statement, she raised an eyebrow.

"Several of the presentations were quite incredible, Linc. And the gowns were positively luscious."

"No way. Mark my words, Kat. We pulled it off."

We? What arrogance! I worked sixteen hours a day on this presentation. Doesn't he ever give anybody credit for their efforts?

She dropped Linc's hand and placed both of hers in her lap. The audience burst into applause again as the emcee stepped out from between the curtains, and she joined them.

"Ladies and gentlemen, the winner of this year's competition..." He looked at those in the front seats and gazed out over the crowd before opening the envelope. "...is..." He smiled, drawing out the moment. Kat held her breath and glanced at the Frenchman and his designer sitting two rows in front of them. She knew they were anticipating a win just as everyone was. "Wolf International Fashions for *Starry Summer Night*."

The crowd roared, stood, and applauded. She turned to Lincoln as the spotlight almost blinded her.

Lillian could see Lincoln in the spotlight. Her eyes clouded. *I should be the one holding onto his arm, standing beside him.* Now she could only hide, hoping no one recognized her. Her heart sank beneath its weight of sorrow. She turned away, not wanting to see the look on Lincoln's face. She had known that look so well, but this time it wasn't aimed at her.

Katarina doesn't know she has a swollen-headed, unfaithful little boy in man's clothing on her hands. He's my kind of man. I know how to handle him.

A spark of resourcefulness ignited inside her. She raised her chin.

I may be down, lady, but I'm darn sure not out. If you think you can replace me, you're in for one big surprise.

The audience continued to stand and applaud. They were escorted on stage to accept the trophy and the over-sized faux check.

Lincoln placed a hand on the small of her back. Someone in the crowd shouted, "Give the lady the check."

Bowing to more applause and roars of laughter, he made a salute of surrender and handed Kat the check. Pride radiated from her glowing gaze, and he wanted to win another thousand competitions just to have her look at him that way. She seemed unaware of the trophy, of the money they'd won. If it weren't for the flush, the tremble of her body under his hand, he would never have guessed the limelight wasn't her second home.

They beamed at each other, then threw the audience a kiss. Nothing had ever felt so right Their synchronicity continued as they waved good-bye and he escorted her off stage.

Behind the curtain in the left wing, Lincoln pulled her close to deliver a victory kiss. Before he got the chance, a stagehand motioned them back on stage to appease the audience's demand for another glimpse of the winners.

With reluctance, Lincoln pulled her to center stage. As they straightened from their bow, he thought he saw a familiar figure. He'd know that stance, that cock of the head, anywhere. He stiffened.

What in the devil is she doing here? She's supposed to be at home.

His past flashed before him and, for the first time, frightened him. He gripped Kat's hand and led her off stage.

"What's wrong, Linc?"

"Kat, there are things you need to know, but not right this minute. I'm putting you in a cab and sending you back to your hotel. Stay in your room and don't open the door for anyone until I get there. I'll explain later." He wiped away the dampness on his forehead with his handkerchief.

If Lillian somehow managed to talk to her first, he could forget any possibility of capturing Kat's heart.

Kat's exhilaration drained away as though someone had pulled the plug. Annoyance bordering on anger rose in its place. This was *her* evening. Oh, yes, Linc had given her the chance to be here. But it was *her* design—her *Starry Summer Night*—that had captured the top prize.

Now he was snatching away the accolades that were to come, the recognition that would give her boutique the impetus it needed, sending her off to her hotel instead of taking her to the gala celebration to which all participants, their parties, and the buyers were invited. She'd worked too hard to miss this opportunity to mingle with the greatest designers in the world.

"Shouldn't we be celebrating our victory?" Her tone carried an edge.

"And we will. I just need to make sure of some things. Trust me on this one, Kat. And do what I say." She heard a stronger edge creep into his voice.

"Make sure of *what*?"

"I thought I saw someone I know. It...uh...may have been Lillian... I'm not certain."

"Excuse me? I'm not concerned about Lillian Rae. These are *my* designs that won, not hers."

"I realize that, but...no more now. We'll talk when I pick you up at your hotel to take you to the celebration."

"Yes, Linc, we'll talk. Then we'll decide whether we attend the gala *together*. Meanwhile, I'm not leaving here until you tell me what's going on. What are you hiding that's so important and so secret that you're sending me away on the biggest night of my life?"

He gripped her arm, ushering her toward the door. "Don't push, Kat. Just do as I say. I have my reasons. Now let's not argue about this." The hard line of his mouth flawed his handsome face. "I don't want to issue an order here, but I will if I have to."

"An *order*? I beg your pardon!"

She tried to stop, but he propelled out the stage door and hailed a nearby cab. Holding her arm securely until she was seated, he closed the door, gave the driver the address, and paid him. The taxi pulled away from the curb.

Okay, Linc. If that's the way you want it, you've got it. I can leave this town and you the same way I came.

Lincoln hurried through the door and to the spot where he'd seen Lillian. He shuddered, hoping the only reason she had been there was to watch the competition.

Since the suicide attempt, he would put nothing past her.

CHAPTER TWENTY-THREE

In the iron grate behind the screen, the fire flickered; and the winter chill crept into the room. Dawson stoked the flames back to life, then added logs. Sparks flew up the chimney in a sudden flurry. He stuck the poker in its rack and settled into the wingback chair beside the hearth. His thoughts focused on his sister. He couldn't allow her to continue believing the cheater was prince charming.

If you don't choose to tell Kat about yourself, Lincoln Wolf, then I will.

Surely, she'd listen and believe. Surely, she wouldn't go rushing into the mongrel's arms.

Dawson shook his head, looking over at Granddad, who snoozed in the opposite chair beside the fireplace.

He walked over and touched the old man's shoulder. "Granddad, why don't you go on to bed. I'll wake you when the winner is announced."

"I wasn't asleep, Sonny. Just restin' my eyes." He took a big breath and yawned. "I'll lie down on the couch for awhile, but wake me when it's time. Don't wanna miss Kitten's win." He pushed himself to his feet and shuffled over to the couch.

Dawson grinned. People didn't snore when they were just resting their eyes. Granddad's step lacked the spryness of a few years ago, but he still stood strong and tall as the Kahill family patriarch.

The fashion show was well underway; Wolf International's presentation had to come soon. Turning back to the television, remote in hand, Dawson heard a knock at the door. It was too late for visitors.

"Who's there?"

"It's me, Val. Please let me in. It's freezing out here."

What in the world is she doing here?

"What do you want, Val? I'm getting ready for bed," he lied, hoping she'd leave. But when he opened the door a crack, she shoved past him into the living room. The familiar scent of her cologne floated behind her, bringing back memories of the day they met. How pretty she'd been...

"I thought maybe you'd like some company. We haven't talked in a long time." She loosened her scarf, threw it on the chair, and strode to the fireplace. She removed her gloves and warmed her hands in front of the fire.

This could only mean one thing. She planned to stay awhile.

"You thought wrong, Val. You've done enough talking to our attorney's, or maybe I should say enough *lying*."

She turned and looked Dawson in the eye. "I'm sorry about all those nasty things I said."

Her forlorn look raised a host of red flags. She needed to leave before he said something his lawyer would regret.

"You must want something. What is it?"

She tilted her head, something close to pleading in her eyes. "Just for us to get along and maybe stop the divorce—you know—try again. We loved each other once. Couldn't we rekindle that flame?"

Strolling to the small kitchen that opened to the living room and pouring a cup of coffee, he tried to soften his voice, to inject a note of polite finality. "It's too late." *I'll not go through the heartache of making up only to end up where they were right now—or worse.* "What brought this on, Val? This is very hard for me."

"So is life...and then you die." Her eyes shot daggers. She turned her back to the fire. "I can't help it, Dawson. Sometimes I hear voices that make me do mean things, and I get all mixed up. But the medicine is helping—I promise—and I'm taking it every day. I'm not like I...I used to be, you know, crazy, mean, and all. I'm getting better. And I love you. I don't want to lose you."

Her voice sounded smooth, even, but the wild look in her eyes he'd seen so many times came and went. She was on the edge, maintaining precarious control. Dawson muted the television. The fashion show would only set her off if past behavior meant anything. He'd been taping the program, so if he didn't get to see it live, at least he'd have it on video.

"Less than two weeks ago you told your attorney that I cheated on you, that I beat you several times and you had pictures to prove it. Was that an intentional lie or one of the voices speaking?"

Tears streaked down her face, and her eyes softened. She made a gesture with her hands as though to reach out to him. Her mouth moved, shaping words, but they were so low that he couldn't hear.

"I love you, Dawson." She walked forward, standing in front of him just inches away.

"What?"

"I love you, Dawson."

"I wish I cared, Val, but I don't anymore." His jaw tightened. "I want a life, peace and quiet, and a little bit of happiness. What will it take for you to let me have that?"

Valorie's tender look slipped into a silent glare. She strode toward the door. Hand on the knob, she glanced over her shoulder at him, her eyes bright with the brooding malice he'd grown to fear.

"The only thing that will stop me," she said with a twisted grin, "is a bullet."

He stood speechless, staring at her back as she disappeared out the door. She'd said the medicine was helping, but he doubted now she had even taken it. After locking the doors, he poured another coffee, turned the television back up, and stared at the screen.

Maybe I should call Hannibal. But what can he do? More than likely, she's just spouting off. Maybe I'm making too big a thing of it.

But he couldn't shake the dark cloud that had settled over him. He didn't know what to do.

The thought of Kat with Lincoln snapped him out of the dilemma. He turned up the volume on the television.

"Wake up, Granddad! They're about to announce the winner!"

The old man sat up, rubbing his eyes. "Did I hear Val's voice, or was I having a nightmare?"

Dawson frowned. "I wish I could tell you it was a nightmare, but she just left."

"You oughtn't let her in here, Sonny. You know what Hannibal told ya."

"I know, but she pushed past me when I opened the door. I didn't dare touch her, what with all the claims she's already made."

"I hear ya, but...look there, Sonny, the emcee's about to tell us who won."

Dawson turned back to the television.

"The winner is...Wolf International Fashions for *Starry Summer Night*." Dawson watched the spotlight sweep through the audience and land on Lincoln and Kat. He saw them embrace before they were escorted to the stage.

"Who's that fella our Kitten's huggin'?" Granddad wasn't smiling.

"That's Lincoln Wolf. He owns the company she did the designs for."

"Looks to me like she's under his spell. Also looks like he's workin' her like a puppet on a string."

"That's quite an assessment for a sleepy old man who just got a glimpse of Mr. Wolf."

"Trust me, Sonny. You don't live more'n nine decades without learnin' a whole lot about people. And that one's no good. We gotta get Kat outta there."

Dawson frowned. "That might be easier said than done. She's a grown woman, in case you haven't noticed."

"Oh, I've noticed. And that Wolf fella's noticed, too."

Dawson's eyes were riveted to the screen as Kat and Lincoln made their way to the stage. Rage against the man who guided her so possessively boiled up inside him.

Tell her tonight, Lincoln, because you won't get another chance.

CHAPTER TWENTY-FOUR

Kat locked the door and tossed her handbag on the chair. What had gotten into Lincoln? How dare he rush her offstage and into a cab without a single explanation?

Retrieving her suitcase from the closet area, she tossed it on the end of the bed and opened it up, shoving her lingerie and other personal items in the large zippered space in the top.

Had he killed someone? Did he owe money to the mob?

She shook her head at the silliness of those thoughts. They were silly, weren't they? If so, why weren't she and Linc at the gala, celebrating their win?

Pulling open another bureau drawer, she grabbed her sweaters, knit tops, and slacks.

She tried to reason on the whole upsetting episode. Only it wasn't just an episode. Linc had been hiding something from her all along, and she was no nearer to knowing what it was now than when he first mentioned that he needed to tell some things about his past. In her heart, she wanted to believe him, to love him. But he wouldn't let her. *Why?*

A part of her feared for him, but a bigger part was angry. She was tired of the secrecy. Whatever the problem was, it stood between them like a stone wall even though he'd told her he loved her.

You don't keep secrets from the woman you love, Linc. So what's going on?

Right now, however, she could do nothing but sit and wait.

She needed solace. Of course...she'd call Dawson.

"Were you watching the show?" she asked as soon as he picked up the phone.

"Granddad and I were glued to the tube. I was just going to call and congratulate you, Sis. The show was wonderful, but you were the absolute best. Your designs were terrific. I imagine Mr. Wolf is sitting on top of the world." Dawson strolled with the cordless to the kitchen. "If it weren't for you, he might not be in the winner's seat."

"Thanks, Daw. It's been an experience—one I wouldn't have missed for the world." She tried to keep her voice cheerful, but her mind wandered back to Lillian Rae. Would Wolf Fashions have won this year with *her* designs?

"Are you celebrating? What's going on?"

"We're...uh...taking a quick break. The victory party will start soon. I'll tell you all about it when I get home."

"You sound a little uptight. Is anything wrong, Kat?"

"Nothing, really. Just the excitement of the evening and all the hours that went into the presentation. I'm fine. You going to meet me at the airport tomorrow?"

"Sure am. Looking forward to seeing my best girl." She heard the tenderness in his voice and knew he was telling her the truth—no secrets with Dawson. "Enjoy your victory party tonight, and remember, I'm standing right beside you all the way. Don't do anything rash."

Kat plopped on the bed. "Rash? What in the world are you talking about, Daw?"

"You know, like anything you'd be sorry for tomorrow."

Kat chuckled. "Don't worry, big brother. I'm not a little girl anymore. I can take care of myself. And If I run into trouble, I'll just give a whistle."

"Promise?"

"Cross my heart." Kat went through the motion. It felt good to have someone to lean on. She changed the subject. "Anything new on your divorce?"

"Not much. These things seem to take a lot more time than they should."

"I know you'll be glad when it's over. Our trip to Mexico should give you some down time. Give my love and thanks to Bonny and Deb. I suppose things are fine at the shop?"

"Yep. Bonny said—"

"Wait a minute, Daw," she interrupted. "Someone's at the door." She heard Linc call out to her. "It's Lincoln. I better go now. See you tomorrow."

"Be good, Sis."

"I will."

Kat opened the door and let Lincoln in. "What's going on, Linc? What happened tonight?"

"It can wait, sweetheart. Don't worry your pretty head about it. Now take a few minutes to freshen up."

"Would you stop all this mystery? *Why* won't you talk to me?"

"Trust me, Kat. I'll tell you everything you need to know, but not now. We have a party to attend, and we're already late." He looked at the suitcase on the bed. "What's this? Are you leaving?" His hurt expression reached out to her heart.

"I...I should've told you before now, but with all the last minute preparations for the show, the time was never right."

"Told me what?"

"Dawson and I are going on a business trip to Mexico in a few days. I found a fabric outlet I want to check out."

"Really? How long will you be gone?"

"A couple of weeks. We'll visit Dad if he hasn't taken off to unknown parts like usual." Lincoln didn't look happy. "You don't mind my going, do you?"

"I guess not. Your job doesn't end with the show, you know."

"As I recall, our contract states that I'd do the show; and you would pay me as soon as it was over. We were going to see how things would go from there, remember?"

"What do you mean, see how things—"

"Look at the time, Linc. I better get a move on." She started for the bathroom.

"Uh...sure go ahead. But I didn't bring my checkbook."

The victory party was even more spectacular than Kat had imagined. Linc guided her around the dance floor, twirling her into a world of bliss to the orchestra's renditions of the old standards intermingled with the sounds of the new millennium.

The soft buzz from the champagne contributed to the surreal atmosphere. Tomorrow she would think about Lincoln and her future with him. Tonight was her time to meet and network with buyers from around the world. Without exception, each one praised her designs. In one sweeping moment, she had made the leap from unknown novice to leader of the pack.

One more dance around the room, one more glass of champagne, and Lincoln let her know it was time to leave this magical playroom. Maybe he would tuck her into bed then go his way, or maybe he'd stay long enough to send her to the land of sweetest dreams.

"Just one more glorious dance around the ballroom, Linc, pleeeease!"

Lincoln took her in his arms. This time he held her tighter, his hand on the small of her back pulling her against him. She was startled at his quick and forceful movement, but she followed his lead. Breathless, she let the warmth spread out from her heart until it engulfed her whole being. Lincoln whirled her around the floor in time to the music. Never had she danced like this. Never had she *felt* like this. She wanted this dance to last forever; she wanted to stay in his arms for the rest of her life.

Pleasantly high from champagne, she allowed him to lead her to the limousine. The night was no longer young. She was going home early tomorrow.

Lincoln insisted on seeing her to her room, but she kissed him goodnight at the door and slipped inside alone. She wanted him to stay, but at the same time knew she would not allow it.

Too many questions needed answers.

Lincoln stood outside the door for a few moments, and then he walked away, smiling. This has been one profitable day. After her initiation into the glamorous world of fashion, he felt certain Katarina Kahill would be ready to leave that one horse town and stay in New York with him.

Thanks to the excitement of the evening, he had avoided the conversation that still hung over his head. Why had he ever alluded to his past with her? Why hadn't he just kept his mouth shut? Now the relationship that held such promise was in jeopardy, and he felt powerless to guarantee its positive outcome. She was becoming more resistant to his lead, more inclined to speak her mind. This wouldn't do. He needed to get control of the situation. Even more than that, he needed Kat.

She was kind and good and everything he wasn't.

If he didn't tell Kat about Rebecca—how he'd drugged her, committed her, and stolen her inheritance—he knew Dawson would.

Dawson had been in New York, had come to Wolf International Fashions, had visited a private investigator. How did he know?

Dawson Kahill wasn't the only one who employed a PI.

Let him tell her. She wouldn't believe him. Lincoln could appear appalled that anyone could have taken a small, misunderstood incident and blown it so out of proportion. He could say he was afraid she wouldn't understand what really happened. Or he could even deny the majority of it.

He suddenly felt old, no longer in charge of his life. Why did the main character in the children's story of Chicken Little pop into his head? Was the sky really about to fall?

CHAPTER TWENTY-FIVE

Kat stood near the metal detectors, looking out the window as storm clouds gathered. The promise of snow had been announced on the weather channel before she left the hotel, and the thought of flying home in bad weather made her uneasy.

Lincoln must have seen the worry lines around her eyes. "Everything will be fine. I've flown in weather a lot worse than today will be."

"Dawson will be waiting for me." Uncomfortable as she was about the weather, she was more so about the possibility that the flight could be grounded until the front passed.

He frowned. "You and your brother are very close, aren't you?"

Did he sound jealous, or was she imagining it? "He's my best friend. He always tells me the truth, and we don't keep secrets from each other."

Now that she was here, she couldn't wait to get home. She hadn't been away from Dawson this long since Cable took him to Mexico when they were kids.

Lincoln gave her a lonely puppy look. "I'll miss you, sweetheart." He wrapped his strong arms around her as though he wasn't going to let her go. "Will you call me as soon as you get back from Mexico?"

"First thing. But I make no promises about when that will be. We may stay longer...uh...if it works out that we get to see our dad."

"I wish you'd stay longer with me."

One thing he would never understand, Kat thought, was how much she loved her home in West Virginia. Nor would he comprehend the reasons why she'd probably never leave it.

"I'm hoping I can get ready to go in two weeks. You remember that I've been away from my boutique way too much recently, and I haven't given my house a good cleaning since before I left." Kat grinned and shrugged her shoulders.

"Listen, sweetheart, I've got a few things I need to talk to you about. The first night you're back, we'll have a nice candlelight dinner at the penthouse where we can talk. Okay?"

"You keep saying that, Linc, but you never tell me anything. I'm tired of the innuendos. Tell me what you have to say or just forget it."

"Not now, there's not enough time. But do me a favor. Don't listen to gossip about me, not ever, from *anyone*. I promise I'll tell you everything when you get back. Deal?"

"I don't know, Linc. But I do know—"

"No buts. If you're going to be my woman, you must have faith in me. And remember that I love you."

Who said I was your woman? Just because I've shown some interest doesn't make me your possession.

"You make it sound so—so dramatic, so serious."

Lincoln looked into space. It was a long moment before he took her hands in his own. "Some of it is awful. But let's not dwell on that now." He grinned and winked. "I want you to have a great time even though it's a business trip. And don't let any of those Latin lover's smooth talk you."

Kat laughed. Struck once more by his almost perfect good looks, she marveled that he was attracted to her. He could have any woman he wanted.

"I'll miss you, Linc."

She didn't have to go to Mexico, not really, but she wanted to. Dawson needed the diversion. And she needed time to put her thoughts together, to decide how she *really* felt about Lincoln Wolf.

"You'll be on my mind constantly, Kat." Lincoln took her in his arms and delivered a kiss she would not soon forget.

Her blood raced to her head. "Keep that up and I won't want to go anywhere."

"That's the idea." Lincoln raised a provocative eyebrow, grinned that daring half grin, and started to kiss her again. Laughing, she pulled back.

"I was kidding. But I *will* miss you." She leaned close, whispering, "Goodbye for now."

His eyes didn't smile when he looked at her. "I'll call before you leave."

She touched his face, kissed his cheek, and stepped back. Halfway to the metal detector, she turned and started to throw him a kiss; then she stopped. Butterfly kisses were for Dawson. They were too personal, too precious, too private, to share with someone else—particularly someone who evoked as many mixed feelings as Lincoln did.

Gray clouds turned black. She wished she could book another flight, but Dawson would be waiting at the other end. Right now, more than anything else, she wanted to see him. And she'd been away from the boutique much too long.

Lightning flashed and thunder cracked. At times it seemed as though the plane would break in half as the storm tossed it back and forth across the sky. The "fasten seatbelt" sign came on just before the captain made the announcement, and the plane rocked and bounced until Kat was sure she'd never see West Virginia again. After what seemed an eternity at the mercy of the elements, they landed.

Outside, it had grown much colder. She shivered at the sound of the wind even though it couldn't reach her as she hurried through the telescoping corridor into the terminal. A grinning Dawson stood in the front group of people waiting in the reception area to meet deplaning passengers. As soon as she saw him, Kat knew her decision to come straight home had been right.

"Seems like I haven't seen you forever. I missed you so much," he said, hugging her.

"Me, too." She held him an extra moment, basking in the security she always found in his presence. They collected her baggage and headed for the pickup.

"Now fill me in on everything," she said as they pulled out of the parking area.

"Okay. Starting with Snow White."

"Snow White? Is anything wrong?"

"Not now. She took sick, and Bonny and Deb took her to the vet. Dr. Lightfoot pumped her stomach and filled her full of vitamin K. He's pretty sure she'd gotten into something poison. But she's fine now."

"Where could she have gotten into poison? There's nothing around the boutique like that."

"I don't know."

"Who's Dr. Lightfoot? Where's Dr. Osborn?"

"Dr. Osborn retired last month. You didn't know?"

"I've been out of town, remember? Do you like the new vet?"

"Ask Bonny about him. She'll tell you." Dawson grinned.

"Why ask Bonny?"

"You'll see."

Kat shrugged. "I'm just glad Snow White is okay. You don't think anyone could have hurt her on purpose, do you?"

"We thought of that, but Bonny and Deb didn't find any evidence of someone's entering after hours. All the customers seemed legitimate. Besides, they knew most of them. I suppose if someone had a key, he or she might have gotten in without leaving any trace of the visit. I can only think of one person who might want to wreak havoc on your shop." His sidelong glance told her who that was.

"Valorie? Come to think about it...I remember the decapitated rooster and the other animals at the farm. I couldn't make myself believe it was her, but now I wonder. We all know I'm not her favorite person, but how would she have gotten a key?"

"I don't know...unless she had mine copied. I might have left it on my dresser one day when I went out on the property. I'm so sorry, Kat."

"Don't worry about it, Daw. You couldn't have known she would do that. We'll just have the locks changed."

"Proving she did it would be difficult if not impossible. I thought of having her watched. What do you think?"

Kat looked out the window at the white countryside. A sense of calm, a sense of home, of belonging, came over her despite the disturbing news about Snow White.

"It might be a good idea to have someone keep an eye on her. Who knows what she'll do next? Did you report any of this?"

"Nothing to report, really. I didn't want to come out and say that my wife's crazy, and she hates my sister, and I think she poisoned her cat. Besides, I can't prove it. If I'm wrong, it could get twisted in court."

"So how's the divorce coming?"

"It's in limbo right now. Valorie thinks she's going to get her hands on Willow Walk. Hannibal say's no way. And you know what I say—over my dead body. And that's where it stands. Doesn't seem like progress to me, but Hannibal says it won't be long.

"So many crazy things are happening: Snow White, your trouble with Valorie. What next? It frightens me."

Dawson touched her shoulder. "Do you want me to stay at the house with you until this is over?"

"I'll be okay. We can't give Valorie more mud to sling. She already thinks we're having some kind of incestuous affair. If I need to, I'll get Bonny and Deb to come over for a couple nights. It'll be like our college days."

"I'll rest easier if I know you're not alone." Dawson sighed. "If the devil buys souls, Valorie's been bought. I just wish I understood why she does such things."

Because she's full of hate, that's why. She's the only one with a motive, no matter how bizarre it seems. Kat wouldn't put anything past Valorie. Things could always be worse, but right now, she didn't know how. It was a good thing she'd come home. She'd never have forgiven herself if something had happened to Snow White or, even worse, to Dawson or Granddad. Add Lincoln's secrecy to the mix, and the whole world appeared to be in a tailspin.

"Now tell me about the show," Dawson said

"Oh, Daw, the settings were spectacular. I wish you'd been there. I feel bad that Lincoln doesn't know I may not stay with the company. I wanted to tell him, but it's hard to explain. I told him about our trip to Mexico. He warned me to stay away from all those handsome men." She laughed at the idea. "I told him he had nothing to worry about with you along. He looked at me so strange. I got the impression he doesn't like you. Of course, I know the feeling's mutual."

"So—he hasn't spoken with you?"

"Spoken with me? About what?"

"Nothing...we'll talk about it later. We're almost home."

Not again. "Tell me *now*." She'd come to expect this evasive response from Lincoln, but it was out of character for Daw. He never hesitated to talk with her about anything.

"I'm not evading the issue, Kat. We just need some time to sit down together and talk."

"You sound just like Linc."

"You know better than that. I'm honest, and I tell you the truth."

"What's that supposed to mean?"

"It means I always have your best interest at heart...which is a lot more than I can say for your employer."

"And how would you know that?" Anger rose in Kat's throat. "You've never even met the man."

"You're right, I haven't. Did you get the big paycheck he promised you before you left New York."

"I—" She hesitated. "I was so eager to get home that I forgot all about it."

"How could you forget about fifteen thousand dollars?"

"Linc will mail it to me. I'm sure he will. He's a respected businessman, Daw. Don't even try to suggest otherwise."

Dawson changed the subject. "I meant to tell you that Bill said he'd arrange for a patrol car to drive by the boutique at closing time to see that you and the girls get to your cars safely, just in case somebody does have it in for you."

She and Bill, who was chief on the police force, had gone through school together.

"Seems you have everything under control." Her anger disappeared as quickly as it had come. "I don't know what I'd do without your help, Daw."

You know I'd do anything for you."

"You're the best brother a girl could have." She leaned across the seat and gave him a quick kiss on the cheek.

"Bet you're anxious to see the girls." Jumping out of the truck, he dashed around to open her door. "I've got to check some fences and call Hannibal. Bonnie and Deb picked up your car this morning and parked it behind the shop." He plucked Kat's luggage from the back seat and walked her up to the boutique door.

"Drive carefully. Love you."

Dawson sent a butterfly kiss whirling through the air." Kat caught it with an open hand and placed it to her lips.

He charged down the road with clouds of dust flying behind. Kat entered the shop, still laughing at Dawson.

"Welcome home!" Bonny shouted when she saw her.

"Congratulations!" Deb grinned wide. "Our celebrity owner has returned to the fold."

Several customers glanced their way as the excited girls embraced, then returned to their shopping.

"It's so good to see you guys." She'd missed everything even more than she thought.

Deb hugged Kat again. "I can't wait to hear all about the show. But I've got to help that lady over there." She nodded in the direction of the gowns.

"How's Snow White doing, Bonny?" Kat looked around for the elusive kitten.

"She's great now and just as frisky as ever. Sky's the greatest."

"Sky?"

Bonny laughed. "Sky Lightfoot, the new vet in town. He's a dream. Comes from the Cherokee reservation in North Carolina. Oh, Kat, I think I'm in love."

They both laughed. "Bonny, you haven't known him long enough to be in love."

"How long does it take to fall in love with a perfectly gorgeous man?"

"In your case, not long, it seems." Why did that seem like a hypocritical statement? "Do I get to meet him?"

"When we get Snow White spayed, maybe you can go with me."

Hours later, an empty teapot sat on the coffee table. The girls had finally run out of questions, and Kat was hoarse from talking so much.

"It's five-thirty," she said, looking at the clock. Let's call it a day."

Should I ask them to spend the night? No! I've never been afraid in my life, and I'm not going to start now.

She'd always felt safe in the two-story farmhouse Mama Suzanne left her and Dawson.

"You sure you don't want some company tonight?" Deb asked. "We could bring a pizza and run the tape of the fashion show."

"Let's do it another time. The flight was rough, and I just want to close up here and go home to soak in a warm bubble bath. Then I'm heading for bed."

"Works for me," Bonny said. "I may even have a date."

"Wouldn't be that good-looking vet, would it?"

"Depends on whether he's in town or out delivering a reluctant calf or a colt that's turned wrong."

"I guess you could change careers and become a vet's assistant." Kat grinned at her friend. "That way you could go with him."

"Not a bad idea," Bonny agreed, putting on her coat. "I'll give it some thought."

The girls headed out the back to the parking lot, and Kat began to tally the day's receipts. It felt good to get back in the swing of her own business, the one where *she* was the boss. She finished straightening the racks of clothing, and she couldn't wait to phone Lincoln when she got home. If only she could be with him for a little while. She missed his conversation, his touch, everything about him—except his secrecy.

Locking the door, she had almost reached the counter when a knock drew her attention. A figure backlit by the streetlights motioned for her to come.

"Ms. Kahill? May I come in?" the woman called through the glass.

Kat turned the key and opened the door a little. "I was just closing for the evening. Would you mind coming back tomorrow?"

"I wish I could. But I've come all the way from New York, and I have an early morning flight out. Could I look around for fifteen or twenty minutes? I'm in need of a special gown, and I couldn't find what I wanted in New York. I've heard so much about you and your unique designs that I had to see if you might have what I'm looking for."

Kat opened the door and stepped back. The woman entered. Dressed in winter white with a floppy black-brimmed hat that shrouded her face, she looked very chic, very vogue. Kat couldn't help but admire her style and the butterscotch hair that peeked out from the hat to frame her face. If the woman hadn't been stoop-shouldered, she would have stood at least five foot eight.

Studying her even features, Kat saw the stress lines that lent a haggard shadow to her beautiful face—almost invisible under the carefully applied makeup.

"Yes, please, do come in. You mean the big city is talking about Fashions by Kat? She felt honored that anyone would travel so far to visit her boutique.

"I saw the competition on television last night. You looked exquisite, and Lincoln went on and on about how your designs put him right back in first place where he belongs."

"You know Linc?" She tried to hide her growing confusion.

"Oh, yes. We've been close for years. Although I'm not sure you'd call us friends."

"I see. Well...look around all you like. I'll finish up my paperwork."

"Thank you."

Kat watched the woman meander through the rows of gowns. Except for the worn look, she appeared ageless and carried an air of grandeur that seemed second-nature, almost as though she had been born into it.

"I'll be more than happy to help you if you wish." Kat offered.

The lady smiled. "Thank you, but I think I've found what I'm looking for." She took from the rack a low cut caramel gown and coat trimmed in fox fur.

"Do you have time for a fitting, Ms. Kahill?"

"I'll take the time." Kat offered her most professional smile.

After measurements were recorded, the woman offered a credit card for her purchase. Kat ran it through the processor and handed it back.

"Please mail it to this address." She reached in her purse and handed a personal card to Kat.

Glancing at the name and address, Kat looked up, then back to the card. Had she read it wrong? Frowning, she looked again at the woman.

"Rebecca Wolf?"

"Yes. Didn't Linc tell you about me?"

"Uh...no...I'm sorry...we...uh, I...was so busy getting ready for the show that we talked of little else."

"No matter," the woman said, a warm smile washing over Kat, heightening her confusion. "He'll get around to it sooner or later."

"I don't...understand."

Kat's stomach flipped over. She couldn't breathe.

"Don't worry, Ms. Kahill, everything will be fine. These things have a way of working out." The woman walked toward the door. Her self-assured elegance added to Kat's bewilderment. "I realize my visit must come as a shock because you don't know me—but you will."

Kat started to speak, but her words caught in her throat. Rebecca Wolf closed the door behind her and disappeared into the night.

Kat took several short breaths. Why was Rebecca Wolf's name familiar? She hadn't met any of Linc's family; she didn't even know whether he had a family.

"Rebecca Wolf," she mused aloud.

Then she remembered—in Lincoln's office the day of the interview—the piece of paper she'd found lying on the floor by his desk. She had picked it up, not intending to read it. But the words had jumped out at her: *The Comfort House. Rebecca.*

Who was Rebecca? Linc's older sister? A cousin perhaps?

Her heart pounded in the silence. Head swimming, she gripped the counter.

Could Rebecca Wolf be Lincoln's wife?

CHAPTER TWENTY-SIX

Kat rolled restlessly from one side to the other. Rebecca Wolf's image swirled in a sea of black, distant at first, then almost close enough to touch. Lincoln's tormented face followed close behind. His mouth moved, but only bits and pieces came out.

Something to tell you... My past... No time to talk...

Clammy and agitated, she sat up in bed with a start. After a couple of deep breaths, she lay down again, drifting back into the nightmare of faces.

Shafts of morning sun woke her, driving away the disturbing images still milling about in her mind. The sheets and blanket dangling from the side of the bed and the twisted pillowcase provided evidence of her struggle to sleep.

The aroma of fresh coffee from the automatic pot reached her as she splashed her face with cold water. She would need the caffeine to get her moving. The prospect of a full day at the boutique seemed overwhelming as she stoked the embers in the fireplace, adding kindling and two small logs to get it going.

Sipping her coffee, she could almost see her mama puttering around the kitchen, scolding Dawson for tromping in with muddy boots. The memories were interrupted with recollections of last night's visitor.

Could the lady from New York have come from a different Wolf family? Possible, but unlikely—this one seemed to know Lincoln quite well. More likely, Rebecca Wolf was the cause of his procrastination, the reason why he always made excuses not to answer her questions. Rebecca had to be his wife, or...

That's it—she must be his ex-wife. Don't be silly, Kat, you don't really believe that.

She couldn't—she wouldn't—accept sleepless nights, not knowing the score, and fears that she could be falling for somebody else's husband. She needed to know the truth *now*. Once again she had to admit she knew very little about Lincoln Wolf beyond his ability to turn her insides to warm butter when he touched her. But the more she learned, the less she liked.

Maybe Dawson could shed some light on her visitor last night. Was his intense dislike for Lincoln based on something he knew that she didn't? Then again, would he like *anyone* she took an interest in?

All big brothers are protective.

She dialed his number at the guesthouse. No answer. Taking a chance, she called the big house.

After the fourth ring, Valorie answered.

"Val...uh...how are you doing?"

"Since when does it matter to you?"

Kat hesitated for a moment. "I didn't call to upset you. Is Dawson there?"

"Isn't he with you—as usual?"

Kat let Val's caustic remark slide. "No, he's not. That's why I called."

"You'd better be grateful I'm not as wicked as you think I am. You have always had some sort of abnormal hold on Dawson."

"What is so abnormal about a brother and sister caring about each other? I know you never had siblings, but you're aware that Dawson practically raised me. Of course, we have strong ties. Why do you inist on making something unnatural of it?"

"Because I see the look on Dawson's face when he talks about you, and he spends more time with you than—"

The smugness in her sister-in-law's tone was too much. "That's an ugly thing to imply. You need professional help, Valorie. For your own sake and Dawson's, I suggest you get it. I'll not listen to any more of this nonsense. Good-bye."

Kat couldn't wait to leave for Mexico. Between Lincoln's deception and Valorie's insinuations, she was ready for a break.

Dawson pulled into the drive right after she hung up the phone. Icy rain had turned to a driving snow, and he jumped the porch steps two at a time.

"You look a bit damp," she said, closing the door behind him. "Get out of that wet coat and let me hang it by the fire."

"I know I shouldn't be here because of Val's dirty mind, but I wanted to talk to you...face to face."

She hugged him. "You spoil me." Brushing a wing of wet, sandy hair from his face, she looked into his eyes, which deepened in color from some emotion she couldn't read. They walked into the kitchen, passing the pantry where Dawson made her hide from their father many years before. That was the day she learned to hate Cable Kahill.

She poured two cups of coffee. "I just called you at the farm, and Valorie gave me a long spiel about your not being there and always being with me. Her innuendos are becoming downright accusations."

Dawson growled his annoyance. "Worse yet, she told her attorney our relationship is immoral, and somehow everyone in town got wind of it. Rumors are flying everywhere. I should have realized the moment she took that picture of us at the Lobster House that she was up to no good."

"Surely, you don't think people will believe such lies. We've grown up here...they know us." She shook her head. "What kind of impact do you suppose those stories will have on my business?"

Overwhelmed by Valorie's accusations, Lincoln's secrets, the mysterious Rebecca, and the check she had yet to receive from Wolf International Fashions, she couldn't imagine what else might go wrong in her life. Crossing her arms, she stood at the window, looking out and fighting the tears that filled her eyes.

"Okay, Sis, calm down and tell me what more is going on."

"I had a visitor last night at the boutique. The card she gave me identified her as Rebecca Wolf." She turned to look at him, hoping for some reaction. His face revealed nothing. Whatever had made her think Dawson could know anything? "There must be a reasonable explanation. If Lincoln were married, he would have told me."

"Would he, Kat?" He twirled a piece of napkin between his fingers and looked at her. "I didn't want to be the one to tell you about Rebecca Wolf. But yes, she *is* his wife.

"*What!*" Her arms fell to her sides. Fire rose from her chest to her face; anger and disbelief washed over her. "And just how do you know that?" She looked away from him, staring again at the falling snow. "Did you check on him without my knowledge?"

"As a matter of fact, yes. I didn't tell you because...I felt it only right that he tell you himself."

She turned back to face him. She spoke slowly, her speech rhythm even and emphatic. "You mean you...you saw him? In person? Where? When?"

"No, I didn't see him. I went to his office with the intention of talking to him, but I decided at the last minute not to. I walked away."

"I see. So how did you get all this information?"

"It's just like I thought, Kat. He's lying to you, and you deserve better than that. I want what's best for you, which doesn't happen to be playboy Wolf of the smart cart."

"Answer my question, Daw. *Where* did you get this information?"

"It doesn't matter. That it's true is what counts."

Kat paced the floor. "Let's get something straight, Dawson Kahill. This is *my* life. If I need any spying from you, I'll ask for it. How do you know Rebecca isn't his ex-wife? Did your informant also tell you that Lincoln said he loved me? Oh...and whether or not I believe that is *my* business."

"I don't doubt that he loves you, Sis. You're beautiful and smart and kind—everything a man could want. Unfortunately, I doubt that marriage is in his plans for you. The truth of the matter is you don't posses a fortune to entice him."

Kat turned on him. "Now you're playing judge, jury, and executioner. Everything is *not* black and white, Dawson, there are a million shades of gray in between."

"Listen, Kat, I'm not judging. Let's review the provable facts. He committed his wife to an institution on questionable grounds, keeps her there under the care of a private doctor who's not on staff, lives a grand lifestyle on *her* money—which he now controls. Wolf International Fashions was funded and operated by none other than his wife Rebecca when they first married eleven years ago."

"How dare you go behind my back and come up with these unbelievable stories? I can't believe you interfered in my life like this, Daw.

I'll ask Lincoln myself and get his side of the story. Until then, call off your spies."

All her reservations about Lincoln Wolf flooded her mind while Mama Suzanne's warnings rang in her ears. She shook her head, trying to dislodge them, but they wouldn't go away.

"No spies. It was a one-time thing, Sis. I was afraid you'd take it like this. I don't know what that guy did to you to make you so blind...and I don't *want* to know. But you can't claim ignorance anymore. What you do with the truth is up to you." Dawson set his coffee down in the sink and stormed out the front door.

Kat followed behind him. "Daw, please don't leave. I just don't understand." His truck door slammed. "Come back!" she hollered.

She hated it when they quarreled. But how could he have so little confidence in her? The nerve of him to have Lincoln checked out!

On the other hand, she couldn't shake the memory of that memo about Rebecca. Or the elegant woman herself who had come to the boutique. Or Linc's refusal to discuss the matters in his past that seemed to be so important. Dawson wasn't to blame. She should have done it herself, like he advised...if not before signing a contract for the show, at least before becoming emotionally involved. But then Lincoln never gave her a reason to doubt him. True, she'd seen qualities in him she didn't like—and his controlling nature annoyed her—but that didn't warrant having the man investigated.

What if Dawson was right? She dialed Lincoln's number at the penthouse.

"Good to hear your voice, Kat. I'm working on some displays for Sax. Sure wish you were here to help. We have a huge account with them."

She couldn't care less about Sax right now. "Yes, I know. Who is Rebecca Wolf?"

A long pause. "How did you come by that name?"

"She came to my shop last night."

Silence prevailed for several seconds too long. "Listen, Kat, I don't want to talk about this over the phone. Sit tight. I'll catch the next flight out. Are you at home?"

"Yes." Why hadn't he answered her question? It wasn't that difficult.

I'll rent a car, so don't worry about picking me up."

"I *wasn't* worried." His reaction seemed to support the accuracy of Dawson's information. Again her anger flared, and this time it wasn't at her brother.

"I'll call you back and let you know what time I'll arrive. I love you, Kat. Just remember that. I can't say more now, but I'll explain everything when I get there."

She hung up without saying goodbye and almost burst into tears. Instead she wiped her eyes and poured herself another cup of coffee. Whatever got into her to make her doubt her brother? He was never wrong.

In a few minutes, Lincoln called back. "I got a flight leaving here in a couple hours. I should reach your place in time for dinner. Will that be too late for you?"

"No."

"Sit tight, sweetheart. Remember, I love you."

Had she made a mistake in allowing him to come? She would rather have talked over the phone, but something this serious should be discussed face to face. Everyone deserved to be heard. She clung to a shred of hope that all those things Dawson's spy told him weren't true.

The rumors about her and Dawson hadn't slowed business at the boutique—at least not yet—and a steady stream of customers kept her busy all day. When the girls offered to close up for her, she took them up on it.

The doorbell rang as she finished making herself a salad. She glanced at her watch and knew it was Lincoln. She'd be glad when this night was over.

Opening the door to him, she walked to the sofa before he could reach out to hug her. It was hard to look at him and even harder to sit beside him. Saying nothing, she bit her lip and prayed for composure before she reached in her purse and handed him Rebecca's calling card. She wished she could slap her hand for shaking and slap his face for causing it to shake.

"Before this conversation gets started, I have something for you." He reached into his pocket and pulled out an envelope with her name on it. "Here's your check as stated in our contract. I want you to know that I'm as good as my word."

She took the envelope and tucked it into her pocket. "Your word was in writing, Linc. It was *enforceable*."

"How can you think so little of me after all we've been to each other? I've looked out for you in all kinds of little ways and even made it possible for *your* name and *your* designs to become known throughout the industry. How can you doubt me after that?"

She refused to be intimated or obligated.

"We'll see how I can doubt you. *Who is Rebecca Wolf?*"

Silence hung heavy in the air as he bent over, putting his elbows on his knees and holding his head with both hands. Those actions gave him away. The woman who visited Fashions by Kat was not his sister, nor a sister-in-law, nor a kissing cousin...nor an *ex*-wife.

"I'm so, so sorry you had to find out this way. She never tires of making me miserable." He rubbed the back of his neck and stared across the room. His voice was almost a whisper. "Yes, Rebecca is my lunatic wife. She's crazy, Kat, on drugs and suicidal. Thinks I'm trying to take her possessions and accuses me of taking over Wolf International Fashions.

"Have you?"

"Have I what?"

"Taken over Wolf International and confiscated her fortune?"

He sat up straight. The power returned to his voice. "I run Wolf International because I'm capable and she isn't. She signed over a few stocks and bonds to me because she wanted me to have them. I didn't hold a gun to her head."

Lincoln wiped his forehead with his handkerchief.

"I see." Kat raised an eyebrow,

He's guilty, and he's trying to cover up.

"Oh, great! Now you're on her side. What kind of lies did she tell you?" His hands shook as he ran his fingers through his hair. This wasn't the Lincoln she'd known.

"Actually, she told me nothing." Kat wanted to get this over with.

"She's on heavy dosages of anti-depressants. Her doctor suggested we commit her until she stopped the threats to do herself and others bodily harm and until she could be weaned off the drugs. I didn't want to, but I had no choice. Do you happen to have a brandy?"

She wanted to believe him, but Dawson had told her it was all Lincoln's doing. The doctor was only the means to accomplish the end. Lincoln must have manipulated him just as he did everyone else. She reluctantly got up and poured him a brandy.

You better enjoy it, Lincoln, because this is the last service you'll ever get from me.

"Go on...I'm listening." She sat down, hoping she could stay calm.

He took a slug of brandy and said after a wistful pause, "I'm going to get a divorce, Kat, if she'll give me one. That's where I stand now. I wanted to tell you all about this sordid mess, but the time was always wrong. At least I told you I'd committed misdeeds."

Ignoring his pleading stare, she remained silent. No matter what excuse he offered now, he'd led her to believe he was free to pursue her Nothing he'd said or done implied he was encumbered by a wife...and a sick one at that.

He turned toward her and took her hands in his. She pulled them away.

"I hope to start divorce proceedings as soon as my lawyer says it's okay to go ahead. By the time you and Dawson come home from Mexico, it should be in the works. Can you ever forgive me for not telling you?"

"The fact that you lied about your marital status is only one of the reasons—"

"I never told you I wasn't married." His indignant tone surprised her.

"When someone comes on to me the way you did, that man's actions indicate he's *available*."

"Excuse me?"

She stood up and paced the floor. He had misled her, used her, taken advantage of her trusting nature. Thank goodness Mama Suzanne had brought her and Dawson up to respect themselves enough not to fall into bed with anybody who came along. She felt her color mounting. She stopped in front of him and glared.

"You lied to me, kept secrets from me. Do you know how much that hurts? I've never been anything but honest with you. How could you do this?" She threw her hands in the air. "I could never love a man who has proven so...so untrustworthy. Please go. I want to be alone."

She fought the urge to slap him. She wanted to run, to get as far from him as possible, to eradicate him from her mind and her heart. The attraction that once consumed her no longer existed. She knew Dawson had protected her once again. Lincoln could never compare to Dawson's caring. Love without friendship was not true love. It could never last.

"Kat, come here. I don't want us to part this way. I promise you, this trouble will pass, and then we'll get married." He stood and reached out to her.

"How dare you?" Her eyes stung; her mouth felt like a desert. Lincoln dropped his arms to his sides. His mouth fell open. "You're still taking me for granted, aren't you? You have no *right* to ask me to marry you, let alone assume I would say yes."

Kat shook her head. How could she ever have thought she might be in love with this man?

"Sweetheart, you're just confused and shocked. Let me hold you... uh...*please*."

She wished he'd stop calling her that. The endearing term didn't fit anymore. "Not tonight, and not ever. I asked you to leave. At least respect my wishes."

"Kat, listen to me. I want you to think about everything and call me when you get back from Mexico. I love you. Yes, I've done some roguish things during my life, but what man hasn't?"

"*Roguish*? You call this deception and your deplorable treatment of your wife *roguish*?"

"Like I said, what man hasn't done that sometime or other?"

"My brother."

"Your brother? Either you don't know him very well, or he must be a god to you. That's how you see him, isn't it?"

She turned away. "There could not be a man more fair, more just, more loveable, more full of understanding." Tears rolled down her cheeks and dropped onto her shirt.

Lincoln frowned. "Then your brother is my competition."

"No! Your dishonesty parts us, not Dawson. Now I believe Lillian Rae's suicide attempt was because of *you*. I had an inkling before, but didn't want to believe it. If you had been truthful with —"

Without warning Lincoln grabbed her and pulled her into his arms. Before she could protest, his lips crashed down on hers. She turned her face and jerked herself away.

With one swift movement, she slapped him across the mouth. "Don't *ever* take liberties with me. Now *leave*."

He held his hands up and backed toward the door. "I'm going, but if you believe nothing else, believe that I love you." Lincoln's head drooped and his voice cracked, but she didn't care. "Goodbye, Kat."

She locked the door behind him, numb, exhausted, dazed by the hopeless outcome. The couch by the warm stove should have been comfortable, but it felt as cold as she did, inside and out. Her brother was right again. Now she believed everything his informer had said.

Lincoln claimed he wanted a divorce, but what did that matter now? She could never justify building her happiness on the ashes of another woman's pain. Besides, how long would it be before he cheated on her the way he had on Rebecca? And what about Lillian Rae? Had he once made the same promise to her?

Right now, she needed Dawson and the comfort of feeling safe, having neither to weigh thoughts nor to measure words.

She'd invite him over for dinner and fix his favorite, fried chicken and mashed potatoes and apple pie.

She'd tease him and make him laugh, and they'd make up like always.

CHAPTER TWENTY-SEVEN

Dawson peered through the windshield into the driving sleet and slowed the truck. His destination lay just ahead.

He'd felt like a huge weight was lifted off his shoulders when Kat invited him to dinner. This spat, like the others in their lives, would pass into oblivion, but the reason behind it gnawed at him.

Kat had a right to be huffy about his butting into her life. He hadn't meant to underestimate her; but regardless of how angry the investigation made her, she had to face facts. He couldn't allow her to fall into the arms of that gigolo without making an honest effort to stop her.

What would it take to make her understand? Chocolates or flowers might be a good choice, but he wanted something more meaningful.

He parked and entered the department store, an ancient building located in downtown Wheeling. Walking up and down the aisles, he remembered the many times he followed Mama Suzanne and Kat along the same path when they were buying school clothes.

He let his feet lead the way and grinned when he found himself in the toy department. What had led him here? He knew as soon as he found the perfect peace offering.

"I'll take this one, Ma'am." Dawson said to the clerk.

Looking at his gift, he envisioned Kat asking him to swing her higher on the tire swing so she could catch the little white kitty in the cloud and put it in her pocket. *No, silly girl, you'll fall and hurt yourself,* he'd told her.

He wrote a note and placed it in the box.

The clerk glanced at him and smiled. "For your little girl?"

"My sister."

"You two must be very close."

"Yes, but we had a disagreement. I need to tell her I'm sorry."

"No better way to say it." She nestled his purchase into a bag and handed it to him. "I think she'll love it."

He couldn't remember a colder, darker, more miserable day. Heavy clouds, gray on the bottoms, scurried across the sky. Pulling the truck into the driveway behind her car, he stuffed the gift under his coat and ran to the front door as he dodged freezing sleet.

"Sis, it's me." He knocked on the screen door and then pulled it open.

"Come on in, Daw. I can't come to the door."

Here goes nothing. She's either mad or she's not.

Kat was in the kitchen at the counter, flour up to her elbows.

"What are you doing?" he blurted.

"What does it look like, silly? I'm baking an apple pie, your favorite, right?"

"Sure is. I thought you were mad at me."

"I am, but you still have to eat. I bet you haven't had a decent meal since you stopped having dinner with me."

He stood behind her, unable to contain his excitement. "Turn around, I have something for you."

"Daw, I just—" She stopped working the dough and faced him. Her gaze fell to the package he held in his hands. She wiped her hands on her apron.

"What's this?"

She looked the way Mama Suzanne had when he surprised her with wild flowers picked from the field next to the house. Suddenly, he felt childish, but he didn't care.

"It's for you. Open it." How amazing she looked, her eyes twinkling.

She frowned and accepted the package. "Daw, what is this for?"

"Just open it...uh...before it melts."

"Before it melts?"

She opened the box and laughed. "Melt, huh?" She put the soft white kitten to her neck and cuddled it. *"I'm* melting now." Tears formed in her eyes. "Oh, Daw, you've melted my heart. The game we used to play—'Kitty in the Cloud,' we called it. I never thought I'd hold that kitty in my arms. But you remembered."

"Something's in the collar."

She found the card and read it aloud. "I'm sorry—Butterfly Kisses." The tears in her eyes spilled over as she hugged him for a long time. Looking back at the stuffed kitten, she smiled. "I'll call him Cloud."

Dawson removed his coat and scarf and hung it on the back of the chair.

Kat ran her fingers through the kitten's soft fur, but her smile turned to a frown and her hands shook slightly. She moved as if on automatic pilot, sat Cloud on the table, and poured two cups of coffee. She set sugar and cream on the table and sat down beside him.

"You were right again, Dawson. Lincoln confirmed Rebecca's his wife, but he said he intends to file for divorce. He also said he wants to marry me. I believe their marriage has been over for a long time, and I've no doubt they're not sleeping together...but...that doesn't excuse his...behavior."

"You're right...it doesn't. So whatever you do, Kat, give yourself time. I didn't want to be the one to tell you he was married, but after Rebecca visited you, I had to tell you what I knew."

"I know you had my best interest at heart. I love you for that, and I'm sorry I got angry. It's not like me, doubting you like that. You're almost always right."

"Almost?" He chuckled. When Kat laughed with him, he knew everything was all right.

"Don't get a big head or I'll have to buy you a new hat." She smiled and winked at him. "Most of what Lincoln told me about Rebecca, I don't believe. He made it sound like *he* was the victim." Kat sprinkled the apples with cinnamon. "I'm so excited about our trip. It's going to be wonderful. And with the best guy in the world."

Something deep inside him sparked alive, a feeling he couldn't define. Whatever would he do without his little sister?

"Daw? Hey, you're a million miles away."

"Sorry. Best guy in the world?"

"You're terrible. I see I'm going to have to buy that hat before we leave." She put the pie in the oven. "I've got so much to do before we leave. I don't know when I'll have time to get it all done."

Dawson gave a sly grin and raised his eye brow. "I'm already packed."

"Oh, hush. By the way, do you know yet when the hearing for your divorce will be?"

"Hannibal says he's shooting for a few weeks after we return. I'll be darned glad when this is over, Kat. I'm so thankful for the guesthouse. But I'd stay in a tent if need be, anything to get away from her. She's becoming more erratic every day. It's frightening."

Kat sat down and rubbed her hand over Cloud. "We'll *both* be glad when it's over."

Dawson remembered the way she used to nestle between all her stuffed animals at night while he read her a bedtime story. A fairy tale princess surrounded by woodland creatures, he'd thought.

"You still want to look for Polly Dee? Dad said she was in the area as far as he knew."

"Sure. We need to see her, Daw—Cable too, if he's there."

"We'll just have to play it by ear. Now that Dad's phone is disconnected, we'll have to track him down." *We need to see Cable? What did she mean by that?*

CHAPTER TWENTY-EIGHT

Four stucco archways led to the veranda, which in turn led to the office of the San Carlos Villas, Cable's last address.

A short man in brown sandals and with a scowl on his face sat with his feet propped on the desk behind the counter. He appeared so engrossed in his magazine that he didn't even look up.

"We're looking for Cable Kahill. Is he registered here? I'm Dawson Kahill, his son."

The man sprang from his chair at the mention of Cable's name. "Oh, *Señor* Kahill. I tell you, your *padre* one mean *hombre*. He leave *mi hacienda* owing money and electric not paid and..."

His arms flailed, his mouth moving faster than the Keystone Cops. "He leaves his stuff, and I tell you, *amigo*, he not get it back till he pay..."

"I understand. I'll pay his debt if you give me what he left behind."

"*Si, señor. Es* good." The landlord disappeared into his living quarters and came out carrying a small box. "Sorry, but your *padre*, he *loco*. He get real mad, shout and holler—but nobody there! Then he get nice again."

"How long has this been going on?" Kat asked.

"Two times since he here, maybe three months ago."

She glanced at Dawson. "Please, if he returns, tell him to call us. We'll be here for seven more days." She wrote their hotel name and room number.

"Now how much does Cable owe you?" Dawson asked.

He paid the amount quoted, adding a few *pesos* for good measure.

"*Gracias, Señor* Kahill."

Dawson felt sorry for the man. The landlord was just another in a long line of people stiffed by Cable. Dawson shook his head and turned to Kat. "It's sad for a man our father's age to be so irresponsible. No wonder Granddad didn't want him to have the farm. I bet he would have sold it and spent the money faster than a cow's tail could swat a fly."

Kat laughed low. "Cable Kahill's running true to form."

"Yeah, but this time I'm worried?"

"Why?"

"I think something has been going on with him for a long time. Why else would his personality be so up and down?"

"Maybe he's bipolar or something."

"I'm no expert, Kat, but he doesn't seem to fit that pattern." He recalled all the inexplicable rages before he'd returned from Mexico.

"Doesn't matter what the cause is. I feel like washing my hands of him."

"Don't say that, Sis. He's our father. No matter what he's done or is apt to do, he'll always be our father. Accept him for the way he is—we don't have to like it, but we can't change it either."

They rummaged through Cable's small box of belongings while sipping lemonades from the hotel restaurant. His meager belongings included an alarm clock, two girlie magazines, a small Bible, three unwrapped cigars, some socks, and a yellowed frame containing a picture.

"Look at this, Daw." Kat showed him a photograph of Mama Suzanne sitting on the farmhouse steps, Kat and Dawson on either side of her. "This must have been taken before Cable took you away. We'd be around five and eleven years old." Kat's azure eyes filled with tears. "I never thought he'd keep a picture of us."

Dawson swallowed hard. "I remember him taking this picture in front of the house."

"If only we could have stayed the way we were in this photo. We all look so happy."

"Dad must have carried this for a long time. Look the way the edges are curled."

She nodded.

In the bottom of the box, covered by a white towel, was a small, worn address book.

"Look here." He read from the book. "Polly Dee Kent. I think we've found her. There's a phone number, but no address." Dawson went to the phone and started to dial the number when Kat laid a hand on his arm.

"Daw, wait. You don't know how she'll react. She might be upset if she hears your voice first. Let me break the ice."

"Are you sure you want to talk to her?"

"If you can forgive her, so can I." Kat sat by the phone and dialed Polly's number.

She looked at Dawson and shook her head. "No one's answering." As she was about to hang up, she heard a soft voice.

"I'm trying to reach Polly Dee Kent?" Kat said, Dawson hovering by her shoulder. She tilted the receiver so he could hear.

"This is she. What is it you want?" She sounded old, almost matronly.

Kat cleared her throat. "I don't know if you remember me, but this is Katarina Kahill from West Virginia. I'm in Mexico, and we—my brother Dawson and I—wondered if you'd consider seeing us. Cable phoned Dawson several weeks ago and mentioned that you'd like to see him."

Kat and Dawson exchanged glances in the silence. He raised a brow. Kat gripped the phone, her fingers knotting the coils.

"Kat and Dawson Kahill?" More surprise than pain shadowed the words. Dawson held his breath. Polly chuckled. "Well, this is a shock. I never thought you'd contact me."

"Is it all right? I mean—can we meet?" Kat glanced at Dawson and looked away. "Dawson, especially, would like to see how you are."

More silence followed by sniffling. Was Polly crying? "I...I...don't know what to say."

Kat waited in silence to let her compose herself.

"Oh, yes, I'd like that very much," Polly said after a moment. "When?"

"Is today good for you?"

"Perfect. Do you want to meet somewhere?"

"What about one of the beaches. We'd like to get some sun while we're here. You know the weather in Wheeling this time of..." She stopped with a chuckle. "You *do* know. Anyway, we've rented a car, so we can meet almost anywhere."

Polly gave directions and they agreed to meet at noon.

They hung up, and Kat rubbed the back of her neck, wiping the palms of her hands on her jeans. "Hope we're doing the right thing. Are you okay with this?"

"A little edgy, but I'll get over it. I'm anxious to see Polly."

Loaded down with beach towels, a blanket, sun screen, shade hats, and a couple coverups, he plodded to the rented car and threw the cargo on the back seat.

"Daw! You look like a regular tourist."

"If tourists break their backs carrying beach stuff, that's what I am."

Dawson jumped behind the wheel and headed west. "Didn't Polly say to take the second dirt road from the city limits?"

"There it is, over there. On the left."

The road led straight to the beach. They parked and got out. Before them stretched incredibly white sand that reached for miles.

Dawson looked around. "She's not here yet. Think she'll come?"

"We're early." Kat eyed him. "You're so tense. As soon as we get settled on the beach, let's take a dip. We've got time."

"Sure—if I can move after lugging all this stuff from the car to the beach."

"Stop complaining, Daw. Give me the blanket. I'll carry that."

"Thanks a lot."

He spread the blanket and followed Kat to the water. She tiptoed in, jumping the tiny waves that scurried onto shore, but he leaped ahead, plunging through the oncoming wave. He surfaced smiling.

"Show off!" she teased, giggling as she splashed him.

The laugh he loved when she was a little girl hadn't changed. She didn't seem to be pining for Lincoln or worried about anything. And she'd grown in ways he never expected.

Twenty minutes later, out of breath and laughing, they returned to the blanket. They sat, arms wrapped around bent knees, staring out to sea.

"How's Valorie been acting, Daw? You haven't talked much about it lately."

He recounted his wife's visit to the guesthouse. Kat shook her head and frowned.

"She's beyond my help, maybe past *any* help. But I've learned exactly what I want in a woman."

"And what's that?"

"Look in the mirror." He gave her a crooked grin.

"Someday she'll come along." Kat cocked her head to the side, a large show of sympathy on her face. Then she bounced up and brushed sand from her legs. "I'm going hunting for shells. Call me if Polly Dee shows."

"Okay, but don't go too far."

She waved and ran to the water's edge. "Don't worry, *Father*, I won't."

Guess I'll never stop being the big bossy brother. Look at her; she's all grown up.

He'd probably be looking after her when she was old and gray and in a rocking chair. He didn't relish the idea of her being with anyone although part of him wanted her to find the right man, have children, and live happily ever after. His fingers fiddled in the white sand beside him, uncovering tiny, rainbow-colored shells. Puffs of ocean mist brushed his face, and he stared out to where turquoise water merged with the blue sky.

Footprints in the sand hinted of life's abundance: Kat's, his own, sea birds, tiny sand crabs running helter-skelter, and coquinas.

A shadow fell on the sand beside his hand. He turned.

Polly Dee stood less than six feet from him.

CHAPTER TWENTY-NINE

Polly Dee's smile, warm and almost shy, caught Dawson off guard. He smiled back, unable to think of anything to say. A different person from the one he remembered stood before him.

Dipping over her forehead, her sun hat barely hid the patch over one eye and the scarred side of her face. *Dad never told me it was this bad.* A handsome boy, taller than Polly and very suntanned, stood beside her. Judging him to be in his middle teens, Dawson couldn't shake the notion that he looked familiar.

"Hello, Dawson."

Her melodic voice surprised him almost as much as her pleasant demeanor. He remembered an irritating twang to her speech.

"Hello, Polly, I...here, let me help you." He reached for the blanket. "I'm glad you came. I was afraid you wouldn't want to."

The boy helped spread the blanket on the sand. Dawson offered him a smile of thanks, and Polly sat down. Dawson returned to his own blanket. He cupped his hands around his mouth and called to Kat. She waved her hand and came running.

"Polly! It's good to see you." Kat said, and reached out her hand. Dawson waited, but Kat's gaze only flickered over Polly's ravaged face. Kat managed to hide whatever shock she might have felt, and he was glad. Her gaze lingered longer on the boy, and he sensed her near recognition, the same feeling he'd had.

She sat down beside him and turned to Polly. "It's good you're here, Polly. How have you been?"

"I'm doing well. I'd like you to meet someone. My favorite fellow."

Polly glanced lovingly at the boy. He looked as though he'd rather be somewhere else.

Kat sent him a bewildered glance, but smiled at the same time.

"This is my son, Cable Darrel." Polly beamed. "Cable, this is Katarina and her brother Dawson. People I...I knew long ago."

The boy mumbled, face reddening, and offered a hand to Dawson. He nodded at Kat. Dawson hoped he was hiding his shock, the strangeness he felt at meeting his half-brother.

The waves that had lapped softly at the sand now crashed along the shoreline, and gentle cries of the sea birds turned to screams. With each passing moment, the noise grew louder and louder until Polly spoke, ending the tension.

"Cable, would you like to play in the water for awhile?" Polly's soft voice enchanted the moment.

"Sure, Mom. Holler if you need me." Polly smiled and nodded.

He kicked his flip-flops off, ran to the water, and dove in. Polly watched until she saw him surface.

Dawson sat paralyzed, afraid to breathe, waiting for some explanation about the boy.

I know what you're thinking. You're wondering if Cable Darrel is you father's child. Well, I'll tell you what happened." Polly kicked her shoes off and looked down at the blanket as though it would make conversation easier. "I'll begin at the beginning. After our—our incident Dawson..."

At the direct mention of the haunting memory, Dawson stiffened and looked away. This was harder than he'd thought, facing her after all this time.

Polly held up a hand. "I want to make something clear before I go any further. You only defended yourself, and I'm glad you did. If you hadn't, no telling how...how far things would have gone. Do you understand?"

Dawson searched Polly's face for signs of blame, but found none. "I think so." He reached into his pocket and pulled out a wad of bills. "But I owe you."

Polly looked startled. "Owe me? For *what?*"

He offered her the money. "I took your booze stash when I left the house. I promised myself I'd pay it back someday."

Polly's deep, rich laugh bore little resemblance to the wicked cackle he remembered from his childhood. She pushed his hand away. "Trust me, Dawson. You did me a big favor. But I admire your honesty." She took a deep breath and began her story again. "Cable visited me in the hospital a couple times. He seemed somewhere in limbo. He wasn't on my side, and he wasn't against me. It was as though he blamed himself for not being there to stop me. He's smarter than people give him credit for."

"But Cable didn't know what happened. He wasn't home," Kat said.

"No, he wasn't home; but we both knew Dawson was too good a kid to do something like that without reason. Later, when Cable wouldn't let up, I told him the truth. I left the hospital a different person. The little bad girl no longer wanted to be bad. I was grateful to be alive—even scarred—and so...so terribly ashamed. I didn't think I could ever face you, Dawson; and I'm surprising myself by being able to talk about this." Polly wiped her eyes with the edge of her coverup.

"I know how you feel." Dawson laid a hand on her shoulder.

She sniffed. "I ran away from the hospital before they released me. I had to get away from people and their prying eyes. I stayed with your father for a while and then fled to the backcountry—to the family of a gal I met in the hospital. She offered me shelter and friendship. I had no money—I had nothing. But I carried Cable's child."

"You were pregnant when...when we fought?"

"Yes, I was, about two months. And again, I tell you, Dawson, it's turned my life around and made me a better person. Now promise you won't blame yourself another time."

Dawson nodded, but said nothing.

"I met a man. Now comes the funny part. Darrel lived far up in the mountains. Despite this ugly face, he offered to take me in, fed me, and took care of me, asking nothing in return. When there wasn't time enough or money enough for the hospital, he helped deliver Cable. I love him very much."

Her face softened. "We moved here when Cable started school. I even took some classes. Darrel's an artist. He's good, too. He sells his paintings, which provides us all with a decent living."

173

"Polly, how old is Cable Darrel?" Kat asked, watching the boy jump in and out of the surf.

"He's fifteen, and he does very well in school. Looks just like his pa, don't you think?"

Dawson smiled and nodded. "He resembles Dad a lot. I thought he looked awfully familiar, but I had no idea."

"He knows very little about my past, and I would like to keep it that way. As far as he knows, Darrel is his father. Even though you owe me no favor, I ask you to please understand. My son respects me. If he knew the truth...I'm not sure what he'd think. He doesn't need to know that bad girl." She put her hand to her face and ran her fingers over her scar. "It's better now. Darrel saw to it that I had some plastic surgery, but I still need more. But being beautiful on the outside isn't important anymore. It's what's inside that counts."

"Polly you're... well, you're just...remarkable." Kat glowed with forgiveness. Dawson wanted to hug her for it.

Dawson agreed. "Yes, you're exactly what Kat said and more."

"My life's much different now, and I'm thankful." She hesitated. "As far as Cable's father goes, I never told him."

"You mean Dad doesn't know he has amother son? Do you think that's fair to him?"

"He doesn't know. That's *my* choice, and I want to keep it that way. Hearts could be broken if Cable Darrel knew. And it's not worth it. Time tells the tale. Why ruin the present and the future by things past?"

"You needn't worry, Polly. We'll honor your wish," Kat assured her. "Maybe the three of you could come to the States to visit someday. I think Granddad would be really pleased to see his fine grandson."

The rest of the day was spent getting acquainted and enjoying nature. The sky dominated everything: the open space, the beach, the powdery sand, the smell of the ocean, the squalling sea birds demanding to be heard—all glorious, but not as glorious as the wonderful tears and smiles and laughter among them. At sunset, Polly hugged them good-bye.

"Keep in touch!" Dawson hollered as Polly and Cable Darrel walked away.

CHAPTER THIRTY

Kat eased back in the seat and sighed. Clouds drifted by the giant jet's window. If only they were pink... How they looked like the cotton candy that stuck to Dawson's nose and cheeks when they attended the street fair held once a year at home.

"What're you thinking about, Sis? You're out there is space somewhere."

"I wish we could've stayed for another week. Our vacation was gone almost before it started."

"You know what they say—all good things must come to an end."

She smacked his arm, then grinned. "You and I've had a great thing going since we were kids, and I never like to see the good times end. I couldn't ask for a better brother even if I'd been doing the picking."

"Yeah, but we had a bumpy ride with that Wolf character. I'm not sure that one's over yet."

"It's over, Daw, you can count on that. But it still hurts a little." She paused and looked down at her lap. "The hardest thing to accept is how gullible I was. I just assumed Linc was free. In my heart of hearts, I never even considered he might be married. He appeared to be so...so honorable. Not all men are like you and Granddad, I guess."

"I would have done anything to keep you from the hurt. But some things we have to learn on our own."

"I'm sorry I worried you...but I think I grew up a little. I know I won't be so vulnerable next time."

Dawson's face relaxed. He kissed her hand and laid it in her lap. She caught his unspoken meaning. He was proud of her.

He laid his head back and closed his eyes while she watched the cotton candy clouds and listened to the steady rhythm of the engines. Some might bemoan the waxing and waning sound as noise pollution, but she found it calming, like the purring of a cat.

Turning her head from the window, she watched Dawson sleep. How dependable he looked and how sincere—what she saw was what she got. She shuddered at the thought of the awful business of Lincoln and the demanding, harum-scarum life she'd been living the past few months.

Kat squeezed her eyes shut and gripped Dawson's arm as the giant plane landed. Flying didn't bother her until she saw the ground rushing up to meet her; then she wished she were anywhere else but there. She opened her eyes as soon as the engines stopped.

The minute the sun kissed the horizon good-morning, Kat opened her eyes to the soft light entering through her louvered shutters. She tried to go back to sleep, but thoughts of Lincoln tumbled through her mind, driving her out of bed and into the shower. The hot water sprayed over her head and rolled down her, and she let go of the longing for the loving relationship that could never be. She'd call him this morning and let him know she had not—and would not—change her mind.

She knew precisely what she would say. Knowing the truth changed everything. No more blinders, no more being hoaxed or fooled or manipulated. For the first time in her life, she was her own woman. It felt liberating.

Kat picked up the phone and dialed his penthouse number.

"Hello," a sleepy female voice answered.

Had she dialed the wrong number? Could it be the housekeeper he talked about hiring?

"May I speak with Lincoln, please?"

"I'm sorry, but he's in the shower. May I take a message?"

Her chest tightened despite her resolve. The throaty, sensuous voice didn't fit the housekeeper theory.

"In the shower? Who's speaking?" Kat tried not to react, but her heart pounded like a jackhammer.

"Lillian Rae. Do I know you?"

"Probably—but don't let it bother you." She didn't mean to sound so defensive.

"Oh, don't worry, I won't. But I will tell him you called if you give me your name and number."

Kat closed her eyes and took a deep breath. She might have lost her gullibility, but she still possessed her manners and her dignity.

"Just tell Lincoln that Kat said good-bye. And Lillian? Don't worry. I'm no threat to you."

Returning the receiver to its cradle, she sat on the floral sofa across from the large plate glass window, knees tucked under her chin. The phone rang, but she didn't answer. Without ever looking at the caller ID, she knew it was Lincoln. She didn't want to hear about Lillian, and she didn't want to listen to any excuses.

As soon as she arrived at the boutique, she filled Bonny and Deb in on everything that had happened in Mexico and with Lincoln.

Deb scowled. "He's not worth another thought or a single tear. But how are *you*, Kat?"

"Not bad. What I felt for Lincoln was infatuation. I know that now. But I was attracted to him big time, and it still smarts a little."

Bonny hugged her. "With all you've got going for you, you'll find the right guy someday."

"Thanks, but for now, my only concern is the boutique—and maybe expanding into New York."

"What?"

"What!"

Kat laughed. "You two sound like twin magpies."

"Did we hear you right? Expanding? New York?" Bonny twirled on one foot and beamed from ear to ear."

"Whoa. Wait a minute." Kat laughed "I'm not sure yet. It's only a thought so far."

"I can remember when Fashions by Kat was no more than a twinkle in your eye. And it wasn't that long ago."

"Fifth Avenue, here we come!" Deb threw her arms in the air. "Watch out. New York. You ain't seen nothin' like these country girls from West Virginie."

"Slow down, slow down." Kat chuckled and tried to turn their focus back to the day at hand. "I've got a bunch of designs to pull together, so I'd better get started. Is there anything we need to discuss first?"

"Not much. Bill Perry came in and asked me to go out Saturday night. I said yes, of course." Deb blushed.

You two make such a cute pair." Kat grinned.

Deb groaned and rolled her eyes. "Maybe, but I don't know how much more *cute* I can take."

"You two go on," Kat said, putting her finished designs into the large black folder. "I'll lock up."

She heard the door close behind them. Getting home and back to her own shop had been so good. She'd almost forgotten the satisfaction at the end of a successful day. With Lincoln out of her life, those days were bound to come in abundance.

Stepping outside the rear exit, she secured the deadbolt and turned toward her car. She stopped in her tracks.

Parked next to it was Lincoln Wolf's Mercedes.

CHAPTER THIRTY-ONE

Lincoln leaned against Kat's car door. He flicked the lapels of his overcoat, his smug expression grating on her nerves like a screeching tomcat on an alley fence.

I wonder what part of goodbye he didn't understand.

Rummaging in her purse for her elusive keys, she wished he'd disappear. "What do you want, Lincoln? Didn't Lillian relay my message?"

"Yes, but give me a chance to explain. You owe me at least..."

"No!" Her azure eyes shot daggers. "I owe you nothing. It's over. Just leave me alone."

Keys in hand, she slung her purse strap over her shoulder and reached for the door handle. Lincoln's big hand beat her to it.

"Just like that? After all, we've been to each other? Listen, Kat...I was in the shower when Lillian let herself in. It means nothing! And you know as well as I do that Rebecca's a mental case and..."

Kat rolled her eyes upward. "It's all so simple for you, isn't it? You only care about two things—what you have and what you want. Don't you get it? It isn't *just* about you; it's about doing what's right, what's...oh, never mind. I don't need this. You'll never understand anyone's need but your own."

"Need? You know what need is? Remember this?" He grabbed her shoulders, swung her around, and pulled her to him. His mouth slammed down on hers.

She twisted her face away from his kiss and shoved him backward.

His hands dropped to his side. "Kat, I'm sorry. I don't know what got into me. I..."

"I couldn't care less *what* got into you." Hot tears threatened to spill over her cheeks. "You make me sick."

She swung her car door open and stepped inside. Turning the key in the ignition, she opened her window.

"I guess you won't be wanting these then." He reached over and grabbed a large box off the hood of his car and shoved it through the window into her lap. "They're imported...Europe's finest chocolates. But I guess they'll be wasted on someone who's *sick*."

She rolled up the window, and put the car in gear. Not looking back, she pulled away, rivers of tears streaming down her face.

CHAPTER THIRTY-TWO

Lincoln's shoulders drooped. Anger oozed from his pores. *Then be sick and go to the devil.*

She shouldn't have rebuffed him like that. Not after all he'd done for her. When before had an inexperienced upstart taken top honors at an international fashion event? Never. Not until Lincoln Wolf took Katarina Kahill under his wing and nurtured her onto the top level of the fame game. Why, if it hadn't been for him...

But this wasn't a game. Yearning for hope but unconvinced that Kat *could* still be his, he flew back to New York.

Settling back in his recliner with the largest martini he'd ever attempted to drink, he weighed his options. They didn't look good.

Women existed for three reasons only—to be conquered by a man, to satisfy his sexual desire, and to produce his children. That's what Daddy had said.

Kat proved his father wrong. He wanted her because...because he loved her. The whole idea scared him.

The third oversized martini made him dim-witted, but it numbed the pain. He fell into bed fully clothed.

Lincoln woke with a walloping headache that almost blinded him. Coffee and a couple aspirins went down hard and did little to dull either the physical agony or the emotional anguish.

Nothing improved after arriving at his office. He attempted to review some sketches for autumn apparel. Failing that, he tried to create a theme that would propel Wolf Fashions' fall line above the competition. How could he achieve anything when he couldn't handle his own life? Even if he came up with another designer, how could he come even close to the stunning success of *Starry Summer Night*? Staring at the drawings in front of him, he saw only Kat's face.

What have you done to me, Kat? All my life I could control women. Even my mother did my bidding for as long as I can remember. But not you. And you're the one I want, whether you do my bidding or not. I just need you in my life.

He had to do something, even if it was wrong. Contemplating the clutter on his desk, he swept both arms in opposite directions, scattering papers everywhere. He looked up when the door swung open.

"Good heavens, Lincoln, what's wrong?" Carla rushed to his side. "You need some coffee, right?"

"Coffee won't do this time, Carla. Get me a brandy."

She blinked several times and hurried to the liquor cabinet. Lincoln watched her pour a healthy glass of brandy and then kneel on the floor to scoop up the files, sketches, and assorted forms. He studied her.

With a sigh she finished the task and stood, arms full, gaping at him. "*What* are you staring at?"

Taking a gulp of the brandy, he realized he had allowed his gaze to lock on her abundant exposed cleavage. And why shouldn't he? After all, he knew her likes and dislikes in *all* the situations that mattered.

"Go back to work, Carla." He had no intention of taking his nightmare out on her. She didn't move, but continued to stare at him. "I said *go back to work!*"

Carla blinked. "Okay! Okay! I'm going." She laid the papers on the desk and marched through the door, mumbling gibberish and waving her arms.

He couldn't sit here all-day and brood. Apologies were not his strong point, but he could live with an enticement to show Kat the honor in his good intentions.

How about financial assistance to expand her boutique? No, money could buy most people, but not Kat.

He never thought he'd see the day when neither his tactics nor his money would work. At a loss for the first time in his life, he slammed the empty brandy glass down on the desk and walked out of his office.

"Lincoln!" Carla almost shouted as he passed her desk. "You have an appointment in ten minutes with—"

"I'll leave the excuses to you," he interrupted. With a wave of his hand, he walked out.

When he got inside the Mercedes, his energy bled away. He crossed his arms over the steering wheel and rested his forehead on them. What had he done to deserve Kat's wrath?

Her words echoed in his head. *You make me sick.* Winning Kat's forgiveness was all but impossible unless he could finagle her into giving in. He raised his head and gazed out the windshield into the drizzling rain and fog. His reflection stared back, blurred and clouded like his future.

Then there was the problem of Rebecca. She could report him for fraud—if she knew about it. According to the drug-induced state he kept her in, he didn't think she had enough working faculties to decipher his false earnings reports to the Internal Revenue Service. Yet she had been able to fly from New York to visit Kat and present herself as a credible individual. Just how did *that* happen?

Putting her in and taking her out of The Comfort House had to stop. Not that the good Dr. Brill wouldn't continue to play along, but the staff was beginning to ask questions. *That* he didn't need.

To make matters worse, Kat's half-brother seemed bent on keeping them apart. Lincoln sighed. Who knew? Maybe the guy was right. Maybe he *wasn't* good enough for her.

He turned the key in the ignition and maneuvered the Mercedes onto the street. He'd take the highway to Winslow House. Neither his favorite route nor the most direct, it was the fastest.

His insides churned. The throbbing in his head nauseated him.

I'll make you mine, Kat. You just wait and see.

He pounded the steering wheel with his fist. His foot pressed on the accelerator as he entered the fast-moving traffic on the highway.

Had it not been for Lillian's set of curves dominating his thinking and making putty of his spine, none of this would have happened. Lillian knew better than to answer his phone. It was her fault.

Like a robot, he wove in and out of traffic. Groaning low in his throat, he fought the burning tears that pulsed behind his eyes.

Where do I go from here? The exit sign loomed on the right. *Guess that's where I'm going.*

Slamming the accelerator to the floor, he shot across both lanes of traffic. His tires hydroplaned on the wet pavement. He tried to regain control, but the wheels didn't reconnect with the blacktop surface. His gaze, riveted on the rearview mirror, watched an eighteen-wheeler barreling toward him. His chest expanded and retracted from the pounding of his heart.

A horn shrieked in his ears at the same time the greatest pain he'd ever known hammered into his neck and back like a railroad spike. Hurled by the huge rig, the black Mercedes catapulted down the highway past the exit and toward the embankment.

Lincoln couldn't stop his body's momentum, couldn't keep his head from drilling into the steering wheel. His breath came in spurts. Something wet and bitter cascaded over his eyes and into his mouth.

Airbags deployed and immediately deflated. The world flipped upside down, then right side up as the doors sprung open. Gunmetal gray sky and a glint of black tar followed brown earth and yellowed grass.

He landed in the ditch on rain-soaked sod, a massive weight wedging him against the ground. He wanted to throw up, but he didn't know whether his stomach was still there. He was afraid to look.

The sleek Mercedes, once the symbol of wealth and prestige, pinned him under its crushed and broken carcass. The great—or was that the *late* great?—Lincoln Wolf had lost his edge.

Where are you, Kat? I need you right now. Please, Kat...

Sirens pierced the air. Arms, legs, nothing obeyed his brain. Eyes still functioned, moving from side to side, up and down, blurring at times. He searched the unfamiliar faces of men in blue uniforms and bystanders, looking for her in the gathering crowd. A shadowy movement caught his attention, then two...and three.

"Ka-a-a-at. Ka-a-a-t!"

"What's he sayin', Charlie?" one of the shadows asked.

"I'm not sure. Sounds like he had a cat in the car with him. Hey, Brian, look around for a cat. This guy keeps saying something about a cat."

What's the matter with you idiots? Not cat! Kat! The woman I love. Don't you know what she looks like?

He opened his mouth to tell them. No words came out. Something encircled his neck. He couldn't move his head, but the pain eased for a moment. Voices echoed in his ears.

"Easy now. Careful!"

"Can't...too tight."

More sirens.

He heard something else, but he couldn't turn his head. Sounded like some kind of tool. The weight of the car eased off his lower half.

"We got it!" somebody shouted off to the side.

"Okay, you guys, easy now. Get the backboard under him."

Lincoln felt himself being lifted. Up he went. Moving faster, bumping, rolling along, then up again—higher this time.

Wherever he was, the rain had stopped. It was warm. Someone spoke, but he couldn't make out the words. A man at his side did something with his arm. A siren whined. The ground moved below him.

Somebody...anybody...please take away this hurting. Where's Kat? Doesn't anyone hear me?

Excruciating pain threatened to devour him. But he couldn't let go, not until he found her. He battled the beast determined to drag him into the tangle of darkness. But the darkness came, covering him like a shroud.

He seesawed between oblivian and one last strand of awareness. The voices haunted him while he drifted in space.

"I can't believe this guy survived."

"Yeah. He'd better be thanking somebody higher up that the full weight of the car didn't land on him."

"Maybe, but he might not be so grateful six months from now—if he makes it that long."

"Can it, Brian," the first voice warned. "That's not our call."

"You're right—it's his," came the retort, "and he already made it."

CHAPTER THIRTY-THREE

The ringing phone startled Kat awake. She propped herself up in the bed and switched on the light. Rubbing her eyes, she looked at the clock and tried to kick her mind into gear.

Who could be calling at one in the morning? Had something happened to Granddad or Dawson? It'd better not be Lincoln.

With a snort of annoyance, she answered.

"Katarina Kahill?"

"Yes. Who's this?" A hint of familiarity nudged at her memory.

"It's Rebecca Wolf. I hesitated to call you so late but...but...something terrible's happened."

"What is it?"

Wide awake, Kat sat up and swung her legs over the edge of the bed. Lincoln's wife didn't sound like the cool, elegant woman who'd been in her boutique.

"It's...it's Lincoln. There's been an accident." Her voice broke. "It's Lincoln," she said again, louder.

"Why are you calling *me*?"

"The doctor doesn't hold much hope for him. They said he changed lanes in front of a semi. I just left the hospital. He's asking for you, Katarina."

Kat's breath caught in her throat. Running a hand through her hair, she pulled it back from her face and around her ear. She wanted Lincoln to leave her alone, not die. Calling her name? *Why?* But could she ignore his plea in the name of protecting her own heart?

"I can't imagine what help I can be, but I'll catch the first available flight. Please tell Lincoln I'm coming."

"He's in and out of consciousness, but I'll call and ask the nurse to tell him. I don't know details of your relationship with my husband, Katarina, and it doesn't matter anymore. But I do know he loves you. That's why I asked the doctor to allow you to see him."

"Thank you, Rebecca. But I want you to know something. There *is* no relationship between your husband and me. I was infatuated with him when I was in New York, but it was over the moment I learned about you. And we *never* slept together."

Kat waited for what seemed an eternity before Rebecca responded.

"Thank you for telling me. I lost all feeling for Lincoln long ago. To tell you the truth, I just stopped caring about his infidelity. I...I didn't mean to sound like I was accusing you of anything."

"I'm truly sorry, Rebecca, for the heartache he's caused you. No woman should have to go through that."

"Don't blame yourself. I know Lincoln well enough to know he didn't tell you about me. I also know it was probably a first for him when you didn't fall into his bed." She hesitated. "Maybe...maybe we could have lunch together sometime?"

"I'd like that. Will I see you at the hospital?"

"I doubt it. Lincoln Wolf has been dead to me for years. I don't need to witness his physical passing."

Kat stifled a gasp at Rebecca's response. "We'll...plan to do lunch... soon. And thank you so much for letting me know about Lincoln."

Sitting on the edge of the bed, she curled her toes into the carpet just like she did as a little girl when things went wrong. She took a deep breath and booked two seats on the earliest available flight. This was one trip she didn't want to take alone.

Then she phoned her brother. "Lincoln's been in a terrible accident. Rebecca just called. He's critical and calling for me, Daw. I wonder if you..."

"I'll throw some things together and be there in a few minutes. Get us tickets."

"I already did."

"Good. You're doing the right thing, Sis."

She slipped on her robe and went to the kitchen to make coffee. Pacing the floor, she remembered all the harsh things she'd said to

Lincoln. But they were true. He must have gone through women like a kid went through candy.

Why should she believe he loved her? Maybe she should have been a little less abrasive, but she couldn't excuse his actions. Nor could she rationalize the havoc he'd caused and the lives he'd stomped on.

Within a few minutes, Dawson arrived.

"What happened, Sis?" They sat on the sofa, facing the fireplace. Flickering flames filled the room with strange shadows.

"I don't know any more than I already told you." She lowered her head. "He's asking for me. I should go."

He put his arm around her, and she rested her head on his shoulder. "I understand," he whispered. "It's okay."

"I want to forgive him, Daw, but it's too soon since I learned the way he deceived me. And it's too late for us to ever have a relationship. I just feel sorry for Rebecca. You should have heard the anguish in her voice."

Dawson wrapped both arms around her and held her close. Minutes passed before she sat straight up and looked into his eyes. "We broke up."

"I figured as much." They stared into the fire for a long time. "Do you love him, Kat?" His voice was soft

She scanned his face. "I...uh...at one time I thought I did." She hung her head. "But now I don't think it was love. But a certain feeling came over me when—"

"Physical attraction?"

"Maybe, but thank goodness I never acted on it. And I knew before we went to Mexico that my feelings weren't true love."

She heard her brother's sigh of relief. "Then I guess we both have something to be grateful for."

"Both?"

"You because you'd be nursing an even bigger hurt, and me because I'd be...hurting for you."

"It must have been really hard for Rebecca to call me. If I'd just listened to you, Daw, I wouldn't be in this mess."

He gave her a squeeze and glanced at his watch. "I'll throw the bags in the truck while you get dressed. We'd best be on our way. I don't think they'll hold the plane for us."

The night was clear, and the traffic, light. Dawson turned onto the highway.

"You're too quiet, Sis. What's going on in the pretty head of yours?"

"I wanted to tell you that Lincoln showed up at the boutique after we got back from Mexico."

"Here?" He glanced at her. "What was *that* all about?"

"I called to tell him I would never change my mind about us, and Lillian Rae answered the phone. He came to convince me she popped by while he was in the shower."

"Yeah, right. He didn't waste any time, did he?"

His words stung her heart. A tear trickled down her cheek.

He reached over and patted her knee. "When I found out what a two-timing jerk he was, I wanted to give him good reason to stay far away from my sister. But what good would that have done? You're not a little girl anymore. I can't go around beating up every guy who pulls your braids like I did when we were kids."

"Maybe, but it was so neat to have a big brother I could always count on to protect me."

"I have to stop treating you like a child because you *aren't* a child. I've got to let go, let you live your own life. You need to...find someone to love, someone to marry and...and have children and build a life. You're a beautiful, dear woman, Kat, You need to be appreciated."

"I'll find someone someday, but for now *your* appreciation is all I need."

Kat shuddered as they walked down the hospital corridor toward the intensive care unit. The rank smell of death mixed with the sweet odor of saving lives almost overwhelmed her.

A nurse flipping through charts looked up as they approached. "May I help you?"

Her voice soothed Kat's raw nerves like liniment on a wound.

"Yes, I've come to see Loncoln Wolf. He—"

"Are you Katarina Kahill?"

"Yes. May I see him?"

"Please come this way." She turned to Dawson. "You can wait in the sitting area at the end of the hall."

He let go of her hand. "You know where I'll be."

"Are you aware of his condition?" the nurse asked as she and Kat walked past the sliding glass doors that gave access to the critical care rooms that surrounded the nurses' station.

"Not really."

"Mr. Wolf has suffered very serious injuries."

"You mean...you mean he could die?"

"I'm afraid there's little we can do except make him as comfortable as possible." The nurse frowned. "Ms. Kahill, you should prepare yourself. Mr. Wolf won't look the way you remember him."

She wished Dawson had been allowed to come with her.

The odor of antiseptic, filtering from the rooms of the sick and injured, made her light-headed. Fluorescent lights reflected off the shiny chrome of hospital equipment. The air echoed with sounds of monitors and respirators. Towering medical apparatuses loomed over immobile flesh and blood beings.

Her stomach flip-flopped when the nurse abandoned her in Lincoln's doorway. *Why* had she agreed to come?

Her hand darted to her mouth to stifle a gasp. The walk from the doorway to his bedside seemed to go on forever as she forced one foot in front of the other. Her eyes brimmed with tears.

She stood motionless, staring at the man she had known only as handsome and vital. Tubes ran in and out of him; the heart monitor beeped while a jagged line ran up and down across its screen. Under all the medical paraphernalia, he lay pale and motionless, his head swathed in bandages and his face swollen beyond recognition.

I can't hate you Lincoln. All I can manage is pity. Pity—for you, for Rebecca, even for Lillian, who didn't want to live without you and who probably loved you more than anyone.

"Linc, I'm here. Can you hear me?" Kat brushed the ends of his fingers, and they twitched. His mouth moved. She leaned closer.

"Ka...at?" Purple lips strained to speak her name. His eyes opened in a blank stare that didn't seem to focus on her face.

"Yes, Linc, I'm here." She brushed his fingertips with her own.

"I...I love you...Kat." He choked. "Forgive me."

She touched his face and waited for him to breathe, watched his chest, watched his mouth. Kissing her index finger, she touched it to his lips. She felt no breath coming from his nostrils.

"Lincoln? Lincoln?"

The intermittent beep of the heart monitor stretched into a solid, mournful sound. Within seconds, medical personnel rushed into the room and began working feverishly. She pressed her back against the wall, watching wide-eyed as the flat line on the monitor failed to convert to the moving one that would announce the restarting of his heart. Seconds slipped into minutes before the doctor looked up one last time and shook his head. Everyone sighed and moved away.

"Would you like a moment with Mr. Wolf?" The gentle words came from the nurse who had left her at the door. She pulled the cover back over Lincoln as the trauma team filed out of the room.

Kat moved closer, looking down at the face she once thought she loved. Still it didn't look like the man she'd known, but it didn't look pained anymore. She reached out and touched the hand that was still warm but didn't move.

"I'm sorry, Lincoln," she whispered, "so, so sorry."

Tears welled up in her eyes and cascaded down her cheeks. She rushed from the room.

Dawson stood as she entered the waiting room. Her eyes still overflowing, she laid her head on his chest and cried.

"It's okay, Sis. I'm here to take care of you."

"Lincoln's dead."

Her brother kissed the top of her head just as he had when she used to fall down and bang her knees. Only this time it was her heart. "I know you didn't want it to end this way."

When there were no tears left, she took a deep breath and let it out with a shudder. Backing away from Dawson's comforting shoulder, she looked up into his caring eyes.

"Take me home, Daw. I've got a boutique to run, and you've got a divorce to get."

CHAPTER THIRTY-FOUR

Judge Parker cut a striking image—stern, sober, and gray haired. Half-glasses sat low on his nose, allowing him to look over the rims when he wasn't reading. He reminded Dawson of Benjamin Franklin.

Valorie presented a classic picture of old-fashioned propriety. Hiding behind her carefully styled hair, fashioned into a bun at the back of her neck, and her sweet, innocent smile, she looked far more like a wronged woman than the mentally ill maniac he knew her to be. Dawson felt like he'd taken a quantum leap into *Little House on the Prairie*.

The judge gestured to Hannibal to begin.

"Your honor, you have the depositions, so I'll make this short and simple. We're prepared to offer a fair and just settlement to Mrs. Kahill." Hannibal's voice rose and he paced back and forth in front of the judge. "Mr. Kahill has agreed to provide a home of her choice, not to exceed three hundred thousand dollars, and a monthly sum of four thousand dollars, in addition to health and medical insurance benefits. Further, we request that Mrs. Kahill forfeit all claims to Willow Walk, the acreage, existing inheritance, stocks, bonds, and bank accounts. If Mrs. Kahill remarries, monthly support will cease." Hannibal stopped pacing and looked Judge Parker square in the eyes. "This is our offer."

Judge Parker looked down at the submitted paperwork and then peered at Valorie's attorney. "Mr. Walker?"

Valorie inched to the edge of her chair, hands clenched and eyes narrowed at Dawson. He thought she might explode, but then she sat back in her seat, eyes watery, as though she wanted to cry.

Thomas Walker rose and glanced from Hannibal to Judge Parker, acknowledging each. "Judge Parker, Hannibal, I'm afraid we see things a bit differently. My client could never survive on Mr. Kahill's offer. Mrs. Kahill has been at Willow Walk since the marriage some eight years ago. She's maintained and cared for the home and now deserves a portion of it."

Dawson fidgeted in his chair, fear rising in his chest despite all of Hannibal's assurances. Valorie's name appeared nowhere on the deed or any other legal papers, yet horror stories of unfair divorce settlements raged through his mind. If Valorie won the judge's favor...

"We suggest that Willow Walk be sold and the profits, along with all liquid assets, be divided equally."

Dawson wiped his sweaty palms on his pants and whispered to Hannibal, "Tell them Willow Walk is my heritage. It isn't now—nor has it ever been—any kind of community property."

Hannibal stood, flexed his shoulders, and looked at Judge Parker. "As you know, your honor, the homestead has been in the Kahill family for generations. It was a gift to Dawson's grandfather, Jedidiah Kahill, from his grandfather, and before his grandfather, from his great-grandfather. Not only is it his heritage, the farm is his livelihood. We made Mrs. Kahill a very fair offer."

Judge Parker fixed dark, knowing eyes on Dawson, frowned, then glanced at Valorie and her attorney. He swiveled his chair to face the window, turning his back to the group. An unnatural quiet filled the room. It seemed forever before he turned around and picked up the thick file that was Dawson's life and his future.

"First, I'm aware that Willow Walk is an ancestral homestead. Second—Hannibal—I'm sure you're aware that *I* will be the one to decide whether your offer is fair."

"I *can't* lose the farm," Dawson hissed through clenched teeth. Hannibal nodded and looked straight at Judge Parker.

"However," Judge Parker's voice deepened, "I'm going to advise you, Mr. Walker, to reconsider and prompt your client to settle."

Valorie shot a sharp look at her attorney. She clasped her hands to her breast as though she'd been shot through the heart and screamed, "Bull crap!" Her face turned blood red, and she leapt from her chair. "All of you can go straight to the devil. I deserve Willow Walk, and I'll get it one way or another."

She came at Dawson. "I'll see you dead before you get away with this." Obscenities flew off her tongue like lightning flashes. "And just for the record, I've changed my mind. I do not...I repeat...I do *not* intend to be the *ex*-Mrs. Kahill. Don't even dream about a divorce, Dawson. I'll fight it to my death." She stomped toward the door.

"Just a minute!" Judge Parker's tone demanded her attention. She turned to face him. "You keep one thing in mind. This is *my* courtroom, and Mr. Kahill's petition for divorce has been properly filed according to the law. Whether or not it is granted is now *my* decision. Is that clear, Mrs. Kahill?"

Laughing hysterically, she spun around and exited the courtroom. Dawson drew a sharp breath. Stunned, he saw his reaction mirrored on the faces of the other three men.

Hannibal grinned just slightly, breaking the tension. Val's attorney shook his head.

Judge Parker looked at Dawson over his glasses, his long face sympathetic. He nodded at Walker. "I suggest, counselor, you inform Mrs. Kahill to take the offer and be glad of it. I might not be nearly so generous as Mr. Kahill."

He raised his bushy eyebrows and turned a direct gaze on Hannibal. "Based on the medical reports that accompanied Mr. Kahill's petition and from what I've seen today, I suggest you obtain a court order to have Mrs. Kahill evaluated by a competent psychiatrist." The judge closed the folder and stood. "Thank you gentlemen, it's been an interesting afternoon."

"What do you think, Hannibal?" Dawson asked as they walked down the courthouse steps.

"I'm willing to bet they'll take anything they can get at this point. If you want to do as Judge Parker suggested, I'll help you file the necessary papers. Keep in mind, Dawson, this woman is capable of anything. You could be putting yourself *and* your sister in danger by not following his counsel."

Dawson frowned. "I'll think about it."

A bad feeling picked at the short hairs on the back of his neck. The first time he'd felt this way, Cable showed up to haul him off to Mexico. The last time—before now—was when Kat went to New York to work for Wolf Fashions.

CHAPTER THIRTY-FIVE

"Twilight comes early this time of year." Kat watched the last inch of the sun disappear behind the mountains.

Bundled in layers of heavy clothes, she sat with Dawson on the old porch swing that hung from the rafters. Snowflakes drifted to the ground beyond the porch, laying a blanket of white. Gray shadows cast from the giant weeping willows and the elm tree where their tire swing used to hang.

This time of day always seemed to bring a sense of delicate peace, like a sleeping baby.

Frowning, Dawson seemed unmindful of the view.

Kat tried again for a response. "Don't you think evening comes so much faster this time of year, Daw?"

"Sure does."

"You're awfully quiet tonight. What's on your mind?"

Shoving his hands in his pockets, he stared straight ahead over the porch railing. "You wouldn't believe the way Valorie acted at the preliminary hearing. She swore at everyone and promised we'd all be sorry. Even I was shocked. But she knocked a big hole in her credibility."

Kat gave him a sad smile. "Is that what Hannibal said?"

"Not in so many words, but Judge Parker's glasses almost fell off his nose, and poor Walker, her attorney, turned three shades of red." Dawson chuckled.

"I'm glad it's going your way." Her sad smile turned to a grin as she adjusted one of the two scarves around her neck. She imagined the judge's glasses slipping from his nose and his fumbling to put them back on. "But what's going to become of Valorie? She's so sick."

"Maybe, but she's more unpredictable than ever; and that makes me very uncomfortable. You should've seen her. She was...wild."

"What do you mean by wild?" Kat grasped her elbows. Her stomach lurched with fear. A year ago, she wouldn't have thought much of Val's behavior, other than to dislike it. But Lincoln had taught her well the deplorable depths to which humans can sink.

"She reminded me of a cornered animal." He paused, his jaw tightening, his gaze shifting from the falling snow to her face. Then he shrugged. "I don't know. It's probably nothing."

"Level with me, Daw."

"Judge Parker suggested a psychiatric evaluation. Hannibal said he'd do the paper work if I wanted him to."

"Cruel as it sounds, it may be the best thing for her. With the proper medical therapy, she might even learn to enjoy life. You could be doing her a favor."

"Maybe, but I doubt she'd view it that way. But I do want to help her."

Kat shivered as a gust of wind whistled around the corner of the house and swept across the porch.

"You look like an Eskimo, Sis. Why don't we go down to the coffee shop and get one of their special warmer-uppers?"

"Right...and we'll be awake all night. C'mon inside and I'll fix us some hot chocolate."

"Nah, I need a change of scenery. Talking about Valorie puts me in a mood, and I want one of those super shot mint mochas to pull me out of it."

"What kind of excuse is that?" She suppressed a grin.

"Ouch! I'm hurt that you'd think such a thing, much less *say* it." He grabbed her hand. "But excuse or not, it sounds too good not to get one. So let's go. It's not that far...less than a block from Fashions by Kat."

Raising an eyebrow, she gave him a look. "I *know* where it is, Daw. My daily pick-me-up comes from there."

"Hmmm. I guess you don't fix *everything* you consume in the lunchroom."

She stuck her tongue out at him and swung her legs into the cab of his truck.

They heard the sirens before they turned the corner. The fire trucks were blocking the way to the coffee shop.

"What's going on, Daw. It looks like—"

"The boutique's on fire!" He finished her sentence.

"No!" She heard herself scream, but she couldn't seem to stop. "No, Daw! My dream's going up in smoke!"

Tears gushed down her cheeks as her brother parked the truck as close as he could get. He pulled her next to him and held her tight.

"Stay calm, Sis. Whatever's happening here, we'll deal with it."

"Oh, Daw! The whole thing's going to burn. Where's Snow White?" She scurried from the truck, only to be stopped by a fireman.

"Sorry, ma'am, you need to step back."

"I'm Katarina Kahill. This is my shop. Please...did you find my cat?"

"Not yet, ma'am."

"If you'll just let me go down the alley here to the back, I know exactly where to check for her."

Dawson moved up beside her and took hold of her arm. "Kat, I don't think—"

An explosion shattered the air.

"No!" Kat screamed.

The front window shattered, glass and flames bursting from the gaping hole in the wall. Breaking away from her brother's grasp and running toward the boutique, she ducked under the safety-tape and reached the fireman closest the door before Dawson caught up with her.

"My cat's in there!" she shouted, grabbing the fireman's arm. "Please...please get her out."

"Get back, lady!" He yanked his arm away, holding onto the fire hose with a tight grip. "We'll go in as soon as we can. Your cat is *not* the only one in there."

"What! How do you know?" She turned to her brother. "Are Bonny and Deb in there? They left before I did." Kat started for the door, but Dawson pulled her back. Tears gushed as she fought to free herself. "Let me go!"

"Kat! Listen to me!"

He grasped her shoulders, holding her firmly until the hysterics ceased. "You've got to let the firemen do their job. You'll only get in the way."

"I don't care!" She struggled, but Dawson was too strong.

The assistant chief approached them. "Ma'am, you'll have to stand on the other side of the tape. Right now, *please*."

She turned to face him. "How do you know somebody's in there? How could anybody get in without a key? Did they break in? Please tell me...I'm the owner."

"We don't know *how* someone got in. We only know that someone did because we heard a voice from inside. And we heard laughter."

"*Laughter?*"

"Yes, ma'am. Now you must move back." The assistant chief clutched Kat's other arm as he and Dawson escorted her to safety.

"I'll take care of her now," Dawson said.

Kat gave the fireman a pleading look. "How did this start?"

"We're not sure yet, ma'am. A passerby saw a small fire inside and reported it. We arrived within five minutes of the call."

"My brother and I heard the sirens right before we got here."

"We'd just hooked up our hoses when we had flashover."

"Flashover?"

"Yes, ma'am. A fire normally doubles in size every three minutes. This one went much faster, so an accelerant may be involved."

"I don't understand."

"Did you keep any flammable substances inside? Oil paint or petroleum-based cleaning products? Fluids to remove spots from the clothing or anything like that?"

"Not anything that would feed a fire." Kat watched a grim expression cross his face. "Are you saying someone *set* this fire?"

"We won't know anything until we complete our investigation."

"What about whoever's inside?" She leaned against Dawson. "Can't you go in with fire suits or something?"

"We're working on that right now. It would be a big help if you could provide us a layout of your shop."

"I designed the floor plan for the interior," Dawson said. "The large room in front is the showroom. Behind it, inventory is kept in a storeroom, and there's an exit door onto the alley to accommodate deliveries. A small lunchroom sits to the right of the storeroom. It contains a stove, a refrigerator, a table and chairs, and a couple cabinets. Neither room has any windows, but both have interior doors that can be shut."

"How about false ceilings?"

"We dropped the ceiling when we did the remodel."

"That's what we need to know." The assistant chief turned and hurried back to his platoon.

"I'm so scared, Daw. This can't be happening." Kat's eyes searched the gathering crowd for her friends. "Bonny and Deb just *can't* be in there...can they? What if they came back to iron the new arrivals or something?" Her knees wobbled. She thought she was going to faint.

Dawson supported her. "Don't assume anything, Kat. Besides, why would they laugh while the place burned?"

"You know those two when they get together. They're always giggling about something. And if they were in back, they might not have known about the fire."

"They'd know now. And they'd be getting out."

"If they could—" She looked up at him, then turned back to the boutique. "What's that?"

"What's what, Sis?"

"*That!*"

An eerie scream from inside the burning building pierced the air.

The woman watched chunks of fire drop from the ceiling to dance across the ceramic tile floor. *Why* was this happening?

Valorie hadn't meant to scream. Nor had she meant to still be here. And she *wouldn't* be here if she hadn't gone into the lunchroom and seen that beautiful box of unopened chocolates on the table. She opened it and shoved two in her mouth. Ahhh...she'd never tasted such delectable confections.

Reaching for another piece, she watched a flaming hunk of the ceiling break loose on one side and dangle over the sweets. Grabbing the precious confections just before it crashed onto the tabletop, she tried to pop one more into her watering mouth. It melted in her fingers.

A blast of heat from overhead pressed down on her as another slab of the burning ceiling tumbled downward. She replaced the lid on the box and hugged the treasure close.

Gasping for air and confused by the fire and smoke, she dropped to the floor. The air was cooler there, and she could take a small breath without choking.

Where was the door? The smoke made it almost impossible to see. She had what she came for and a bonus, too. Kat's cherished dream was fast becoming ashes, and she held in her hands the most delicious chocolates she'd ever tasted. She inched her way to where the door should be, but where was it? Running her hand along the wall, she belly-crawled along the floor's edge. She couldn't find it.

The lack of oxygen and toxic smoke made her dizzy. Her mind began to play tricks on her.

Meow.

What was that? It couldn't be Kitty. Kitty was dead. She had killed her beloved kitten herself when she was seven.

Meow.

There it was again, louder this time. Her mind slipped backward.

Mama lay crumpled on the floor at the foot of the bed, a pistol lying beside her hand. She was so still. Her pretty white dress had turned red.

"Mama!"

She rushed to her side, kneeling down and shaking her as hard as she could.

"Mama, wake up, please! Daddy's coming to get me." Her breath caught in her throat as she looked up. Her father stood in the doorway, tossing a knife from one hand to the other. He staggered toward her.

"Mama! Help me!"

She picked up the gun and pointed it at him.

"Don't come any closer, Daddy!" She could already smell the stench of the whiskey. "Go away, Daddy! Leave Mama and me alone."

"Whatcha mean, Val?" he slurred. "Now come to Daddy like a good li'l girl." He kept tossing that knife back and forth. "I promise I won' hurt you."

"You already hurt me!" she shouted. "You hurt Mama, too. And you made me shoot Kitty."

He took a menacing step toward her and reached for the gun.

She aimed at his mid-section, then pulled the hammer back just like he'd taught her to do.

"You promised you wouldn't hurt Mama and me anymore if I killed Kitty. You lied! This is for Kitty!"

She closed her eyes and squeezed the trigger. The gun banged and bucked, and her arms flew up. She opened her eyes. Daddy had stopped, his mouth open and his eyes wide. He held his stomach with both hands, red like Mama's dress oozing between his fingers. She pointed again.

"And this is for Mama!"

Another bang. Again her arms flew upward. She threw herself across her mama's body.

"Mama, I'm sorry about Kitty. I only did it to save you. But Daddy lied. He hurt you anyway. It's okay, 'cause I hurt him, and he won't never do it again. You can wake up now, Mama. I've got something special for you. I opened your box of chocolates."

She bumped into something. It felt...like a refrigerator.

Meow.

The sound was coming from behind it.

"Here, Kitty. Here, Kitty. Come to Valorie. I won't hurt you again, I promise."

A ball of fur rubbed against her hand. Reaching out, she picked up the kitten and cradled it against her breast.

"My sweet Kitty. I'm so glad you really did have nine lives. Now I can take good care of you like I couldn't before."

She stroked the fuzzy black head with her thumb while the kitten's heart pounded against her palm.

"I know you're scared, Kitty. I'm scared, too. But I'll get us both out of here and take care of you just like I promised."

A flaming piece of ceiling tile crashed beside her. Acrid smoke rolled over her, filling her lungs. She coughed and gagged. Tucking the kitten in the inside pocket of her coat, she inched her way backwards the way she had just come.

"We just have to find the door, Kitty."

From somewhere nearby, she heard a pounding, like someone chopping wood.

"Oh, oh, Kitty, Daddy's coming! But I won't let him make me hurt you again."

She heard another sound, like running water—a dam or a waterfall.

"And I won't let him drown you either."

She put her free hand over her coat pocket to hide the kitten.

Now the pounding was closer. It was at the lunchroom door.

"Anybody there?" a deep male voice called out.

"Don't you come in here, Daddy!" She stood up. "Kitty's not here. Mama's not here either."

"We're coming in for you, lady. Stay down low where you can breathe."

Two more heavy blows, and the door collapsed.

"Don't hurt us again, Daddy." She stood up and stepped backward into the depths of the heat and smoke. "No, Daddy! No, Da—"

A firemen rushed up the alley toward the waiting ambulance. The woman in his arms lay limp and still, her skin ashen in the beam of the streetlight.

"Daw, it's Valorie!" Kat tried to break free from Dawson's hold, but couldn't.

Gasps from the crowd rose above the roar of the flames and water hoses.

Kat and Dawson watched from behind the yellow ribbon safety barrier. "We have to go to her, Daw. Hurry!" Kat screamed.

"No! Listen to me, Kat." She tried to free herself, but Dawson's firm hold commanded her to listen. "The paramedics will take care of her. We'd only be in the way."

"But she needs us, Daw."

"We don't even know that she's alive." He held her tighter as she sobbed. "There's nothing we can do for her now."

"Ms. Kahill."

She looked around to see the assistant chief. "The lady had this in her pocket."

He handed her Snow White.

Kat reached out for the kitten that leapt into her arms, mewing frantically.

"She probably saved the kitten's life by protecting it inside her coat. But the woman herself might not be so fortunate. My men found her on the floor, but she apparently was standing before they got in there. She inhaled a lot of toxic smoke."

"You mean—"

"I mean she'll be on her way to the hospital in just a few moments. You don't know who she is, do you?"

"She's my wife," Dawson said in a low voice. "We'll follow the ambulance."

"Oh...I'm so sorry," the fireman said. "You go now. We'll contact you later regarding the investigation."

"Thank you." Dawson turned to Kat. "Let's go, Sis. The ambulance is leaving."

Dawson stared at Valorie's grave. He covered his mouth and cleared his throat. What was he feeling? Sadness? Pain? Relief? Maybe Kat would know. He'd ask her.

The trauma of the last few days washed over him. First. Lincoln's death, now Valorie's. Who would be next? His thoughts turned to Granddad. He was an old man, but he was still healthy and vital. Dawson wasn't ready to let him go. Not yet...

He held Kat's arm and bowed his head.

Kat placed her hand over his, and a sense of belonging and peace overcame him. It was short-lived. Valorie interrupted even in death. Her screeching voice rose, grating on his memory.

Admit it! You love your sister more than you love me.

He turned to Kat and saw only goodness and beauty, inside and out.

For once you're right, Valorie. I do love my sister more than you. Because she's everything you weren't.

CHAPTER THIRTY-SIX

In Valorie's car, Dawson had found scores of photographs—Kat and Dawson holding hands, walking down the street together, sitting on the porch at Willow Walk, even one shot of her hugging him goodbye at the airport. Scattered among them were pictures of dead animals, mostly small livestock from the farm they suspected she had killed.

Kat shook her head and swallowed hard, laying them back on the kitchen table. "She saved Snow White, so I know there had to be some goodness there."

Bonny and Deb sipped coffee at the breakfast bar.

"Maybe there was...once upon a time," Deb said, "and maybe again at the end. Who knows? So...when are you going to start on the new boutique? We've got a great customer base, and it's growing all the time—particularly since you placed first in the New York competition. We were getting more and more out-of-town patrons who made a special trip to Wheeling just to come to your shop."

"You *are* going to rebuild, aren't you?" Bonnie raised her eyebrows.

"I don't think so. Not now. Maybe never."

Deb scowled. "What do you mean...*maybe never?*"

"I sank most of my inheritance into Fashions by Kat. That was my dream, my income, my life. Now it's gone."

"What about the insurance?" Bonnie asked. "I know you were covered."

"The insurance settlement will help when it comes, but I have to wait until after the investigation's finished."

"That can't take forever," Deb said. "Unless you plan on working for somebody else or have been hiding the fact that you're independently wealthy, you're going to need an income soon."

"I suppose you could go back to Wolf International," Bonnie suggested, a dubious expression on her face. "Working for Rebecca Wolf should be a lot safer than working for her late husband."

"Yeah," Deb agreed. "And they'd probably welcome you with open arms. After all, your designs propelled them back into an enviable position in the fashion industry."

Kat gave her friend a hard look. "I don't think that's an option."

"In that case..." Deb grinned.

"Point noted." Kat walked over to the coffee maker and picked up the pot. "Who wants more?"

Both girls held up their cups.

Dawson walked in as Deb and Bonny pulled out of the driveway. "Are you making plans for the new shop?"

She ignored the hopeful look on his face. "Not yet."

"C'mon, Sis, it's time to think about new beginnings."

"First, Bonny and Deb, and now you. What is this, a conspiracy?"

He put his arm around her. "You know better than that, Kat. It's just that we all love you and think it's time you quit moping around here and went back to work."

"I'd love to go back to work, Daw, but every time I close my eyes, I see my dream going up in smoke. And I see Valorie's white casket topped with that spray of pink roses and baby's breath. I can't let go of it, and I can't rebuild something that caused so much pain."

He held her close until her tears stopped.

"The boutique didn't cause the pain, Sis. It was Valorie. Even in death, she's running our lives. Don't you think it's time to put a stop to all her negativity and move on?"

"She was sick, Daw."

"Yes, but *we* aren't. And we have our whole lives ahead of us."

She sniffed and stepped back to look at him. "Maybe you're right. I'll have to think about the boutique, but maybe I can start here." Granddad stepped into the room as she spoke. "Let me go through Valorie's things for you."

Dawson gave her a pained look.

"I'll help her, Sonny," Granddad said. "Best we get it done 'cause it ain't gonna get no easier."

After several seconds, Dawson nodded. Then he turned and walked out of the room.

Dawson steered clear of them while they sorted through the remnants of Valorie's life.

"You know he's hurtin', Kitten," Granddad said. He held the box open while Kat put the last of Valorie's clothes into it.

"I know. At one time, I think he loved her. I remember when he was so hopeful that he could help her past her problems. And then I watched his optimism fade into despair."

Granddad frowned. "I watched, too."

"Do you think he'll ever move back into the main house?"

"Someday soon I think he will. He really loves this place. He just needs some time."

"And we need to rid it of Valorie's presence. This is the last of her things. I'll take them to the women's shelter drop downtown. Valorie had nice things, and those poor women often leave their homes with nothing but the clothes they're wearing. Then they don't have anything decent to wear when they go job-hunting."

Granddad nodded. "Yep. Sonny would like that, I think. Better that his last memory be of Valorie helping someone, not of her trying to hurt you. He needs that. You know he's feelin' responsible for what happened 'cause he's the one who brought her into the family."

"That must be why he hides out in the barn most of the time."

"Could be, Kitten. Let me help you carry this box to the van."

She marveled at the old man's strength. Even in his nineties, he could still do a day's work and heave a bale of hay.

He's a rare one. What will we ever do without him when he's gone?

She fought the tears surfacing at the thought of that inevitability, which would come one day in the not-too-distant future. By the time she came to the five boxes of chocolates in the refrigerator, she couldn't hold them back any longer.

"Now, now, Kitten," Granddad said, his arm around her shoulder. "Sometimes things happen for the best, even though we may not see it at the time."

Kat sniffed and wiped her nose. She tossed the candy into the trash.

"It's so sad that a meaningless box of chocolates was Valorie's only comfort. And so ironic that her single comfort also brought about her end. Did you know that, when the firemen pulled her out of the kitchen, she had Snow White in her pocket and was clutching the box of chocolate's Lincoln gave me to her chest?"

Granddad frowned. "Sonny didn't tell me 'bout that."

"I can't help but think that if I'd put that candy in the trash instead of on the lunchroom table, Valorie would still be alive."

"Now don't you go blamin' yourself for that woman's obsession. She was where she wasn't supposed to be, doin' what she wasn't supposed to be doin'. I think that's called somethin' like breakin' and enterin', trespassin', arson, and probably a number of other things that put her on the wrong side of the law. I knew she was trouble the first time Sonny brought her home. I tried to tell 'im, but you know how stubborn that boy can be."

"I know, but none of that makes her any less dead, does it?"

Granddad's expression softened. "No, it doesn't, Kitten. Neither does it tell us why she had such a dark side. But you mark my words, that woman came to us damaged. Somethin' terrible happened to her 'for we ever knew her. I'm guessin' that's what *really* killed her."

Kat sank down at the kitchen table and covered her face with the dishtowel.

"Get it out of your system, girl. You've had way too much grief."

She looked up at him with watery eyes. "I'm crying for Valorie. She's the sister-in-law I never knew and the sister I never had." He patted her shoulder. "Lincoln, on the other hand, doesn't deserve any more tears. He's a chapter in my life I'm glad to close."

The breezy sixty-four degree temperature felt like spring—and new beginnings. Kat threw open the windows, grabbed her car keys, and headed down the long drive. At the floral shop in town, she bought every bouquet that didn't remind her of a funeral. She filled the backseat of her van and hurried back to Willow Walk.

Granddad met her at the door. "Kitten! What in tarnation are you trying to do, give an old man pneumonia?" He followed her to the kitchen, waving his cane in the air while she juggled several bouquets of flowers.

"Now, Granddad, fresh air is good for you. Why don't you sit down, and I'll fix us some tea. That'll warm up those bones that don't know spring's almost here."

"Tea, you say? Naw. If I can't have a nip o' brandy, I don't want anythin'. I'm goin' for my morning nap, now. Seems you want me to catch my death down here. If you need any help, you call me. I love you, girl—even if you do try to make an icicle out of me."

Kat laughed for the first time in weeks. She'd almost forgotten how good it felt.

After arranging the bouquets in vases and placing them throughout the house, she stood at the kitchen window and looked out, letting the crisp breeze blow away the pain of loss. Dawson's truck sat next to the barn. He must be inside, catching up on all the chores that didn't get done during all their trauma. Seems he had a lot to do in there because that's where he'd spent a good part of the past couple weeks.

The promise of spring reached out to her. She had to get off her duff and start planning for a new boutique. If only her heart were in it...

As the sun lost its strength, she went from room to room, closing windows. She returned to the kitchen just as Granddad stomped down the stairs, all bright-eyed after his nap.

He glanced around at all the bouquets. "Looks like a dad-gum garden in here. You must have spring fever the way you're puttin' smelly flowers all around the house and openin' windows and all."

"Just brightening up the place a bit." Kat smiled. "Want to sit on the porch swing for awhile?"

"Yes, ma'am. Been meanin' to talk to you about somethin' real important, and now's the time, Kitten."

"Okay...you go on, and I'll bring some hot cocoa."

Kat chuckled when Granddad donned a long coat, scarf, and gloves. The temperature had reached a record high, but still he needed to insulate his bones.

She sat beside him while they sipped steaming chocolate topped with tiny marshmallows and stared beyond the railing. "What was it you wanted to talk about?"

He turned to look her square in the eyes. "I'll say it right out. You know I never beat around the bush, and you know I love you very much—so here it is. Don't say I ever held anything—"

"Granddad! Please...get on with it." Kat grinned and shook her head.

"Listen up now. You stop feelin' sorry for yourself, girl. There are people in this world a whole lot worse off. So you lost what you had. It's nothin' you can't replace if you just get to it and do it. You got a fine architect at your disposal, one who thinks the sun rises and sets in you. And you've got insurance money comin' any day now, so there's no excuse not to rebuild and expand. What are you waitin' for? You wanna dry up and blow away?"

Kat stared at him. Her mouth dropped open.

"Granddad, you're...you're so right. I've been selfish, being all down and out like this." She bowed her head. "What you and Daw must think of me! I haven't been at all the way Mama taught me to be—strong and brave no matter what. I'm *really* sorry."

"Now, Kitten, I didn't mean to hurt your feelin's." He put his arm around her and pulled her head onto his shoulder, planting a kiss on her hair.

"I love you, Granddad. You always tell me the truth. I just wish all this had never happened."

"I know. I know. But you can't un-ring a bell. It's time to move on with your life."

She kissed him on the cheek. Out of the corner of her eye, she spied Dawson coming from the barn.

Trying to hide a smile, he twisted his mouth in a way that made his dimple sink in and give him away. "What are you two up to?"

"Never you mind, Sonny. We got secrets." Granddad winked at Kat.

"Come to the barn with me, Sis. I want to show you something." Dawson sounded excited.

"What is it Daw?"

"Come and see!"

"Why so mysterious, Daw? Are you making a magic potion or something? Don't tell me you got a new tractor."

Granddad laughed. "He's concoctin' somethin' alright."

He followed several steps behind, raising his voice so they could hear. "He's brewin' some good ol' white lightnin', Kat; that's what he's doin'. Said he's gonna keep the sheriff stocked up so he'll leave him alone on the road."

Dawson turned around. "I am not! But it's a darn good idea. I'm sure you'd volunteer to be my taster, Granddad."

Kat stopped. "Hurry up, you slow pokes."

Set up in a corner of the big red barn was a long workbench. On it sat a large plank of wood covered with a sheet.

"Come closer, you two."

While Granddad and Kat stood staring down at the sheet, Dawson grabbed it and with one hand pulled it off.

Kat's mouth dropped open.

"Daw, oh my..." And then louder, "Oh, my!"

She rubbed her hand over the sign.

"Daw, it's beautiful." Looking through her tears, she read it aloud: "*Welcome to Fashions by Kat.*"

The black script lined in gold was the prettiest she'd ever seen. Her black cat insignia had been worked into the design.

He was grinning like he used to when they were children and he'd done her a special favor. "You like it?"

She flung her arms around his neck and hung on. "*Like* it? I *love* it! I feel like hanging it up right now. This is more than a gentle hint to get myself out of a rut. It's a blow to my silly heart." She wiped her eyes again. "I'm ready to get started on those new boutique plans anytime you are."

Granddad beamed. "Nice work, Sonny. You outdid yourself. I told you she'd snap out of it when she saw the sign."

"Oh...I see now...you two were in cahoots." Kat grinned. It's a gorgeous sign, Daw. It far surpasses the one that..."

"That burned?"

"Yes...that burned." Kat took a deep breath.

They strolled back to the house, Kat in the middle with her arms around Dawson and Granddad.

"What do you think of a vaulted ceiling for the boutique?" she asked. "Just inside the entrance, we'd place a huge fountain, water cascading down rocks with a rainbow of shimmering lights. And live plants and trees all around it. We could even have—"

Granddad interrupted. "My girl's back. There's no stoppin' her now."

Kat looked up at the old man and grinned. "Remember to be careful what you ask for because you might get it."

"I remember, Kitten, and I'm always careful 'bout that. And I been askin' a whole lot 'bout this one."

All through supper, caught in a tidal wave of ideas, she brainstormed. It felt wonderful after such a long drought. Afterward, Granddad and Dawson talked by the fire while Kat did the dishes. When the phone rang, she dried her hands and plucked the receiver from its cradle.

"Kat? Polly Dee here."

"Hi. Polly. This is a surprise. Is everything okay?"

"I have bad news. Cable's in the hospital. He called and begged me to get him on a plane to the States where he could be with you and Dawson. Said if he had to be in the hospital, he'd do it there. I think he really wants to talk to you both."

"What's wrong with him?"

"I went to see him, but he won't tell me the results of the tests. So I just did what he asked and found a flight into Pittsburgh tomorrow morning. Will that work for you?"

"Yes...of course."

"He's pretty frail. The flight will be hard on him."

"Is he well enough to travel?"

Polly sighed into the phone. "No, but you know how hard-headed he is. I think he'll crawl to the airport if I don't take him. He's determined to see you two, no matter what it takes."

"I can't thank you enough for helping out like this."

Polly gave her the flight information and hung up. Shivering, Kat stared at the handset. The sun had gone down, and a chill permeated the air.

"That was Polly Dee," she said a moment later, sinking onto the couch in front of the fire. "Cable called her. He's in the hospital, but he wants to come home. There's something he wants to talk to us about. What do you suppose it is, Daw?"

Dawson shrugged. "It could be anything."

Granddad frowned and rubbed his chin. "That boy's probably got the creepin' crud or somethin'. He never did 'mount to nothin'."

"Granddad! He's your son no matter what. And he's sick."

"I care about him, Kitten. He's just disappointed me so much. He can't hold a candle to you, Sonny." He nodded at Dawson. "I got the best grandkids in the world. Guess who they take after?"

Kat raised her eyebrows and gave him a look.

"They take after me. And I'm goin' to have the best great-grandson in the world, too...if you ever find yourself a good woman, Sonny."

Kat suppressed a grin before rescuing Dawson from the path Granddad was traveling. "We'd better get to the airport early. We don't know what shape Dad'll arrive in."

Granddad frowned and narrowed his eyes. "I'm goin' with you."

"But you just said—" Kat began.

"I know what I said. But like *you* said, he's my son. And knowin' him as I do, I'm thinkin' somethin' must be mighty wrong for him to be makin' so much effort to come home when he never did before."

"Okay, if that's what you want."

"Thank you kindly. I'm goin' to bed now." Granddad stood and rolled his eyes. Kat thought he was going to wave his cane at them, but he didn't.

She watched him walk away, tapping the cane on the floor with each step but putting no weight on it. Most times he could walk just fine on his own. Maybe he figured he'd earned the right to lean on it during those moments when the notion or the need arose. And he certainly had.

But what about Cable? What rights did *he* have in the family now?

She couldn't shake the feeling that this unexpected visit would somehow change their lives forever.

CHAPTER THIRTY-SEVEN

They left earlier than necessary for the airport. Several times during the hour-long drive, Kat tried to start a conversation. Each time it fell flat. Finally, she gave up and stared out the window. Even the awakening spring all around them couldn't dispel the gloom that hung over the truck's crew cab.

They waited inside the new Pittsburgh Airport's Terminal A, watching as passengers met loved ones or scurried alone toward baggage pickup. Kat looked at her watch. Where was Cable? Had he missed the plane? Or, more likely, changed his mind about coming? Her nerves wound tighter. What kind of a game was he playing this time?

Dawson stopped pacing long enough to scan the newest set of travelers. "Isn't that Dad? The man being pushed in a wheelchair?"

Kat grabbed Dawson by the arm and stared through the crowd. "It can't be, can it? He looks *awful*."

Granddad, standing behind them in the crowd of waiting people, walked toward them.

Cable waved weakly—dropping his hand when his father approached. As the attendant pushed him closer, Kat saw the hollows in his cheeks and the great dark circles under his eyes. He looked almost as old as Jedediah.

Dawson took the wheelchair from the attendant, who nodded and left. "Polly was right, Dad. You're sick."

Cable raised his head and looked to where his father stood. He eyed him as though he were a stranger, then smiled. His face became skeletal."

"Let's get you to the hospital, Dad." Dawson said. Cable seemed not to hear him.

"Son?" Jedediah's voice broke. He walked toward Cable, his arms outstretched, pools of liquid spilling over the rims of his eyes onto his cheeks.

As though that one word was all the permission Cable needed, he pushed himself into a standing position and flung his arms around his father's neck. Kat blinked back her own tears as she watched the years of pain and anger and guilt melt into forgiveness and reunion.

Granddad took over the wheelchair, pushing Cable to the truck. Dawson put his one small suitcase in the bed and helped him into the cab's back seat. Granddad crawled in beside him.

"You rest now, son," Jedediah said.

"Yes, Dad, you rest," Dawson echoed.

Kat turned to add her agreement, but she said nothing when she saw his eyes were closed.

Dawson pulled up to the hospital's emergency entrance and ran inside. He came back with two orderlies, one pushing a stretcher. They rushed Cable into a cubicle.

"Please wait outside until the doctor evaluates him," a nurse said.

Cable's limbs began to jerk under the light coverlet. "I want to stay with my boy," Jedediah said. "It's been so many years—"

The doctor who had been paged hurried past them.

"We'll let you know what's going on as soon as we know," the nurse assured him. "But you need to go out now so we can do our job."

"He's not going to make it," Granddad said in a low voice as he sank into a chair in the waiting area.

"You don't know that, Granddad." Dawson said.

"Oh yes...yes, I do, Sonny." Jedediah's eyes drooped and glazed over as he looked up at Dawson. "I've seen enough death in my lifetime to know when a body's dyin', and my boy's dyin' real fast. I'm just glad we made our peace, 'cause I can let the past go now." Granddad's voice cracked. He cleared his throat. "I can let him go, too, and remember the good times when he was a young'un."

Kat put her arm around him, but he shrugged it away. "It's okay, Kitten. I was afraid I'd see this day if I lived long enough, but it just don't seem right. Parents shouldn't outlive their children."

She couldn't think of any words of comfort, so she picked up a magazine from the table in front of them and thumbed through it, trying to read an article on a movie star she liked but giving up after failing a third attempt to get into the story. She couldn't get her mind off the father who had left her with little except bad memories. Time seemed to drag by as people came and went and they waited and waited.

Finally, the doctor approached them. "Are you the family of Cable Kahill."

"Yes," Dawson answered, standing. "What's happening?"

"He's had a seizure. We've administered an anticonvulsant. He's stable now. We're admitting him, and he'll be in a room as soon as he comes back from x-ray. Check with the front desk in a few minutes, and they'll direct you."

Kat followed Dawson and Granddad as they walked down the corridor that would lead them to the information desk. Thoughts of Cable continued to race through her mind.

When he took Dawson, she thought she'd never forgive him, much less care what happened to him. But the man she'd seen today wasn't frightening—even though he was the same man who'd taken Dawson away from her. She'd despised him then. But she couldn't now. He was so sick and feeble...dying, Granddad said. She'd carried the burden for years, weighed down by her hatred for her father. But finally, at long last, she was liberated.

Two hours passed while they waited for Cable to return from x-ray. Jedediah, restless and tired, fussed at the nurses one minute and joked with them the next. Finally, two male attendants brought Cable to the room and lifted him into bed.

The doctor followed behind, motioning them out of the room and into a small office down the hallway. "We found a tumor at the base of the brain consistent with what he told us he learned in Mexico. Considering his condition and the size of the tumor, it's amazing he's awake and coherent. Just be aware he won't stay that way for long."

"What about surgery?" Dawson asked.

"We've called in a neurosurgeon, but I've seen several similar cases. Surgery may not be an option."

"Can you tell how long he's had this tumor?" Kat asked.

"Some of these tumors grow very slowly. At this point it's too early to say in his case, but some of them may grow for years before the seizures begin."

"What are the symptoms?"

"At first they may be vague, coming and going without warning. They could include headaches, personality changes, vision problems, seizures, loss of balance and hearing."

Kat's eyes met Dawson's, and she assumed they were thinking the same thing. This explained so much.

"I thought something physical might be working on him, but never this," Dawson said.

Granddad's eyes clouded. "I'm a foolish father. Should've figured the boy was sick the first time he contradicted the Kahill way."

"You didn't know, Granddad. Don't blame yourself for what you couldn't even have imagined. You gave Dad all kinds of chances over the years to straighten himself out."

"Right now, knowin' that don't help much, Sonny."

"If you don't do surgery, what then?" Kat wanted the doctor to get to the part where they'd cure him with medication and treatments.

"Let's wait and see what the neurosurgeon has to say. Meanwhile, we're treating his symptoms and making him as comfortable as possible. I do recommend you spend time with him and enjoy his company while he's lucid."

"Keep him out of pain," Granddad said. "That's all I ask. Can you do that much, doc?"

"We'll do our best, Mr. Kahill."

"Your best'd better be good enough," Granddad said, frowning. "I don't want him sufferin' no more."

"Thank you," Dawson said. Kat nodded. Granddad stood and, leaning on his cane more than usual, hurried back to Cable's room. Kat thought she saw tears in his eyes.

She took Dawson's hand, and they stood still, staring after him. "Oh, Daw, do you realize this may have been the cause of his behavior? If only we had known, maybe we could've understood him better. Maybe we could've done something to help him."

Dawson started back toward Cable's room, Kat in tow behind him. They stopped just inside the door.